The Darkies Gold

On the Trail of the Bushrangers Booty

Max Barrington

For the love of my life,
my darling wife and my inspiration,
Lynette

First published in Australia in 2024 by Etteleah Books - Cairns Australia
This edition printed in 2025

4

Max Barrington

Contents

"Gold is never just metal; it's a mirror, reflecting not only the sun but the sickness in a man's soul.
 Greed doesn't glitter; it devours."

But, none! Shall have, The Darkie's Gold.............

San Francisco

Wesley and Adina Ahrens were practically vibrating with excitement, their joy twitching just beneath the skin like a current of electricity. It wasn't the kind of excitement you felt when buying a new car, or finally springing for that fancy espresso machine you'd been eyeing. No, this was deeper. Darker. A delicious, unsettling mix of awe and trepidation. They had done it, they'd won the auction. By some twisted blessing of fate, they were now the legal owners of the Twilight Star Saloon on Brannan Street, a crumbling old husk of history wedged between the steel-and-glass arrogance of modern San Francisco.

The bidding had been brutal. A modern-day knife fight fought with raised paddles and chequebooks instead of Bowie knives and pistols. The air in the auction room had been thick with tension, every eye gleaming with the lust of conquest. But in the end, the Ahrens's had emerged victorious. Or maybe "survivors" was a better word.

The Twilight Star was more than a building. It was a memory carved in wood and brick and soot-stained wallpaper, a ghost dressed in architecture. Built in 1876, it had been a rowdy beacon for sailors, drifters, dreamers, and the damned. A saloon on the ground floor where the whiskey had flowed like the bay tides, and a row of modest rooms above where travelers laid their heads, and sometimes, never woke up.

It all ended in fire.

The blaze came in 1902, whispering through the upper levels like a vengeful spirit with unfinished business. It charred the walls, blackened the ceilings, and left the rooms upstairs uninhabitable. The building survived, but it never recovered. The upper floor was sealed off, shuttered like a tomb. Over time, it became a convenient dumping ground, the forgotten attic of the city, filled with crates, dust, and echoes of a louder, bloodier past.

But it wasn't just the creaking bones and scorched memories that had drawn Wesley and Adina in like moths to a flame. It was the stories. God, the stories.

There were whispers about one of the early owners, a man who spoke with a slow, measured drawl and kept his left hand wrapped in a filthy bandage. Supposedly, he was an Australian bushranger on the run, having fled the sunburnt outback with blood on his boots and a warrant at his back. No one ever knew his real name. Some said he changed it as often as his shirt, which wasn't often at all. He vanished one night after a brawl that left two men bleeding on the saloon floor and a third carried out on a pine board.

And then there was the one about Wyatt Earp. Yeah, that Wyatt Earp. The legend himself. Said to have sat at the corner table under the mirror, sipping rye and watching everyone like they were entries in a ledger only he could read. Maybe it was true. Maybe it wasn't. But legends, like mould, thrive in places like the Twilight Star.

Wesley had read those stories out loud one night in bed, the glow of his tablet screen casting eerie shadows on the wall. Adina had listened with wide eyes, half-intrigued, half-terrified, and wholly enchanted. By the time he was done, they both knew they had to have the place. Not just for its bones, or its stories, but for the feeling it gave them, like standing at the edge of a deep, dark well and sensing something down there, breathing. Waiting.

By 2012, the Twilight Star Saloon had new stewards, flesh-and-blood inheritors of brick, timber, and time. Wesley and Adina Ahrens stood in the dusty threshold of the old place, hearts hammering like fists on a coffin lid, giddy with purpose and not a little fear. They'd traded in the comfortable predictability of suburban life for something older, wilder. The kind of dream that has teeth.

Their plan was bold. Reckless, some might say. The kind of leap you only take once you've burned the bridge behind you. They'd liquidated their investments, kissed their three-bedroom house goodbye, and watched the familiar life they'd built flicker in the rearview mirror. In the end, they'd scraped together just over a million bucks, hard-earned, hard-saved, and now entirely at the mercy of something as unpredictable as an old saloon with a history soaked in bourbon and blood.

The building had cost them $260,000, a steal, really, given its location. It had been sitting long enough for people to forget it was even there, swallowed by the city's expansion like a rotten tooth ignored too long. Their budget had allowed for a generous renovation fund: $400,000 to pry open the walls, scrape the soot from the ceilings, and maybe, just maybe, uncover whatever secrets had been bricked in with the foundation. Another $100,000 would cover the liquor license, bar stock, and whatever surprises the city inspectors decided to throw at them.

And there would be surprises. There always were.

Their enthusiasm bordered on obsession. Wesley, with his precise, mathematical brain, part engineer, part gambler, could already see the blueprints in his mind's eye, the way light would hit the back bar, how the scent of aged oak and fresh varnish would dance with the perfume of top-shelf spirits. Adina was the anchor, the realist, the one who made lists and double-checked the fine print. Her hands were calloused from past projects, her eyes sharp enough to catch a lie before it finished forming on someone's tongue.

They weren't naïve. No, not that. Life had chipped away at them too often, too cruelly, for that. But they were hopeful, and sometimes that's even more dangerous. Hope is what gets you to walk into the dark with a candle, thinking you can banish the shadows.

They believed in the saloon. That it could be beautiful again. Alive again. That they could make it so.

What they hadn't yet considered, not really, not deep in their bones, was that sometimes, places like the Twilight Star didn't want to be brought back to life. Sometimes the dead have their own ideas about staying buried.

But for now, Wesley and Adina stood in the quiet gloom of their new purchase, hands clasped, breath fogging in the cold air. The building groaned softly in the wind, as if shifting in its sleep. The dust on the floor whispered with movement, though neither of them had taken a step.

Wesley Ahrens had come into the world beneath a hard, white sun in Be'er Sheva, Israel, a place where the dust gets into your bones and the wind doesn't so much blow as grind. He was raised in a tight, unyielding knot of family, where secrets didn't have far to travel and grudges were passed down like heirlooms. The Ahrens didn't speak of emotions, not really, but they felt them all the same. They just swallowed them whole and let them calcify.

At eighteen, Wesley, like every Israeli youth with a beating heart and a national ID number, found himself conscripted into the Israel Defence Forces. No choice. No questions. You put your boots on and did the work. But Wesley had always been the kind of boy who liked to fix broken things, radios, engines, wounded birds, and war, it turned out, broke a lot. So he leaned into the structure, followed the rules, and found himself admitted to the IDF Medical Academy. In the field, blood had a way of making time bend. He came to understand how fast life could leave a person, and how sometimes it hung on by a whisper.

By twenty-four, Wesley wore the title of surgical specialist. He had learned to cut and stitch and extract shrapnel from the meat of men while artillery rattled the world beyond the tents. In that same hot crucible of military service, he met Adina.

She was fire where he was stone.

Adina wasn't destined for medicine. She'd chosen a different path, a harder one in its own way, an officer's commission with the Israel Police Force, specialising in criminal investigation and counterterrorism. She didn't talk much about what she saw during her training. But once, just once, after too much red wine and not enough sleep, she told Wesley about a boy with a bomb sewn into his backpack. "He was eleven," she said. Then she didn't say anything else for a long time.

They were young, sharp-edged, and hungry for meaning. That shared gravity, service, purpose, the daily brush with things most people never see, drew them together like two loose pieces of metal on a magnet. And so they married, quietly, without fuss or ceremony. Just two souls trying to find shelter in the storm.

The early years were a blur of sterile white corridors, long briefings in sandbagged rooms, and whispered conversations in the hours just before dawn. Wesley's hands stayed slick with blood, while Adina's grew familiar with a pistol's grip and the weight of suspicion. They saw one another in fragments, breaks between deployments, seconds stolen in crowded mess halls, but somehow, that was enough. Maybe even more than enough. Because their love wasn't built in candlelight or poetry. It was forged in fire.

Then Caleb was born.

And everything changed.

The child came red-faced and wailing into a Tel Aviv hospital on a Tuesday that felt, for a moment, like a gift from God. He had

Adina's eyes, sharp and green, like something alive in the underbrush, and Wesley's quiet intensity. Holding him, Wesley felt something uncoil inside his chest, something he hadn't realised had been wound tight for years. For the first time in a long time, he saw a future not covered in gauze and gunmetal.

But here's the thing about peace: it's a delicate animal, quick to flee.

By the time he turned thirty, Wesley Ahrens had patched enough hearts to know that the human body was as fragile as a dry leaf in a stiff wind. He'd seen how life could vanish in a blink, how a single misstep in a scalpel's arc could mean the difference between triumph and tragedy. And though he didn't say it aloud, not even to Adina, he felt something begin to itch beneath the skin of his ambition. The battlefield surgeries, the long nights, the ghosts he carried home like invisible stowaways… they had done their job. Now it was time to do something else.

So, he made a decision. A big one. The kind that doesn't just alter the course of your life but lifts it off the tracks entirely and sends it hurtling into uncharted territory.

He applied for migration to the United States.

It wasn't a gamble, not with his credentials. Within three months, he had a green card and a prestigious offer from Highland Hospital in Oakland, California: a position as a specialist heart surgeon. The kind of role that came with heavy expectations and whisper-soft respect.

Adina, never one to sit idle in anyone's shadow, landed on her feet with the same quiet precision she'd honed back in Israel. She joined the Oakland Police Department as a detective, slipping into the American system like she'd been born to it. Her specialty, digging up truth in the dirt of the city, translated well.

She didn't smile much at work. Didn't need to. The badge did the talking, and the steel behind her eyes did the rest.

Their new life in the States had the clean smell of something freshly unwrapped. It was a good life. A sharp, clean slice of the American dream. They bought a modest home in the Oakland Hills, learned to love sourdough and strong coffee, and settled into a routine that most people would envy. Adina got used to the American way of doing things, loud, direct, and just a bit too proud, and Wesley, with his quiet grace and surgical discipline, began to thrive.

Their son Caleb flourished, too. A bright boy with a wide smile and a buzzcut, he grew into a sharp-edged man. The kind of kid teachers remember long after graduation. He finished his senior year of high school with the sort of promise that sparkles like tinsel, and then, without hesitation, joined the United States Marine Corps. Said it felt like the right thing to do. No coaxing. No dramatic scenes. Just a handshake, a duffel bag, and a one-way ticket to San Diego.

And then, just like that, they were alone again.

Twelve years had passed since they'd landed in America like pilgrims, armed with talent and grit. And now, with Caleb gone and building a future that didn't include bedtime stories or shared breakfasts, Wesley and Adina found themselves in the slow drift of midlife silence. Their careers were solid. Respected. Predictable. But that was the problem. Life had become too known. Too scheduled. They weren't afraid of aging, but they were afraid of boredom. Of inertia. Of dying with nothing more to show than a collection of pay stubs and photos in digital frames.

So when the Twilight Star Saloon showed up in a listing that Wesley stumbled across, half by chance, half by fate, something stirred in him. Not just curiosity. Recognition. A feeling like déjà vu wearing a different coat.

The building stood on Brannan Street like a half-forgotten relic from a dream, its redbrick bones weathered by decades of sun, salt air, and benign neglect. Most people wouldn't have looked twice. But Wesley and Adina weren't most people.

They stood in front of it one grey morning, hands in pockets, hearts strangely loud in their chests. The building seemed to exhale as they approached, like it had been holding its breath for them. Wesley saw past the rot and decay, past the broken windows and the ghost-smeared glass. In his mind, he was already drawing up floor plans, imagining hardwood floors polished to a mirror shine, gas lamps glowing like fireflies, the sharp clink of glasses echoing beneath laughter.

Adina, ever the realist, was already on the phone, lining up contractors, getting quotes, vetting suppliers. She'd always had a nose for people, especially the ones who said one thing but meant another. She moved through the world with quiet confidence, and even the sketchiest contractor thought twice before trying to sell her a line of bull.

They weren't fools. They knew this wasn't going to be easy. Every renovation would come with delays and dust. Every historical detail would have to be fought for, uncovered like bones in a graveyard. But that was the point. They wanted it to be hard. They needed it to mean something.

This wasn't just about building a bar.

It was about building a legacy.

The Twilight Star wasn't just a property. It was a chapter. A second act, maybe even a final one. It was wood and brick and old whispers, yes, but it was also a mirror. And in its dark glass, Wesley and Adina saw their future.

A place where laughter could live again. Where stories could rise like smoke. Where ghosts might walk the hallways, sure, but maybe they wouldn't walk alone anymore.

And if you stood there, just long enough, in the shadow of that old saloon... you could almost hear the music start again.

And now, here they were. Two weary professionals from lives of scalpels and sidearms, about to step into a new role neither of them had prepared for, renovators of a 136-year-old ghost of a building called the Twilight Star Saloon.

The rain had started, soft at first. The kind that felt like the building itself was breathing mist into the air. They stood just outside the sagging front door, its iron handle cold and slightly sticky, like a palm that had forgotten to let go.

Adina glanced at the warped sign hanging above, the paint flaked and bleached by decades of coastal sun and salt air. "What have we done, Wesley?" she said quietly, more to the building than to him.

Wesley looked out at the cracked sidewalk, the pale sky, the huddled storefronts that hadn't seen joy since Eisenhower was in office. He exhaled slowly. "Who cares? No more 3 a.m. call-outs. No more blood in the ER. No more knocking on strangers' doors with a badge and a face full of grief. I'm over it. And I know you are too."

He paused, watching a moth flutter against the cracked glass pane like it was looking for a way back into yesterday. Then he added, softer, with something like finality: "Fuck the money, Adina. I'd rather live a life than be a slave to it."

She laughed, but there was no warmth in it, just the kind of tired chuckle you give when you know you've already jumped off the cliff and now it's just about surviving the fall. "My darling, I think we've got a hell of a lot of slaving left to do right here. And let's face it, we don't know jack shit about renovations."

"Well," Wesley said, his voice light but his jaw set like stone, "that all starts tomorrow. Tonight, we celebrate." He took her hand, and for a moment, there was nothing but the sound of the city humming around them, old and indifferent.

They left the saloon site and began the short walk to the King Street hotel, an old railway-era structure that looked like it should've been condemned years ago, but at least the sheets were clean and the water ran hot. It would be home, for now. At least until they carved a livable corner from the wreckage of the Twilight Star.

They thought they had it all figured out. Or at least, they wanted to believe that.

The saloon's lower level had once been the kind of place where the smoke hung low and the lies came thick and fast. There was a massive bar, a beast of oiled timber that smelled faintly of whiskey and stories. Beyond it lay a cavernous room with uneven floorboards and tarnished sconces, probably once used for cards, dice, and quiet cheating behind a smile. A smaller bar sat beside a curtained dining space, positioned just off a battered old kitchen. They guessed that was what it had been, anyway. Hard to tell now through the cobwebs and decay.

The kitchen itself was a beast of its own, a wide space with cast-iron fuel ranges that had been converted to oil sometime after the war. Too old now, too tired. The smell of grease and soot still clung to the walls like the aftershave of a long-dead cook.

A small reception office squatted near the front, tucked behind a cracked window that had once held a bell. Behind it, a larger office loomed with old cabinets and sagging filing drawers. Another door led to a side room with a single iron bedframe and broken dresser. The manager's quarters, probably. The place where the secrets piled up.

The main stairway was a spine of timber and soot, its rail warped from age and fire. That was where most of the damage was. Smoke-stained walls bled up to the second floor like ink spilled from a bottle. The fire had eaten through parts of the corridor, blackened the ceiling, and left scars that still smelled faintly of ash.

Eight rooms on each side of the corridor. Each one with its own story, or maybe its own ghost.

The roof was ruined, half caved-in and patched with a blue tarp that flapped like a warning flag in the wind. The load-bearing walls between rooms had been compromised, charred to the point of danger. It was Adina's idea, brilliant and grimly practical, to turn every second bedroom into an ensuite. "Just perfect," she'd murmured, tracing the plan with her fingertip. First, third, fourth, and sixth bedrooms would get the upgrade. The rest would remain, a little less glamorous but no less necessary.

Two smaller single rooms at each end of the corridor would remain untouched, positioned beside the communal bathrooms that somehow had survived the flames, the storms, and the silence.

Downstairs, the flooring would need full replacement in spots. Hardwood planks had warped from moisture, some even popped like loose teeth. The entire surface would need sanding, polishing, and sealing. The walls, plaster over old brick, were cracked, flaking, and painted in hues no one could name. Those would need to be patched, scraped, and lovingly restored.

Yet despite the ruin, there were touches of beauty. The bars, both of them, were solid timber. They'd aged like good bourbon.

All they needed was sanding, lacquer, and maybe a little reverence. One of them, the larger of the two, had three bullet holes in the front. Smooth and clean. Like they had been made yesterday.

Neither of them mentioned the bullet holes.

Neither of them wanted to ask what lay behind them.

The bar had its quirks, all right. The kind of quirks that whispered stories when no one was around to listen.

Running the full length of both bars were old refrigerated cupboards, massive, iron-handled things with embossed brass lettering and smooth, icebox-white enamel interiors. They'd been electric, remarkably so, proudly proclaiming their birth year: 1880. That was just a year after electricity lit up the streets of San Francisco, a marvel in its day. State of the art, the sign read in a curling, chipped typeface. The words felt ghostly now. You could almost hear the crackle of Edison-era current humming through their long-dead coils.

But time takes its toll on all things manmade, no matter how proud or revolutionary. The cold boxes were done. Every last one would have to go, just like the old keg-drawing system that once pumped foaming beer from the stone cellar below, straight to the polished taps above. The tubes, like arteries long since clotted with time, lay brittle and yellowed, their copper veins twisted with corrosion and the scent of old yeast.

And then there were the restrooms.

Indescribable was the only polite word for them. And even that felt generous. Adina had stepped into the women's first and come out visibly paler, whispering something about "things that had no business growing in tile grout."

Three total facilities: a male room, tight and claustrophobic, with a cracked urinal and two doors that wouldn't lock; a female

Max Barrington

room with five cubicles, their partitions listing like sunken gravestones; and a third, a supposed unisex facility that looked like it had hosted more crime than convenience. All were to be ripped out to the studs and redrawn. Sterile, fresh, and functional.

The only areas that seemed untouched by time's cruel hand were the reception office and the main office behind it. The reception space was compact but efficient, its tiny kitchenette a time capsule from the 1950s, and the attached bathroom clean, functional, and blessedly mould-free. The larger office was nearly pristine, as though some unseen force had preserved it while the rest of the building decayed. The air in that room was...different. Still. Heavier.

It was the wallpaper that ruined the illusion of elegance.

Dark green. Embossed. Almost scaly. Like it had been peeled from the hide of some ancient creature lurking just behind the plaster wall. It shimmered faintly when the light caught it, not gold or silver, but something older. Something that didn't quite belong. Wesley had run his fingers across it once, and swore he'd felt it pulse.

Still, the furniture was magnificent, carved mahogany, oak, even rosewood. Every drawer slid open with a satisfying shhhk, the brass handles gleaming beneath a thin coat of dust. The chairs were wide and high-backed with curled legs and green velvet seats that had faded just enough to make them elegant rather than garish. The dining tables and chairs in the main room were equally remarkable, pieces you might find in a collector's gallery or an eccentric billionaire's private lodge.

They were worth something, that much was obvious. But Wesley and Adina weren't here to sell history, they were here to live inside it.

So they made the call. The two offices and the smaller side room, the old manager's quarters, would become their temporary home. A makeshift fortress while the contractors descended like ants on the rest of the structure, hammering, sawing, sealing, and sanding their way toward the future.

The barricades had already started to come down, those ugly sheets of plywood pried off the windows and doorways like dead skin. Light poured in. Real, honest-to-God daylight that seemed to push the shadows back. For the first time since they bought the place, the saloon didn't feel haunted. It felt...possible.

Adina, always the first to act, started in the larger office. She moved quietly, reverently, removing paintings and brittle-framed photographs from the walls. Some were strange, Victorian women in stiff gowns standing beside stern-faced men in suits and bowler hats. Others showed the saloon itself, back when the streets were still dirt and horses stood tethered at the post.

She stacked them carefully, like relics being prepared for burial. Then she turned to the wallpaper.

The green stared back.

She peeled the first corner, and behind it, something darker.

It was an accident, really. Most important things were.

Adina had been working her way through the cluttered wall behind the desk, heavy frames, dusty certificates, brittle maps with curling corners, when she reached for a portrait of General Ulysses S. Grant. The frame came off with a reluctant creak, revealing something she hadn't expected: a steel face embedded in the wall, matte black and faintly pitted, as though it had endured a fire and lived to tell the tale.

The nameplate was intact, burnished brass and proud:
Briggs & Son, Rochester NY.

Max Barrington

A thick escutcheon plate slid sideways beneath her fingers, revealing a keyhole large enough to swallow a cigar. The safe was about a foot square, set into the brickwork like it had grown there, part of the original bones of the building, untouched and unnoticed for who knows how many decades.

Of course, it was locked.

She stared at it, heart beating just a little harder than it had a moment before. Something about it...felt wrong. Not dangerous, not exactly. But significant. Like finding a tombstone in your basement.

Her first thought was that the key had to be somewhere, maybe still in the desk, tucked inside an old book or jammed behind a drawer. She spent the better part of an hour combing through both offices, methodically opening every cabinet, pulling out drawers, checking behind panels, tapping along the backs for any false bottoms or hidden catches.

Nothing.

Eventually, she called a locksmith. A local man named Graham Edwards who'd sounded like he'd smoked a pack a day since the war, which war, Adina didn't ask. He'd chuckled down the line when she said the name Briggs & Son.

"Antique safe, that's a good one," he'd rasped. "They built 'em like coffins. Some you can pick. Others, you got one shot before the tumblers seize up for good. I'll be over late this afternoon."

While she waited, Adina returned to the wallpaper. She had avoided the wall with the safe, superstition more than strategy, but resumed her work around it, slowly unwrapping the room like a mummified relic. The paper came off in long, stubborn strips. It flaked in some places like dead skin, and in others tore as if resisting her touch.

The wall didn't like being exposed.

Meanwhile, Wesley had gone full-blown archeologist out in the main rooms. The contractors, two young blokes and an older man with hands like cracked leather, were beginning to strip the saloon of its old furnishings, bar stools, battered benches, broken banquettes, and the odd splintered high-chair or tipped-over bureau. They piled it all in the central space, a dusty hill of history waiting to be sorted: what might be salvaged, what might be sold, and what would be cast aside.

Wesley sorted with a calm detachment. He appreciated the craftsmanship, admired the solid dovetail joints, the aged timber grains, but his mind wasn't on the furniture.

It was on the safe.

He didn't like it either.

Something about it didn't sit right, not the fact that it had been hidden, not even that it was locked, but the feeling he got when he was in that office alone. A pressure. Like someone standing just behind him, waiting to speak but never quite saying the words. He hadn't told Adina, of course. No need to spook her over something that could just be his own nerves. They'd been through worse. Way worse.

But still.

The safe had a presence.

It was like the room had rearranged itself around it, subtly warping toward that small square door like iron shavings to a magnet. It pulled at you. It watched.

Back in the office, Adina paused her work and stared at the thing.

Not long now.

Whatever lay behind that iron face would soon be open to the light for the first time in a century.

She wasn't sure whether to feel excited or afraid.

It had been a big day, at least by the standards of demolition and dust, but Wesley could see little to show for it. The first day of renovations was always chaotic, like cracking open a long-sealed tomb and trying to make sense of the bones. The contractors had been busy, sure, but the saloon still felt more ghost than business.

Three months. That was the deadline.

The grand reopening of the historic Golden Spur Saloon.

The contractor, a wiry man with a nicotine-stained moustache and an eternal smirk, had sworn he'd have everything finished in ten weeks.

"Ten weeks, easy," he'd said, like it was a blessing.

Wesley, ever cautious, had added another two weeks to the calendar. Just in case the ghosts didn't cooperate.

As the sun dipped low, long shadows stretched across the floorboards, and the men began packing up for the day. The air was thick with sawdust and old secrets, and Wesley found himself wandering back toward the main office. The sound of paper tearing reached him before he saw her, his wife, Adina, sleeves rolled, her hair pinned up messily, standing in the centre of the room with a length of vile green wallpaper clutched in her hand like a snake's shed skin.

She was working that wall like it had personally offended her.

He stepped inside, his gaze drawn immediately to the square shadow on the wall, darker than the rest, where sunlight had never touched, where a portrait of General Grant had once hung in perpetual salute. And there it was: the safe.

Squat. Black. Watching.

Wesley raised his eyebrows and gave her a crooked grin. "Found treasure, did you?"

Adina didn't look up. "I don't know yet. Still waiting for the locksmith."

"No key?"

She snorted, a short, frustrated sound. "Spent over an hour digging through every drawer, cubby, and coat pocket in both offices. Found nothing but some dead spiders and a pair of antique cufflinks. Called a locksmith. Said he'd be here today…" she trailed off, glancing at the bare doorway, her voice tinged with skepticism. "But like everything else around here, that promise seems about a hundred years out of date."

As if on cue, because fate is funny like that, a voice called out from the direction of the front bar.

"Helloo?… Anyone here?"

Adina straightened, wiping her hands on her jeans. "In here!" she called, walking toward the voice.

Footsteps echoed, confident but not hurried. A tall, slim man stepped into the room, framed by the doorway like a figure from an old noir film. He wore a canvas coat and carried a small leather valet bag that looked older than he did. His face was lean, lined, and framed by glasses with round lenses that caught the dying light in a way that made his eyes disappear entirely.

"Your foreman let me in as he was leaving," the man said, his voice smooth and quiet. "I'm the locksmith you called. Graham Edwards."

Adina gave him a quick, appraising glance and then gestured to Wesley. "I'm Adina. This is my husband, Wesley."

Graham nodded politely.

She pointed to the wall, where the safe sat like a dark eye in a sickly green face. "That's the monster over there."

The locksmith turned slowly, his expression unreadable as he looked at the safe. He took a few deliberate steps forward, then crouched before it, resting his bag on the floorboards. His fingers hovered over the escutcheon like a priest blessing a tombstone.

"Briggs & Son," he murmured. "Haven't seen one of these in years. Built to last. And to stay closed."

He looked over his shoulder, and for a brief second, his glasses caught the light again, blinding, reflective, like twin moons. When he spoke, his voice dropped an octave.

"Let's see what this old thing's been hiding, shall we?"

The locksmith stepped closer to the wall safe and squinted at the nameplate with the kind of reverence usually reserved for vintage cars and grandfather clocks.

"Ahh, a Briggs & Son," he said, drawing out the name like it meant something personal. "Indeed. This one might be a bit of a challenge. Pommy Milner lock by the look of it. Solid bit of craftsmanship. Not a toy."

He ran a fingertip along the sliding escutcheon with a tenderness that felt almost inappropriate, then looked over his shoulder.

"I'll give it about an hour trying to pick it. If that doesn't work, I'm afraid it's the drill. And if I go that route, you'll need a new lock, those don't come cheap. Not cheap at all." He gave a tight smile, the kind that said you've been warned.

Adina leaned on the edge of the desk, arms folded, expression unreadable. "We've no idea what's in there. Most likely nothing. But it's a handy spot for a safe, especially if we decide to keep using the office."

Wesley chimed in from behind her. "There's another one next door. Bigger. Door's standing wide open though, so hopefully less drama with that one. We'll need keys made for it too."

Graham Edwards nodded once and got to work. The tools from his little leather bag were unrolled on a cloth like a surgeon preparing for a peculiar operation. He inserted a tension wrench, then a pick, and leaned in, the only sound now the faint clicking of metal on metal and the occasional creak from the building settling into its age.

Adina fetched a chair and positioned it a few feet away, curiosity shining in her eyes. She perched on the edge like a kid watching someone unwrap a Christmas gift that might just explode.

Five minutes passed. Then ten. The tension wasn't dramatic, it just simmered beneath the surface like a low fire in an old hearth.

Then,

Click.

It echoed louder than expected in the still office. A sound that suggested not just a mechanical success, but an invitation.

"There we go!" Graham announced with a satisfied sigh, stepping back. "You can do the honours, madam."

Adina didn't hesitate. She was up and across the room in an instant, fingers curling around the safe's small handle. For a moment she paused, just a beat, and then pulled.

The little door creaked open, revealing its ancient belly.

Inside, nestled alone in the dark like a relic left behind in a hurry, was a single item.

A key.

Adina blinked, leaned closer, and let out a quiet sigh. "Well… not quite Blackbeard's treasure."

Wesley peered over her shoulder and let out a short, sharp laugh. "And what a bloody perfect place to keep a spare key, for the safe itself. Genius."

The locksmith gave them a dry smile. "Keeps me in business. Want me to make some copies?"

"Yes, please," Wesley said. "Two, just in case one ends up in a safe again."

Edwards pocketed the key with a practiced flick of the wrist, then gestured toward the door. "I'll pull the lock from the other safe before I go. I'll have your new keys by tomorrow afternoon."

He packed up, the little tools slipping back into their places like they'd never been used. As he made his way out, Wesley watched him go and shook his head with a bemused grin.

Another little job done. Nothing exciting. No gold coins. No lost deeds or cryptic ledgers. Just a spare key in a safe.

But the building was old. And old buildings liked to keep their secrets close.

They just had to know where to listen.

The next morning, Adina was elbow-deep in peeling the last stubborn strip of wallpaper off the office wall. The same wall that held the old safe, cold and silent, like some relic from a different, darker time. The wallpaper, a faded green with a weird, ugly embossing that always made her skin crawl, was sticking like it had a grip of its own.

That's when she saw it, a narrow slit, almost invisible if you weren't looking, running straight down the wall just beneath the safe. It was about seven inches long, like a tiny secret someone had carved out and then covered up, hoping no one would ever find it.

Her hand tightened around the scraper, and she pressed it carefully against the tear. The paper crackled, whispering like dry bones as she pried it open. And there, folded and wedged behind the wall, was a piece of paper. Yellowed and old, the kind of thing that smelled faintly of dust and mothballs even though it was hidden for who knows how long.

Adina pulled it free slowly, like she was handling something fragile and dangerous all at once. She unfolded the paper on the cluttered desk, careful not to crease it. The lines were shaky but deliberate, a hand-drawn map. Jagged lines traced the edges of some place she couldn't recognise, with marks and symbols that hinted at secrets and stories buried deep.

She sat down, her eyes locked on the map, heart beating a little faster, fingers trembling just a touch. There was something about this old building she hadn't figured out yet, something watching just beneath the surface.

"Hey! Wes, come here! Check this out!" Her voice broke through the quiet like a sudden crack of thunder.

Wesley appeared in the doorway, rubbing sleep from his eyes, carrying his usual mix of curiosity and skepticism. "What've you got there? Was it in the safe?"

Adina shook her head. "No, no. It was behind the wallpaper, right below the safe. Here, I'll show you." She stood and walked to the spot, pointing at the slit like it was a wound in the wall.

He squinted, then grinned. "Well, that's something. Interesting, for sure. I'll give it a good look later."

He glanced around the room, the dust motes hanging thick in the shafts of morning light, and then said, "By the way, they're stripping the old roof today. Section by section. Trying to get it done while the weather's still decent. They're putting up a canvas cover so nothing comes in, but if you hear weird noises overhead, don't freak out. It's just the roof coming off."

Adina smiled thinly, her mind still half on the map. "Good to know. I'd better get back to work."

She folded the map carefully, sliding it into the top drawer of the desk, where it lay hidden but heavy with promise. Outside, the workers' hammers and saws echoed through the building, a symphony of destruction and renewal.

But inside that dusty old office, something old and forgotten was waking up, waiting for its story to be told.

The Twilight Star Saloon

Contrary to the contractor's confident promise of finishing the renovations within ten weeks, the Twilight Star Saloon took just a week longer to emerge from its dusty chrysalis. Ten weeks had sounded like a firm deadline at first, but the extra seven days stretched out longer than they should have, each one feeling heavier and slower than the last, as if the building itself was resisting its own resurrection.

For Wesley and Adina, that extra week was a minor setback, nothing more than a wrinkle in their carefully laid plans. They told themselves it was a blessing in disguise, a final chance to perfect every last detail. But late at night, when the contractors had gone home and the silence crept back into the empty rooms, the saloon seemed to settle in around them like a living thing, watching, waiting for something.

The big day was coming, and the couple threw themselves into the next phase, promotion. Bright, colourful flyers were printed, bursting with bold fonts and promises of the Twilight Star's grand reopening. The words almost shouted from the page, a siren call to the neighbourhood to come back to the old place, to step through its doors and be part of something new and old all at once.

Wesley and Adina walked those streets, rain or shine, pounding the pavement with the kind of determination that felt more like desperation. They slipped flyers under windshield wipers, tucked them into shop windows, and handed them out with smiles that were just a little too wide, eyes that flickered too quickly away.

The work was exhausting, the ache in their feet and backs a dull reminder that the dream they had fought for was almost within reach. Yet, beneath the tired smiles, there was a flicker of something else, an unspoken anticipation, a tension they couldn't shake, like the saloon was holding its breath.

Inside, the restaurant and bars were staffed with a bustle of efficiency and nervous excitement. The hotel rooms, each one cleaned and made to sparkle, stood ready to welcome their first guests in years. The Twilight Star gleamed with new life, its polished wood and shining brass fighting to hold onto a whisper of its haunted past.

It was perfect, or as perfect as something like this could be. But in the back of their minds, both Wesley and Adina wondered what shadows still lurked in the corners, waiting for the doors to swing open.

The opening was set for midday on a Friday, a strategic choice, or so Wesley insisted, meant to catch the lunch crowd and build momentum into the evening. Noon came with the clang of the old saloon doors swinging open, the familiar creak echoing down the polished floorboards, and the Twilight Star was officially back in business.

The first wave of customers trickled in like a slow-moving tide, curious locals, a few wandering passersby drawn by the novelty of a reborn legend. Lunch service unfolded quietly, almost hesitantly. Plates clattered, voices murmured, but the energy felt thin, like a house settling into a long-forgotten groove.

By three o'clock, the buzz had nearly evaporated. The saloon's vast rooms seemed to swallow the few remaining patrons whole, leaving only a group of six U.S. Navy sailors at the pool table in the main bar, their laughter bouncing off the walls in sharp bursts. They played their game with careless grins, the only real life in the room.

Adina stood behind the bar, her smile forced, eyes shadowed with disappointment she didn't bother to hide. Wesley, ever the optimist, slid a reassuring hand onto her shoulder.

"Evenings bring a different crowd," he said softly, as if willing it to be true.

And true it was. As the sun slipped down behind the low horizon, painting the sky in bruised purples and blood reds, the Twilight Star began to stir. Shadows lengthened and deepened, but with the dark came a pulse, a heartbeat rising in the rooms upstairs where seven of the hotel's rooms were booked, two for multiple nights, no less. The bars filled gradually, glasses clinking, voices rising, the atmosphere thickening like smoke curling from a forgotten cigarette.

Wesley and Adina moved through the crowd like reluctant royalty, shaking hands, sharing laughs, gauging every expression. They asked quietly, almost too quietly, if anyone had come because of the flyers they'd spent hours distributing, their carefully folded promises of rebirth and revelry. The answers were always the same: no, nobody had heard of them. The flyers, like ghosts, seemed to vanish into thin air.

Still, the growing crowd was a balm, a sign that the saloon was breathing again, filling its lungs with life and noise. By ten o'clock, the bar was comfortably busy, warm laughter spilling into every corner, the scent of whiskey and spilt beer mingling with the faint trace of old wood and something else, something faint, like memory or regret.

Wesley and Adina found refuge in a small, dimly lit bar tucked away in a quieter corner, their bodies finally allowed to slump into chairs, drinks cradled in hands that trembled just a little from the day's tension. They exchanged tired smiles, reflecting on the day's mixed fortunes. It wasn't the triumphant opening they'd dreamed of, not yet, but it was a start. A foothold.

Their conversation drifted, words softening and slowing, when two elderly gentlemen appeared through the haze of cigarette smoke and low conversation. Warm smiles crept onto the men's faces, but there was something in their eyes, an odd flicker, an uncanny familiarity that set Wesley's nerves on edge, though he couldn't say why.

"Good evening," one of them said, voice smooth but carrying an echo of something unspoken. "We thought we'd come see the place ourselves."

And just like that, the past slipped in through the doors once more, like a shadow stretching long over the polished floorboards of the Twilight Star.

The two men settled into the dim corner with a casual ease that suggested they belonged here, or at least had belonged once. They looked to be in their seventies, though their sun-weathered faces told stories that stretched far beyond mere years, a lifetime of labor under harsh skies, of hard-earned wisdom and hard-lived days. Neatly pressed shirts tucked into well-worn jeans, boots scuffed from years of use, eyes sharp and steady like the kind of men who'd seen too much to be fooled by much anymore.

They ordered beers with quiet authority, the kind of order you place when you've sat in this very seat a hundred times before. The bartender poured, the glasses caught the low light, and the men turned their attention to Wesley and Adina.

"You two must be the new owners," said one of the men, reaching out with a hand calloused from years of honest work. "Name's Harry. This here's my brother, Lou. We've been waiting a long time to see this place open again."

Harry's handshake was firm, a grip that spoke of trust but also challenge, like he was sizing them up, figuring out if they were worthy of the old place. Lou smiled softly, a little faded around the edges, like the last embers of a dying fire, and nodded.

The brothers were local legends in their own right, keepers of stories that only people who'd lived here through the good and bad could tell. They spoke of the Twilight Star Saloon's glory days, when the walls vibrated with laughter, when the floor shook with the stamp of boots and the crash of pints raised in celebration or in defiance.

"Back in the day," Harry said with a chuckle that rattled like a loose hinge, "this place was the heart of the neighbourhood. If you wanted a drink, a meal, or just some good company, this was where you'd come. No questions asked."

Lou's voice softened, tinged with something like mourning or reverence. "Used to be packed every Friday night. Wall-to-wall people, shouting over the music and the fights. Folks from all over, not just locals. You've got a good thing going, bringing it back. People just need to hear about it."

Their stories painted the saloon's past in vivid strokes, rowdy nights where strangers became friends and enemies found themselves on the wrong side of a barstool, where music and voices tangled until dawn, where every cracked wooden table held secrets and memories and spilled dreams.

Wesley and Adina listened, buoyed by the brothers' encouragement, feeling the weight of the place settle over them, not as a burden, but as a legacy.

As the night wound down and the last amber drops of beer disappeared from their glasses, Harry leaned in with a kind of knowing look that didn't quite reach his eyes.

"Don't worry too much about today," he said, voice low and steady. "It takes time for word to spread. Give it a couple of weeks, and you'll see. This place… it's got history. And people, well, they love history. Especially when it's right under their noses."

There was something almost too deliberate in the way he said it, like a warning or a promise whispered in a language only the old walls understood.

The brothers stood, settled their tab, and faded back into the shadows of the Twilight Star Saloon, leaving Wesley and Adina alone with the heavy hum of the night, and a feeling that the saloon's past was far from finished with them.

As the last glass was dried and the final barstool straightened, the Twilight Star fell into silence. The laughter, the clink of bottles, the murmur of stories told over pints, all of it faded like smoke into the midnight hush. Wesley and Adina moved through the quiet saloon with tired limbs but lifted spirits, locking the doors behind them with a sense of quiet ceremony. The day hadn't unfolded quite as they'd imagined. It hadn't roared. But it had begun, and beginnings, they both knew, were sacred.

Outside, a cold mist curled through the alleys and along the worn brick of Brannan Street. Inside, the air still held the warmth of bodies, of hope, and of something else too, something older. Wesley paused at the bar for a final moment, fingers resting on the polished timber. Somewhere beneath the surface, he imagined, lay the imprints of a hundred years of elbows and fists, of secrets whispered and tempers flared.

They turned in for the night, retreating to the modest comfort of their upstairs quarters. Sleep came quickly to Adina, her dreams tangled with the rough laughter of Harry and Lou, their weathered faces shining with memory. Wesley lay awake longer, watching the patterns of shadow and streetlight crawl across the ceiling. He thought of the old ledgers, the nameless invoices, the disagreement over whether this place had been the Twilight, the Starlight, or something else altogether.

But as the hours deepened and the city sighed around them, none of it seemed to matter. The saloon had a name now, one they'd chosen together, and that name had been spoken again, loudly, warmly, with clinking glasses and ringing laughter.

Whatever had come before, the Twilight Star Saloon had found new life. It had been awakened. And if the ghosts were watching from the corners, leaning against old beams with crooked smiles, Wesley figured they could stay, so long as they respected the rules of the new owners.

In the stillness, he finally allowed his eyes to close.

Tomorrow, the story would continue.

"You know this was never the Twilight, don't you?" said Gerry, one of the older locals, his voice carrying that dry, tobacco-edged rasp that came with a thousand beers and a hundred secrets. He said it to Adina over the low murmur of the near-empty bar, where the floor still held the scent of stale hops and old wood polish.

Adina looked up, a flicker of surprise breaking across her face. "Oh?" she managed, blinking like someone pulled into a conversation she hadn't expected to have.

Gerry leaned in a little, elbows creaking on the varnished timber. "Two old-timers were in here last night, yeah? Harry and Lou. You probably know 'em, or will. They get around. Anyway, sounds like they gave you the grand tour of memory lane."

"They did," she said. "They talked about how this place used to rock, especially on Fridays. Sounded like something out of a movie."

Gerry gave a low chuckle, but there was no humor in it. "Well, if they remember that, then they're older than God. Because this place? It's been shuttered for over a hundred years. I think you'll find they've got their wires crossed with the old Twilight. That was a different place altogether."

"That's right!" piped up Matt, another regular whose ball cap had more grease on it than fabric. He'd been half-listening while cleaning up some glasses behind the bar. "The Twilight was over on Kearny Street. 'Bout two miles around the coastline. This joint here, far as my old man ever told me, used to be the Starlight. Yeah… Starlight Saloon, that's what it was."

Wesley, who had just walked in from the hallway, froze mid-step. The blood drained from his face, ever so slightly. That wasn't what the records said. That wasn't what the paperwork said. That wasn't what anything had said.

"No," Gerry said, shaking his head slowly like a priest denying absolution. "The Starlight was up closer to Third Street. I'm telling you, my grandfather swore by it. Said Wyatt Earp used to drink there when he was in town, back when San Francisco had grit in its teeth and blood under its fingernails."

"You could be right, Gerry," Matt said with a shrug, offering a kind of truce in the fog of fading memories. Then he turned back to Wesley and Adina, his voice softer now. "It gets messy, y'know? After the '06 quake, whole neighborhoods vanished. Streets shifted. Buildings just… went. It's no wonder nobody can agree on what used to stand where."

Later that night, after the last pint was poured and the doors locked tight against the creeping Pacific fog, Adina turned in. Their apartment was just off the main office, a snug little flat with a lounge, a modest TV, and a bed that still smelled faintly of fresh paint and old ghosts.

Wesley stayed up. He'd claimed the reception office as his vigil post, self-appointed night watchman of a place that may or may not have existed as they believed it did.

Under the yellow hum of a desk lamp, he flipped through crumbling ledgers and day sheets, careful not to tear the brittle pages. The handwriting danced in flourishes from a bygone era, copperplate that whispered of cigars and gunpowder and whiskey bought by the barrel. 1895, 1896, 1897…

No mention of Twilight Star. Not once. No letterhead, no receipt, no supplier invoice. Just "Saloon, Brannan Street." Like the name had never mattered. Like the building had simply been there, nameless, timeless, and waiting.

He sat back in the creaky office chair, the springs moaning like a tired ghost. Maybe it didn't matter. Maybe names were just paint on a signboard. The place was the Twilight Star now, and it would stay that way. He and Adina had breathed life into the bones, called the spirits home.

But still, something gnawed at the back of his mind like a rat in the walls. Why had those old men spoken about it like they remembered?

And more importantly, how could they remember a place that hadn't existed for a hundred years?

They'd owned the Twilight Star Saloon for just over three years now, three long, hard-fought years. Not golden, not glorious, but solid. Reliable. Like the steady rhythm of an old clock that kept decent time as long as you remembered to wind it.

Business wasn't booming, exactly, but it wasn't tanking either. The saloon had settled into a kind of stubborn survival. A heartbeat. Some nights were flush with laughter and full tables, the sound of pool balls cracking off each other like distant gunfire, drinks flowing, jukebox humming with country rock and West Coast soul. Other nights, they'd watch the minutes drag by, polishing already clean glasses and waiting for the next pair of boots to walk through the door.

Wesley and Adina ran the place together, day in, day out. No manager, no middlemen. Just the two of them, like they were trying to keep a campfire burning in the middle of a snowstorm. It was exhausting work, sure. But it was theirs. That counted for something.

Caleb helped out when he could. That is, when he felt like it.

More often than not, he was on the other side of the bar, nursing a beer or a double shot of bourbon, flanked by a handful of Marines or Navy boys from the shipyards or the dockside bases. He had a way of drawing them in, like gravity. When Caleb said, "Come to the Star," they came. The rooms upstairs filled fast when word got out that servicemen got a special rate, a little discount here, a free round there.

Wesley and Adina didn't mind, not really. The uniforms kept the saloon busy and the barstools warm. But Caleb, he was another story.

He wasn't active duty anymore. Hadn't been for almost a year. The limp was slight, almost unnoticeable unless you knew what to look for. A drag of the right leg, a hesitation on stairs. Most people didn't notice. Most people didn't know what to notice.

He'd said it was his tendon, something called the Plantaris, a stringy little bastard of a thing that could wreck a man's stride in an instant. But Wesley had worked construction in his younger days, and Adina had studied kinesiology for a semester back when college still seemed like a thing. They both knew you don't get pensioned out of the United States Marine Corps at thirty years old for a Plantaris injury, not unless there's something else going on.

When they asked, gently at first, then with a little more steel in their voices, Caleb would just go quiet. His face would cloud over, and the light in his eyes would blink out like a dying bulb. He'd look at the floor, sip his drink, and change the subject. And you didn't push Caleb. You never pushed Caleb.

They'd seen what happened when you did.

So they waited. And one night, after too many drinks and a silence thick enough to choke on, Caleb told them. Just laid it out in a voice so low it might have been mistaken for wind scraping against the windowpane.

He'd been special forces, Marine Recon, the shadow walkers. Men who went places they weren't supposed to be and did things no one was supposed to know about. The kind of missions that didn't show up in any debriefs or yearbooks. He'd worn the Green Beret too, which was strange because that was usually Army, but he said it like it meant something, like it meant everything.

And just like that, a torn tendon ended it. Not because he couldn't walk, but because Recon demanded more than a man could give when he wasn't whole.

43

Wesley remembered thinking it wasn't the limp that got him pensioned, it was the way he watched the exits, the way he never sat with his back to the door. The way he listened more than he talked. Like a man who'd learned the hard way that silence could save your life, and noise could get you killed.

Caleb never spoke of his missions. Not once. But every so often, Wesley would find him outside, smoking a cigarette, staring out toward the fog-draped bay like he was expecting something to crawl out of it.

And on those nights, Wesley didn't ask questions.

Because some ghosts don't come in chains.
Some come wearing dog tags, and walk with a limp.

When Caleb first announced he was joining the Marines, his parents looked at him like he'd just declared he was moving to the moon.

He wasn't the sort of kid you imagined in uniform. Hell, he wasn't the sort of kid you imagined outside at all. Pale as a fish belly, skinny as a rake, and built like the runt of a malnourished litter. He weighed in at a hundred and sixty pounds if he'd just eaten a full breakfast and kept his shoes on. And the glasses, those thick black-rimmed monstrosities that made his eyes look like marbles floating in milk.

And when he told them he'd signed the papers, was headed for basic training at MCRD San Diego, they nearly had heart attacks at the kitchen table.

They tried to talk him out of it. They begged him. Suggested college, trade school, maybe something safe like forestry. But Caleb had that look in his eye, quiet, steady, unshakable, the look of someone who wasn't just determined, but called. Like he was trying to prove something, maybe to them. Maybe to himself.

At the train station, Adina wept. Wesley shook his head in a way that meant good luck, son, but you're going to get your ass kicked. And then Caleb was gone, duffel over his shoulder, glasses fogged from his breath, heading toward the hardest damn thing he'd ever do in his life.

The moment he stepped off the white school bus and onto the burning tarmac of the Marine Corps Recruit Depot, the California sun already drilling holes through his scalp, a voice rang out like a bullet cracking against steel.

"What in the name of Jesus H. Christ is this thing?"

That was Drill Instructor Gunnery Sergeant Marvin Bilingsky. A ten-year veteran with forearms like butcher's hams and a voice like God with a hangover.

Bilingsky had seen all kinds in his years, farm boys, gangbangers, cowards pretending to be tough and tough kids pretending to be cowards. But Caleb? Caleb was something else entirely. He looked like he'd taken a wrong turn on the way to a chess tournament.

To Bilingsky's credit, he didn't care that Caleb was Jewish. He was Jewish himself. Had the Star of David tattooed on his left bicep and didn't give a rat's ass who saw it. But he did care that this kid had walked into his platoon like a lamb into the slaughterhouse.

The other recruits noticed right away. They always did. The weak ones, the quiet ones, the different ones, they were like chum in the water. And basic training? It was a shark tank.

Bilingsky knew what was coming. The whispering, the cold shoulders, the jokes that started as teasing and turned into something uglier. Recruits didn't just get broken down by the system, they got broken by each other.

And he hated that. Hated that he'd now have to spend extra hours keeping the wolves at bay. Hated that he'd have to protect this skinny, twitchy kid with the librarian glasses from becoming another footnote in the company's history.

But most of all, he hated the creeping thought he couldn't quite push down: This kid's going to surprise us. And we're all going to pay for underestimating him.

Because sometimes, the lamb walks into the slaughterhouse with a fuse already burning.

And when it blows?
No one walks away clean.

Caleb

The drill instructors roared like lions, their voices ricocheting off the concrete and steel of the parade deck like thunder in a steel drum. It was the kind of chaos that had order to it, a savage ritual made to break down flesh and mind and rebuild it into something cold, hard, and useful. The recruits stood at attention, wide-eyed and terrified, most of them trying not to piss themselves. And for good reason. This wasn't summer camp. This was boot.

It was the usual welcome ceremony, if you could call it that. Like something straight out of Full Metal Jacket, only without the Hollywood glint. There was spittle flying, obscenities spat like machine gun fire, and a distinct smell in the air: sweat, oil, fear. Gunnery Sergeant Marvin Bilingsky had seen it all before. This was his orchestra, and he was the conductor. Every insult a note. Every scream a beat. Every humiliated recruit a goddamned instrument.

Except one.

He didn't call Caleb out by name. Not in front of the others. That would've painted a target on the kid's back the size of Nebraska. No, he waited until the others were herded away like sheep toward their bunks, buzzing with the leftover electricity of panic.

Then, and only then, did Bilingsky lean in close to Caleb, his breath warm with coffee and rage.

"You do not look fit," he said, his voice low, coiled, venomous. "Not fit to be here. These plebes, hell, my plebes, they're going to destroy you. Do you hear me?"

"Yes, sir, Sergeant, sir!" Caleb barked, trying to summon a spine.

"Cut the shit, Ahrens," Bilingsky snapped, his voice flat now, quieter, heavier. "I'm not giving you a pep talk. I'm giving you a goddamn survival manual. We've got a gym on base. You'll be in there every evening after chow. I'll get you the pass. The staff sergeant there knows what you need. You follow his orders like they came from God himself. Because if you don't? These boys are gonna eat you alive, and I won't be there to stop them. You understand me, Ahrens?"

"Yes, Sergeant," Caleb said, quieter now. Real.

That was the deal. No exceptions.

The morning after graduation dawned in shades of brass and gunmetal, the kind of light that catches on polished boots and reminds a man that war never really sleeps, not even on parade grounds.

Caleb stood in formation, spine like a rifle barrel, heart still thundering from the day before. He could still feel the weight of the uniform, the ribbon on his chest, the ghost of the flag that had fluttered above them as they were declared Marines, God help them all.

Then came the voice. The one that had haunted his nightmares, shaped his bones, and somehow, maddeningly, become familiar.

"Ahrens," bellowed Drill Instructor Marvin Bilingsky, like thunder wrapped in camouflage, "Major Hemming wants to see you."

Caleb blinked. That wasn't standard.

As he began to move past, Bilingsky let his voice drop low, barely audible over the shuffle of boots.

"Congratulations, Ahrens. I knew you'd make it."

And just like that, the softness vanished like a ghost in the dark.

"TODAY, Ahrens!" he shouted, back to the bark and bite. "He wants to see you today, if that's alright with you, Ahrens? Now! Move! It!"

Caleb moved. God, did he move.

Major Hemming's office wasn't much, just some oak, brass, and a flag that had seen more history than Caleb's entire bloodline, but there was a weight in the room, like the furniture had judgment in its joints. Hemming himself was a mountain of a man, not in the way of fat or flash, but in presence, calm, immovable, with a face like an old tree that had weathered a thousand storms.

"Stand easy, Private. Take a seat."

The words knocked Caleb sideways. Sit? In an officer's office? This had to be a trap.

He obeyed anyway, his legs stiff, unsure whether to relax or prepare to bolt.

"Were your parents here yesterday, Private?" Hemming asked, almost casually.

"Yessir! Major, sir!"

Caleb shot to his feet like a jack-in-the-box.

"Resume your seat, Ahrens. Go easy."

He did, hands folded like a schoolboy. He had no idea what was coming.

"The postings go up today," Hemming said, his voice still calm but heavy with something more than protocol. "And I'd like to recommend you for Recon, amphibious training. Camp Pendleton."

There it was. The hook. And it went in deep.

"Recon, sir?" Caleb asked, blinking behind his glasses.

"Yes," the Major said. "You'll speak to my orderly, Staff Sergeant Canon. He'll explain what that means."

The Major leaned forward, eyes like twin nails.

"This is a career move, Ahrens. Recon only takes the best. And then they make them better. Their failure rate is sixty-four percent. That's not a typo. You screw it up, you don't die, you come back here. As a trainer. Still a good life, and you'd be one of mine."

He paused, letting that settle in Caleb's chest like a stone.

"You have twenty-four hours. Tell no one. Not your bunkmates. Not even your family. Just Canon. Dismissed."

Staff Sergeant Canon didn't look like a Marine out of central casting. He wasn't cut from the same cold, granite mould as Bilingsky. He had warmth in his eyes. Maybe even a sense of humour, tucked away behind the fatigue lines and the salt-and-pepper brush cut. He looked like a man who'd buried some friends and kept others alive by being just smart enough and just mean enough.

"Take a seat, Ahrens. Let's talk."

What followed wasn't a briefing. It was a recruitment sermon.

Canon didn't mince words. Recon was hell with swim fins. They trained harder, lived harsher, and died quieter than anyone else in the Corps. It was part Navy SEAL, part ghost story, and all edge. Missions deep behind lines. Amphibious insertions, jungle ops, mountain warfare. Psychological training so intense it broke more minds than bodies. You didn't join Recon. You bled for it.

But when you made it? You became something different. A shadow. A storm with a rifle.

By the end of the hour, Caleb wasn't just interested. He was burning.

He saw his own reflection in the mirror of that role, still skinny beneath the muscle, still the kid from nowhere with glasses and something to prove. But the fire was there, and it was hungry.

He signed the acceptance papers that same evening, without fanfare or hesitation.

And just like that, the boy who had once been dismissed as weak had taken his first step into the dark side of the Corps, where only ghosts and warriors walked.

It was only the next day that Caleb Ahrens found himself shipped out like a parcel with a military barcode, bound for Camp Pendleton on a nondescript government bus that smelled of cold vinyl and old sweat. Fifty recruits rode with him, some broad-shouldered and cocky, others jittery and quiet, their eyes flickering like faulty bulbs. No one said much. No one needed to. They all knew what they'd signed up for, or at least they thought they did.

Two days later, the training began.

RECON training wasn't like basic. Basic was a scouring wind, rough, relentless, but predictable. RECON was something else entirely. It was quieter, darker. The instructors didn't bark so much as whisper, and that was worse. The silence was tactical. Surgical. Like the calm of an operating room just before the knife slices open skin.

On day one, six recruits were gone by sundown, disappeared like they'd never been there at all. No farewell, no ceremony, just the slamming of a metal door and the grinding of a truck in gear. Ten more were gone the next day. Some washed out. Others broke down. One simply started screaming halfway through a cold-water infiltration exercise and had to be restrained. Caleb watched it happen from the shoreline, teeth chattering from the cold, wondering how any of them had survived basic. This wasn't that hard, at least not yet. But maybe that was the point. Maybe it was never meant to be hard, just precise. Clinical. A test not of muscles, but of marrow.

There was a rule, unwritten, but ironclad: tell no one. The families of the recruits were to be fed a carefully prepared fiction. Each man was supposedly training to become an instructor in the Marine Corps. That was it. No details. No hints. Just a lie that wore the face of truth like a Halloween mask. The official word was that the deception was for operational security. The real reason, Caleb suspected, was much simpler: if you didn't make it out, there was no need to explain what had gone wrong. The dead were easier to forget when they had never officially existed.

The course lasted twenty-four weeks. Half a year of pain, sweat, and secrets. By the end, only twenty-eight were left standing. They were leaner, harder, and wore their new Green Berets like silent halos. No one smiled during the graduation. Smiles were for civilians. Reco's didn't smile. They endured.

Caleb was placed into a platoon of sixteen, green berets all, forged in the same crucible, and now ready to disappear again. They were deployed to a sliver of land in Arizona that didn't appear on any official map, tucked behind fences so tall and so old they seemed to hum with secrets. The base itself was technically part of a larger Army installation, but the RECON unit operated like ghosts, barely acknowledged, rarely seen.

From there, it was on to the Middle East.

They embedded with a regular combat company, trained the locals in demolition, hand-to-hand combat, and covert tactics. They taught without ego, but with a quiet, unshakable authority. They moved like shadows and spoke in clipped sentences. Most of the grunts respected them. A few feared them. And every now and then, someone would make a joke about the "Reco's" being part of some CIA kill team. Caleb never laughed. Some things were better left unspoken.

They weren't just trainers. They were weapons. They were sent on "tasks" no one else wanted. Kidnapping enemy informants for interrogation. Blowing up safe houses used for surveillance. Quiet things. Bloody things. Things that made sleep harder to find and nightmares easier to summon.

Then came the embassy job.

It was in a neighbouring country, a place America claimed as an ally, though the locals burned flags every Friday after prayers. The embassy had received chatter. Threats. There was talk of a siege. The Reco's were ordered in to help the CIA get the staff out, quietly, efficiently, and without international incident.

It should have gone smoothly. It almost did.

The embassy was still standing when they arrived. The marble floor was scuffed, the walls stained with smoke, but there was no enemy in sight. No shouting, no shooting. Just a thick, ugly silence.

The Reco's swept the building in tandem with a half-dozen CIA agents. That's when it happened.

Caleb was clearing the east wing when he heard it. The unmistakable snap of a gunshot in a confined space. A sound like a firecracker with teeth. And then, pain. Sudden. Searing. Alive.

He hit the ground hard, clutching his right thigh.

Blood gushed between his fingers, hot and slick. The room spun. Somewhere, someone was yelling.

It wasn't an ambush. It wasn't a sniper.

It was a goddamn CIA rookie with a 9mm Glock and a finger that had no business being near a trigger. The kid had been walking around like he was in a Jason Bourne film, waving his sidearm like a toy, nerves jangling. He tripped. The gun went off. And Caleb Ahrens went down.

There was no enemy. Just stupidity. Just a moment of carelessness that cost Caleb a piece of himself.

The mission was still considered a success. The embassy was evacuated. No lives lost, at least not officially.

But Caleb would carry that bullet in his memory long after the scar had faded. Because it wasn't just the pain, or the blood, or the sound of the shot that haunted him.

It was the knowledge that in their line of work, the deadliest mistake wasn't made by the enemy.

It was made by a friend.

It all got a hell of a lot easier once Caleb was full-time at the saloon. Like a missing gear finally dropped into place, everything started to hum. There was just something about him, the way he laughed from the gut like he meant it, the way he looked people in the eye and made them feel seen. Real. Important, even. Folks didn't just like him; they gravitated toward him, like moths to a porch light in late summer.

The saloon, just a narrow sliver of bar tucked into a tired corner of San Francisco, started to take on a new kind of energy. You could feel it in the air, like static before a storm. Caleb made the place rock, and not in the fake, neon-sign, Happy Hour way. No, it was real. You walked in and felt like something could happen. Something good. Something alive. The bartenders caught his vibe like a virus, laughing more, snapping towels playfully, slinging drinks with flair instead of obligation. The regulars picked up on it too. So did the drifters.

The military guys came first. Then the off-duty cops.

The SFPD had a dozen watering holes they could have chosen, most of them closer to the station. But they adopted the saloon like it was a stray dog with a crooked smile and nowhere else to go. And Caleb? They took one look at him, at that squared-off jaw and steady posture that screamed former military, and started calling him "Sarge." It stuck. Fast. Like gum on a boot heel. Pretty soon, even the customers who didn't know his real name were calling him that. So were the staff at the second bar he sometimes helped out at. Just "Sarge." It was easier, maybe. More familiar. More fitting.

Adina and Wesley, owners in name, barkeeps in reality, watched it all unfold with a bittersweet kind of awe. They had been grinding away at the saloon for a couple of years now. Long enough to learn the truth behind the cracked paint and sticky

55

floors. It wasn't a gold mine. Hell, it wasn't even a silver one. It was just... theirs. But it was no cash cow, that was for damn sure.

If the three of them, Adina, Wesley, and Caleb, didn't do the bulk of the heavy lifting, the place would've bled out financially months ago, like a gut-shot deer crawling into the woods to die quietly. And yet, they kept at it. All of them. Not because it made sense. Not because it paid well. But because, what was the alternative?

Go back to the lives they had before?

Adina, with her careful makeup and corporate smile, pushing paper and pretending she gave a damn?

Wesley, always fidgeting in meetings, cracking jokes to hide the boredom, slowly losing bits of himself behind a computer screen?

Caleb, haunted by the echo of gunfire and the guilt that came with surviving it?

No. This was better. Harder, yes, but honest. Each shift felt like a battle, but one they chose to fight. The work was long, and the hours were cruel, but there was something sacred in it, too. Something real.

The saloon had heart. It had grit. And with Caleb behind the bar, grinning like he knew the punchline to the world's longest joke, it almost felt like home.

Almost.

Because in places like this, where the lights are low and the jukebox never quite works right, there's always the sense that something's coming. Something just beyond the reach of the neon glow. Something you can't quite name.

But for now, they poured the drinks, counted the tips, and laughed a little louder than they meant to.

And somewhere, in the dark just outside, the city kept breathing.

It happened on a Tuesday. That kind of night where the wind had a bite, rattling the saloon's old windows like a warning whispered through cracked teeth. The last of the regulars had stumbled out an hour ago, leaving behind the usual wreckage, half-drunk beers, a busted stool, and the ghost of a rowdy night echoing through the wooden bones of the place.

Caleb was tidying up, the jukebox long silent, when he found it.

He was behind the front desk in the saloon's cramped reception office, more of a cluttered cubbyhole with peeling paint and an old wooden chair that creaked like it had arthritis. He had opened the bottom drawer of the desk looking for a pen. What he found instead was something else entirely.

A piece of paper. Yellowed at the edges, brittle, like a leaf too long dead. Folded twice and tucked beneath a warped stack of receipts and takeout menus no one had looked at in years.

He unfolded it carefully, almost reverently, as though some part of him already knew this was no ordinary scrap.

A drawing.

Crude, inked in thick black lines and what looked like charcoal. The style was rough, almost childlike, but there was something about it, something intentional. A shape emerged, jagged and irregular. It took him a moment to recognize what he was seeing.

"A map," he muttered, the word barely more than breath.

Caleb tilted the page under the dim light. He could make out a river, or maybe a road, winding through uneven terrain. Small symbols dotted the edges. A pair of crossed bones. A star. A tree with roots that extended far too long and too deep, like veins. A circle drawn three times over in what might've been blood, if that was the kind of thing he let himself believe.

He didn't hear his mother coming. Adina was passing by the office with a stack of clean dish towels when he called out to her.

"Hey, Mum? What's this?"

She stopped mid-step, pivoted on her heel, and leaned into the doorway.

"What's what, sweetheart?"

He held the drawing up. She blinked, frowned faintly, and stepped closer, narrowing her eyes behind her tired smile.

"Oh! That thing…" Her voice dropped a little, and something in her face flickered, recognition maybe, or the ghost of it. "It's an old map… we think that's what it is, anyway."

"You forgot about it?" Caleb asked, watching her eyes.

"I completely did," she admitted, bending to get a better look. "I found it when we were renovating, remember when we gutted this place? I was stripping the wallpaper back in here and there it was, sandwiched between the layers like someone wanted to keep it hidden, but not lost. Strange, huh?"

"Yeah," Caleb said, glancing at the rough edges of the paper again. "It's weird. There's something off about it."

Adina straightened slowly, as if remembering more than she cared to. "I meant to throw it away. Or maybe I didn't. I honestly don't remember. But it gave me the heebie-jeebies. Like something from one of those dime-store horror stories Wesley's always reading."

"Or something outta The Shining," Caleb said, only half-joking.

She gave him a sideways look, a little too serious for comfort. "Well, don't start following it around or anything. Old maps like that don't lead to treasure, Caleb. They lead to trouble."

But as she walked away, Caleb didn't throw the map out. Didn't crumple it. Didn't burn it.

Instead, he folded it again, carefully, and slipped it into the breast pocket of his denim jacket.

It rustled there like a secret.

Like it was waiting.

60

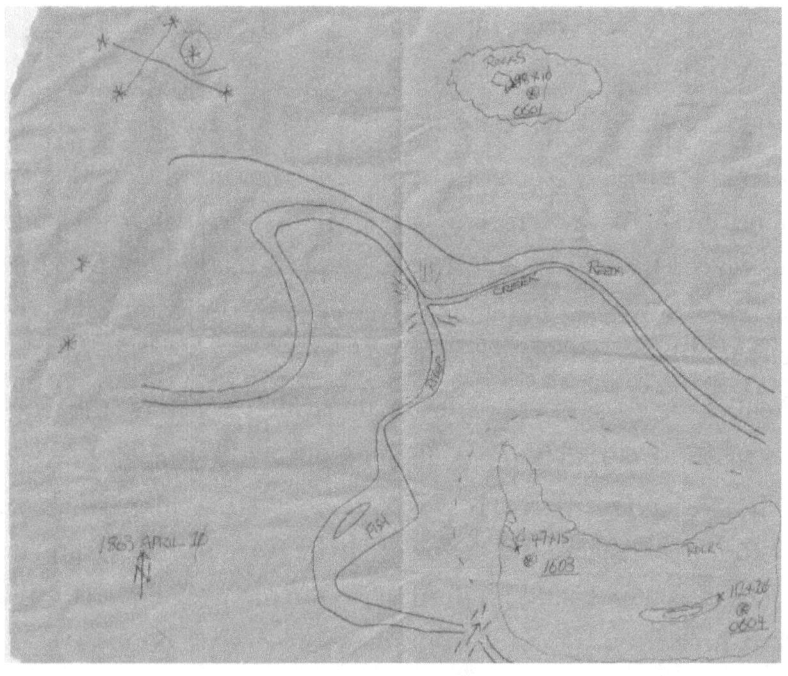

"It's a map alright," Caleb said, more to himself than to his mother, though his voice still carried a thread of disbelief. "But of what?... and where?"

Adina gave a tired shrug as she tucked a strand of hair behind her ear, her eyes already drifting back toward the clink and clutter waiting for her in the bar. "We don't know anything about it. Honestly, we've never really had time to look at it properly, and I'd completely forgotten we even had the damn thing," she repeated, her tone light, but with a vague edge of unease beneath it.

"It was always one of those 'when we get around to it' things," she added, but Caleb wasn't listening anymore. Not really. His eyes were glued to the curling edges of the old map, and his hand was already reaching for a notepad that lay abandoned on the dusty desk. The pen he used scratched softly, rhythmically, as he began to make notes, notations, measurements, guesses.

He didn't even notice when Adina left the room.

The saloon was winding down, ghosts of footsteps echoing in the now-quiet building. Glasses clinked in the distance. Chairs scraped. The neon buzz from the beer sign over the bar was the only soundtrack as Wesley appeared in the hallway, his shift at the reception desk about to begin. He stepped into the office and saw his son hunched over the desk, eyes locked in intense focus, head down like he was decoding some ancient manuscript.

"What've you got there, buddy?" Wesley asked, voice casual, but with a curious glance toward the paper.

Caleb didn't look up. He mumbled something low and unintelligible, his brain clearly somewhere else entirely, far from the reception office, far even from San Francisco. Somewhere deep in ink and imagination.

Wesley smiled, leaning on the doorframe. "Well, stay put if you want. I'm happy for you to do my shift tonight."

Still scribbling, Caleb nodded. "Sure, Dad... Have you seen this?"

Wesley stepped in fully, now genuinely intrigued. "Not really. You think it's real?"

Caleb finally looked up, eyes bright in a way Wesley hadn't seen in a long time. "I'd say it is. Just from the look of it, and from where Mum found it, stuffed behind wallpaper? That's hiding, not forgetting. I just wonder what river it's showing..."

Wesley squinted at the drawing. "Doesn't it say the river name? I thought it did."

"It says 'Fish' in one spot along the bend," Caleb replied, tapping the area with the end of his pen. "It's scrawled in this wider part of the water, maybe it's a fishing spot, or maybe that's the river's name. Could be either."

He stood suddenly. "I'm gonna get my laptop."

Wesley moved behind the desk, eyes fixed on the odd little map. His brow furrowed as he studied the page. Something about it tugged at him, like the half-memory of a dream. He wasn't one for mysteries, not anymore, but there was something magnetic about the map's worn lines, as if they whispered secrets in a language just below hearing.

A minute later, Caleb was back, laptop under one arm, breathless with excitement. He slapped the device down on the desk, flipped it open, and began to type.

"You're going to Google it?" Wesley asked, raising a brow.

"Google Earth," Caleb said, already immersed. "Let's see if there's a 'Fish River' anywhere near here, or anywhere this thing might be pointing to."

The laptop whirred to life, casting a pale, flickering glow on their faces. Outside, the wind had picked up again, pressing against the old windows in a mournful, whining gust.

Neither of them noticed.

The map lay between them like an artefact from a forgotten world. And the search had begun.

Google Earth pulsed on the laptop screen, illuminating Caleb's face in soft, blue-white light. He scrolled through the results slowly, as if handling sacred text.

"Three locations," he said aloud, more to the air than to his father. "One in Namibia. One in South Africa. And one… in Australia."

Wesley leaned over the desk, brows furrowed. "None in the U.S.?" he asked, the words hanging like a question posed in a dream.

"Nope," Caleb replied, shaking his head.

Wesley scratched his jaw, something tugging at the edges of his memory, an old conversation, maybe a half-joking story from one of the dusty regulars who used to haunt the saloon in the early days. He stepped back from the desk. "Wait here. I think I remember something… odd. Something about the guy who originally owned this place."

He turned and left the room, boots thudding softly on the old timber floor. The reception office fell quiet again, save for the hum of the laptop and the murmur of the neon sign just outside the window, flickering like a tired heartbeat.

A moment later, Wesley returned, Adina trailing close behind, wiping her hands on a dishrag and frowning.

"It wasn't a bandit," Wesley said, eyes wide with new excitement. "He wasn't American. He was a bushranger. An Australian bushranger! That's who used to own this saloon!"

"But that doesn't make any sense," Adina said sharply, stepping into the cramped room. "According to those old-timers at the opening night, this place was never called the Twilight Star Saloon until we bought it."

"Exactly," Caleb muttered, eyes flicking between them. "But if the original name was changed, maybe deliberately, then maybe it was the Twilight Star once, a long time ago, and just got buried in history. Maybe someone wanted it forgotten."

He tapped the laptop, the cursor blinking over a satellite view of rural New South Wales. "We'll try Australia first. That's the only Fish River that makes sense with a bushranger connection."

Adina crossed her arms, skeptical but curious. "What do you mean, try Australia first? What exactly are you doing?"

Caleb explained, his words quick, precise, eyes still locked on the screen. "I'll trace the course of Fish River in Australia, inch by inch if I have to. I'm looking for a specific bend in the river, just like the one drawn here on the old map. It's got a smaller creek feeding into it from the west. If I find that, if it matches this layout, then we might be onto something."

He sat back, a small smile curling his lip. "Once I find the right bend, we'll decode the rest of the scribbles, coordinates, landmarks, whatever's there. We'll follow the map."

"Easy," he added, more to himself than to anyone else.

The room fell into a thoughtful silence.

Adina didn't say anything further, but she didn't leave, either.

The next morning came quietly, as all good revelations tend to do.

Wesley found Caleb at the reception desk, already halfway through checking out the five guests who had stayed the night. He was efficient, polite, but his eyes never quite left the open laptop beside him, where Fish River meandered through the screen like an old vein across an ancient body.

When the last guest wheeled their suitcase out and the door swung closed behind them, Wesley leaned on the counter.

"So?" he asked. "Any luck?"

Caleb looked up. There was something gleaming behind his eyes now. Not just excitement. Something deeper. Obsession. Maybe even awe.

"Yeah," he said, nodding slowly. "I think I found it, Dad."

He tapped the screen.

"There's a bend… a creek… just like the map. And near it, something even stranger, a clearing. Like something used to be there."

He turned the laptop so his father could see.

"It might be nothing," Caleb added, voice low now. "But then again… it might be everything."

"I spent forever, Dad. Every inch of that damn river." Caleb rubbed at his eyes, bloodshot and rimmed with fatigue. The screen glow had left its imprint on his vision like afterimages from a flashbulb. "There's a Fish River in New South Wales, yeah. But nothing matches. No bend. No creek. Just scrub and silence."

He slumped back in the cracked vinyl chair behind the reception desk, the old map lying like a curse on the desktop beside his laptop. "And what do these markings even mean anyway? We're guessing. Hell, we don't even know who this bushranger guy was. Could be someone made it all up."

Wesley had stepped in from the hallway with two mugs of coffee, but paused mid-step at his son's tone. There was a hard edge there, frustration, no doubt, but also something more dangerous. Obsession unraveling into disappointment.

"I mean, don't get me wrong," Caleb went on, a note of apology bleeding into his voice. "I want to know what the map's about. I do. But before we get too carried away digging up ghost stories, maybe we should find out who the bushranger actually was."

Wesley placed one mug on the desk without a word, keeping the other for himself. He took a long sip and let the silence settle. He could see it now, Caleb had been up all night, chasing river bends like shadows, chasing answers. The boy had a good head on his shoulders, but sometimes you had to let the dust settle before the picture became clear.

"You're right," Wesley said finally. "No point going on a treasure hunt if we don't even know who left the map behind." He sat on the edge of the counter, the wood creaking under his weight. "Tell you what. Matt and Gerry, those old-timers who drink here every Wednesday? They might know something. Old guys like that, they've got history rattling around in their bones like marbles in a tin. I'll keep an eye out for them."

Caleb lifted his head, the tension easing slightly from his brow. "They come every Wednesday?"

"Like clockwork," Wesley said, smiling. "Usually by two, sometimes earlier if they've got something to get off their chest."

"Good," Caleb said, a glimmer of curiosity returning to his voice. "I hope they show. I've got questions."

And sure enough, the following afternoon, as the saloon clock ticked past one-thirty, the door creaked open and in stepped two figures who seemed to carry the very dust of the past with them.

Matt and Gerry, both draped in threadbare jackets and that comfortable scruff that only comes from years of letting the world wear you down and choosing not to care, shuffled their way toward their regular corner. They smelled faintly of tobacco, leather, and sun-bleached memories. Their voices, already rising in laughter, echoed in the low-slung room as if they'd been part of the woodwork since before the saloon had a name.

Wesley, polishing a glass behind the bar, glanced up and gave a small nod. Right on time.

The past was back, just as expected. And maybe, just maybe, it was ready to talk.

Caleb had been loitering near the bar most of the afternoon, slipping in and out like a man with too much time on his hands and too many thoughts in his head. He checked the door every ten minutes. The clock above the liquor shelf ticked on with mechanical indifference.

Wednesdays were always predictable, quiet foot traffic, a few tourists drawn in by the brass and mahogany charm of the old saloon, and, by mid-afternoon, the arrival of a handful of dusty old regulars. Two in particular.

He had seen them here countless times before. Matt and Gerry. Familiar faces, but never more than that. He'd poured them drinks. Smiled. Nodded. Never cared enough to ask their names, let alone their stories. But today, that changed.

When the saloon door creaked open just after two and the pair shuffled in, shoulders hunched against the late sunlight, wearing jackets too heavy for the season, Caleb moved fast. He slipped behind the bar before the on-duty staffer could lift a hand.

"There you are, gents," he said with casual cheer, sliding two Budweisers across the worn counter. "No friends with you today?"

Matt gave a laugh that rattled in his chest like coins in a tin. "Well! Thank you, Sarge! Ernie and Bruce should be along directly. But Barney won't make it. Doctor's appointment this afternoon." He raised his bottle in a sloppy salute. "Cheers, buddy!"

Gerry raised his own bottle in a silent echo of the toast.

Caleb wasted no time.

"You two ever hear of a bushranger who used to own this saloon?" His voice was easy, but there was a flicker in his eyes, an urgency he didn't bother to hide.

Matt blinked. "Bushranger? Hell, that's going back. My grandfather worked for one, if you can believe that. Bartender. But it wasn't here." He jabbed a finger against the bar. "It was down on Kearny Street. That's where the old saloon stood. Never heard the bloke's name though. Don't think I was ever told."

Before Caleb could press further, the door creaked again.

"Who's that?" said a gravelled voice as a newcomer entered.

"This here's Ernie," Gerry said with a nod toward the man approaching, tall, narrow-shouldered, his boots scuffing against the floorboards as if they'd marched through more than their share of stories.

"What can I get you, Ernie?" Caleb asked. "On the house."

Ernie grinned. "I'll take a beer, thanks," he said, settling in beside the others. As Caleb handed him the glass, Ernie's eyes narrowed. "You're asking about the bushranger, huh?"

"That's right," Caleb replied quickly.

"Well," Ernie began, taking a long swallow, "my father used to talk about him. Said his name was Frank… sometimes Andrew. Not sure which was real and which wasn't. He got the stories from his own father, who claimed he was a friend of the guy."

Caleb leaned in. "A friend? What else did he say?"

Ernie scratched his jaw, eyes growing distant. "There was a book. Not really a book, more of a diary. Written by the bushranger himself. Passed down to my father."

"Do you still have it?" Caleb asked, barely keeping the hope from his voice.

"Pretty sure it was lost in a fire," Ernie said quietly. "Back when I lived on Folsom Street, Mission District. Whole house went up. We lost damn near everything."

He took another drink, slower this time.

"See," he continued, "my father was a rough bastard. Worked part-time for the Pinkerton's. Not the friendliest crowd. Private muscle. Vigilante justice, you might say. Got on the wrong side of someone, or maybe three someones. House got torched. Rumour was, he and my grandfather tracked the bastards down and shot all three. Dead men don't confess."

"That's awful," Caleb murmured. Then, catching himself, added, "I mean about the book."

Ernie gave a dry laugh. "Yeah. Funny thing though. You forget your car keys, but not your favourite book from fifty years ago. I read it so many times, I still remember some of it." He nodded to the door as another man arrived. "Ah. There's Bruce."

Caleb slid a beer across the counter.

"So, Ernie," Caleb said, eyes sharp again, "why two names?"

Ernie set his glass down gently. "Because he robbed a stagecoach in Australia. Gold shipment. Him and two mates. The other two got shot. He got away, vanished into the bush with the loot. Changed his name. Laid low. Eventually made it here, to America. Plan was to go back for the gold once the heat cooled down. Never made it."

"What happened?" Caleb asked.

Ernie looked him dead in the eye. "Got himself shot. Right down at the end of Brannan Street. Near the Embarcadero. That's what my father told me, anyway."

Wesley had joined them silently, arms folded as he listened. Now he spoke.

"Was it this saloon?" he asked. "The one we're standing in?"

Matt was quicker.

"No. Like I said, it was the one on Kearny Street."

"You're wrong, Matt," Ernie said calmly. "My dad always called it the Brannan Saloon. Said it was on Brannan Street. Never once mentioned the Twilight Star, which was on Kearny. Maybe the bushranger owned both. Ever think of that?"

The group fell quiet. The jukebox in the corner clicked and whirred to life, but no one paid it any attention.

Caleb stood still, a thread of something electric beginning to coil in his gut. Two names. Two saloons. One man with gold and a secret. And maybe, just maybe, a trail that hadn't gone cold yet.

Caleb had heard enough from the old pioneers of the local district taverns to light a fire under his curiosity, enough to drag him deep into the dusty, shadowed corners of Australian bushranger history. One name kept gnawing at him, Frank, or

Andrew, whispered in half-forgotten tales over dimly lit bar counters. His fingers flew across the keys late into the night, piecing together fragments of a legend that refused to be forgotten.

The search led him down twisting paths of aliases and stolen identities: Andrew Taylor, Frank Clarke, Frank Jones, Frank Gardiner, and chillingly, The Darkie. Each name like a ghost slipping through the cracks of history, each one linked to the same ruthless outlaw who haunted Australia's wild edges. Caleb's pulse quickened when he realized two of those names, Frank and Andrew, matched the ones Ernie had rattled off so casually over beer. It was no coincidence.

This wasn't just folklore or an old man's tale fading into the background noise of the bar. The history of this bushranger was written in blood and gold. A daring robbery of a 'Gold Escort', money and 2,719 ounces of gold vanished without a trace while his accomplices fell dead, gunned down in cold betrayal. The story was dark, almost cinematic, and Caleb swallowed it all like a dry draught. This was the man. No doubt in his mind.

But the story didn't end there. The outlaw's trail crossed oceans and continents, carried him away from the dusty Australian outback to the roaring chaos of San Francisco. There, the bushranger opened a saloon, The Twilight Star. Caleb felt the weight of the discovery settle on his shoulders, a puzzle piece snapping into place with satisfying finality. He told his father, eyes shining with the thrill of the hunt. His father nodded, equally convinced.

Only one snag: the records said the saloon was on Kearny Street. No mention of the Brannan Street saloon that Ernie insisted upon. The second saloon, yes, it existed, but its name was lost to history. It wasn't The Twilight Star. That much was clear.

And yet, something stubborn inside Caleb whispered the map was real. The puzzle was more than a legend. The shadows of those old streets, the whispered names, the lost gold, they were all pieces of a story waiting to be uncovered. And Caleb was ready to chase it into the dark.

Caleb's late-night rabbit hole into the world of Australian bushrangers had pulled him deeper than he ever expected. The murky history was like a thick fog, but the clues kept flickering through, the kind that make your skin crawl and your heart pound. The bushranger's stomping ground? Somewhere near the Fish River in New South Wales, a detail Caleb had tracked down on Google Maps, only to hit a dead end trying to match the exact location shown on that scratchy hand-drawn map he'd found.

But then, a flicker of something unexpected. While digging through Wikipedia's endless pages, Caleb stumbled onto a tantalizing footnote: the Lachlan River, running close to the site of the infamous robbery, was once called the Fish River. His pulse quickened. Suddenly, the puzzle started to snap into place. With this revelation, Caleb pinpointed the general area that the bushranger's crude map referenced. He even figured out what the large cross on the map might mean, perhaps a nod to the Southern Cross constellation, those ghostly stars that watch over the southern skies, a celestial guide pointing the way to something buried deep.

One evening, over a rare family dinner, Caleb dropped the bombshell casually, as if he were just musing about the weather.

"I'm thinking about going to Australia. To find the bushranger's gold," he said, voice calm but eyes blazing with something unshakable.

His parents froze like the room had suddenly gone cold. They exchanged a look that said What did he just say?

"Really?" they said in perfect unison.

"Do you think the map's even real?" Wesley asked, suspicion thick in his voice.

"And what if someone else already found the treasure?" his mother added, shooting him a look that made Caleb want to grin and shake his head. No one took wild treasure hunts seriously anymore, not in their world.

But Caleb pressed on, the fire inside him refusing to be snuffed out. "Hear me out. I've done tons of research over the past few days. This map's real. The treasure's real. And I'm going to find it."

His parents stared at him, eyes wide with a mix of disbelief and something like dread.

"I've got a friend in Australia, Joanna. We were buddies in the Marines. She's now stationed at the US Embassy in Canberra, right near the Lachlan River. She's a Major, part of the Military Attaché. I've asked her to help me find and recover the gold. She'll get a quarter share of whatever we find."

Adina, his mother, finally softened. "Sounds like a lot of fun, if nothing else. Is your friend as keen as you are? It'll be a nice break for you, too. We'll manage just fine without you for a few weeks. You're not planning to stay there longer than that, are you?"

Caleb smiled, relief bubbling up. "I'm planning on a month. That's all the leave Joanna can get."

"Oh, Joanna?" Adina's tone brightened. She hadn't even caught on to the 'she' part until now. Suddenly, the whole wild idea seemed less like madness and more like an adventure.

Caleb laid out the rest of the plan, careful to temper his excitement with reason. "Most of what I have now is guesswork. But I've spoken to Joanna. We agreed she gets twenty-five percent of whatever we find. She has a car, camping gear. We'll get a metal detector and whatever else we need. She's taking care of the visa and will pick me up at the airport. I just have to tell her when I'm arriving so she can arrange her leave."

Wesley chuckled, trying to mask his envy. "Sounds like you're heading off soon, son. Kind of wish I was going with you. Maybe next trip?"

Caleb felt the thrill ripple through him, the call of the unknown, the promise of a treasure buried beneath foreign soil. It wasn't just a hunt. It was a chance to step into a legend, to touch something old and wild and alive. And he was ready to chase that ghost all the way to the other side of the world.

Australia

It was the middle of June when Caleb stepped off the plane in Canberra, and the cold hit him like a slap in the face. The outside temperature hovered around 9°C, a bone-chilling contrast to the balmy 87°F (about 31°C) he'd left behind in San Francisco. The cold air was sharp and biting, slicing through his light shirt and trousers like tiny needles, and the wind whipped past at a steady 25 kilometres per hour, as if the whole country had been breathing out a chilly breath just for him. For some reason, some stubborn, romantic idea lodged deep in his mind, Caleb had pictured Australia as a sun-soaked, tropical paradise. It wasn't. Not here, not now.

He tugged his shoulders inward, shivering as he reached for his baggage claim, eager to get his hands on the jacket he'd packed. A wool sweater would have to do for now, but the cold was something he hadn't really prepared for.

Joanna Martinez was waiting for him in the arrivals lounge, looking as sharp and confident as ever. It had been years since they'd first crossed paths at the Marine training facility at Pendleton. Back then, she was just a tough-as-nails recruit with a spark in her eyes. Now, she was a fully-fledged Major, battle-hardened and highly decorated after two gruelling tours in the Middle East. Time had only carved deeper strength into her features.

They didn't stop talking as they waited for Caleb's two bags, a Marine canvas travel bag and a battered Marine backpack. Joanna smirked approvingly when she caught sight of his gear. "Good choice," she said with a wink, watching as Caleb rifled through his travel bag and pulled out a thick wool sweater, the rough fabric a small comfort against the Canberra chill.

Joanna's ride was a Jeep Cherokee, its gleaming black paint marked by the unmistakable DC number plates. "Diplomatic Corps," she explained, catching Caleb's curious glance. "We get away with murder with those plates," she added with a mischievous giggle as she unlocked the doors. The clock on the wall said it was just past one in the afternoon.

"I'm officially on leave," Joanna said, sliding behind the wheel with a grin. "Looking forward to spending the next month on what might be one hell of an adventure."

They drove through the quiet streets toward Kingston, a tidy suburb on the edge of Canberra. The city was calm under a pale winter sky, the cold wrapping itself around every corner like a secret. At Joanna's townhouse, they dropped off Caleb's bags. He hurried inside, shedding his light clothes for something warmer, the wool sweater doing little to stave off the chill creeping under his skin.

Once Caleb was bundled up properly, they caught a cab into town. The city's pubs were warm and welcoming, the low hum of conversation and clinking glasses a sharp contrast to the cold outside. Over drinks and dinner, they laid out the plan for their upcoming trip, the excitement buzzing beneath their words. The bushranger's gold was waiting somewhere out there, buried in the wild Australian landscape, and Caleb could almost feel the weight of the treasure, cold and real, calling to him through the shadows.

"Pretty neat place," Caleb said, his voice echoing softly in the spacious townhouse. He wandered through the sunlit living room, eyes tracing the clean lines of the two-storey, four-bedroom layout, each bedroom boasting its own ensuite. "This must cost you a fortune."

Joanna smiled, settling onto the plush sofa with the ease of someone who owned every inch of the space without a penny taken from her own pocket. "Not a penny," she said with a casual shrug. "It's an embassy staff share house, and so far, I've been the only one sharing it. I told my boss you'd be staying for a month, just to be safe, so they didn't dump three other people in here while you're around."

Caleb chuckled. "Good thinking."

She popped open the fridge, pulling out two cold beers. "What do you want to do? We could just kick back for a while. It's quiet here, no blaring traffic or screaming kids. Then maybe head out for dinner around six?"

Caleb nodded, gratefully accepting the beer. "Sounds perfect."

They moved out onto the balcony, a sheltered nook tucked away from the harsh, biting wind but bathed in gentle sunlight. Caleb pulled out the photocopy of the bushranger's map he'd brought with him, he'd spent hours tweaking the contrast and highlights at the copy shop, making the faded handwriting and faint ink far easier to decipher.

Joanna reached into a stack of papers and produced a large topographical map of the area Caleb believed matched the hand-drawn map's location. Spread out on the small balcony table, they hunched over the maps together, tracing the curves of the rivers, the bumps of hills, and the jagged lines of property boundaries.

After a long pause, Joanna pointed to two marked areas. "Looks like those two are private properties. We'd have to find the owners, maybe ask permission. Could even offer a cut of whatever we find."

Caleb grimaced. "I don't like that. What if the gold is everything the legend says? Sharing a treasure like that? And if word got out, would we really want some stranger poking around, thinking it's theirs?"

His mind spun. The gold had been stolen over a century and a half ago, so who did it really belong to? The rightful owners, long lost and buried in history? Or the landowners who now legally held the land, possibly entitled to everything found beneath their feet?

Joanna tapped the map again. "The other target's in a New South Wales State Forest. Illegal to fossick there, or use a metal detector. But it might be the safest bet for now. If the map's real, that is. It could just be a wild goose chase."

Caleb's mother's words echoed in his head, the warning that the treasure might be nothing more than a myth.

They shared a silent look and, with a quiet nod, agreed to play it by ear. If they were chasing ghosts, they'd do it on their terms.

Finishing their beers, they gathered the maps and headed down to the cab waiting outside. The city lights of Civic awaited, the promise of dinner and conversation filling the cool Canberra air as the shadows lengthened into the coming night.

Joanna's gear was impressive. She had a Hillenberg four-person tent, solid as any shelter Caleb had ever seen, with rugged poles and thick canvas that promised to keep the worst of the elements at bay. She owned an Extreme sleeping bag rated for bitter cold, and she'd already bought a second one for Caleb, no compromises when it came to staying warm. The camp stove, cookware, and a massive car fridge stuffed with food and cold drinks were all packed tight in the Jeep. The only thing left on their list was a metal detector, no, not just any detector, a gold detector.

Their research was meticulous, and they both agreed: the Minelab GPZ7000 was the machine for the job. Fresh on the market and heralded as a miracle worker for prospectors, it wasn't cheap, close to ten thousand dollars, but if the gold was there, this beast would find it.

Before dawn the next morning, the engine rumbled to life. They rolled out of Canberra at five, slicing through the cool, dark air toward Yass, then on to the tiny village of Reids Flat. The road curled and climbed, cutting through ghostly forests and empty plains that felt both familiar and wild, a land suspended between myth and reality.

By midday, they arrived at the spot, the narrow ribbon of river where the creek met, just as the hand-drawn map had promised. They were skirting the edge of the State Forest, where they planned to set up camp before nightfall.

The forecast whispered of cold and clear skies. Perfect for stargazing. Perfect for following the Southern Cross.

Dinner was a simple feast cooked over Joanna's portable BBQ: thick rump steak searing beside tender mushrooms, and tin-can whole baby potatoes roasted to golden perfection. Caleb cracked open a cold Australian beer and grinned. "These are second to none," he said, holding one out to Joanna. "I might have to find a way to get these shipped back to the saloon."

The night air was sharp, a chilly wind sweeping away the last traces of fog. Slowly, the Milky Way unfurled across the sky, glittering with countless stars. And there, gleaming unmistakably, was the Southern Cross.

Caleb pulled the map out again and held it up against the night sky. Aligning the Southern Cross with the two pointer stars wasn't easy, but by moving carefully around a wide circle and turning the map, he matched the stars perfectly to the map's illustration.

He crouched down, marking his position on the ground with a small stone, then pulled out a compass. The needle spun and settled. Caleb recorded the bearing on the back of the map in soft pencil, his breath visible in the cold night air.

Joanna did the same, but her reading was slightly off, a subtle difference that Caleb attributed to the thickness of her jacket or the weight of her watch on her wrist.

Two positions. Two separate bearings. Both promising, both needing investigation.

They packed away the maps, the night suddenly feeling thick with possibility, and settled in for what promised to be a long day of hunting the shadows and whispers of a forgotten treasure.

They were Marines through and through, hardened by endless hours of training in the choking heat of jungle canopies and the relentless glare of desert sands. Every muscle, every reflex honed to move silently, unseen, like ghosts stalking shadows. Now, that training came alive in the cool, whispering forest as they crept up the steep hillside toward the big rock marked on the map.

Caleb led, careful not to snap a twig or leave a footprint, his boots finding purchase on moss and fallen leaves, his breath shallow and controlled. Joanna followed close behind, eyes sharp, senses stretched taut like a hunter's bowstring.

About a third of the way up, the forest gave way to a rough four-wheel-drive track cutting through the trees like a scar. They froze at the edge, muscles coiled, ears straining for the faintest hum of an engine or crunch of tires. Nothing but the rustling of leaves stirred by a whispering breeze.

They scanned both directions, the shadows deepening in the afternoon light. After a slow, deliberate count to ten, Caleb gave a slight nod. It was clear, no vehicles were coming.

But caution ruled the day. They veered off, weaving a narrow detour in search of a firmer patch of earth that wouldn't betray their presence with fresh tracks. The paranoia gnawed at them, was it justified? Or just the nervous echo of too many missions and too much caution?

Neither dared dismiss it. The last thing they wanted was an unexpected meeting with another soul out here in the State Forest. This was their secret hunt, their quiet war against time and chance. And for now, silence was their only ally.

After two long hours slogging up the hill, sweating under a sky that offered no mercy, they finally reached the rock, the one Caleb and Joanna had been hunting by the dim glow of stars and the stubborn hope in their hearts. They carried the weight of their gear, the buzz of the gold detector slicing through the thick silence, but so far, nothing. Two more hours spent scanning and sweeping the patch of earth they believed was marked on that maddening hand-drawn map, and still nothing. Not a whisper of treasure.

Joanna, ever sharp, stopped suddenly, the idea clicking like a distant bell in the cavern of her mind. "Wait," she said, voice steady but urgent, wiping a streak of dirt from her brow. "Maybe we've been looking at this all wrong."

Caleb, standing nearby, looked a mess. His shirt clung to his skin, his face flushed from the climb and the disappointment. He was blaming the detector, sure, maybe he hadn't set it up right, but Joanna's eyes, fierce and calculating, cut through his frustration.

"What if," she began, hesitating just long enough to let the suspense build, "we should have taken the compass reading from the rock? The stars' bearing from that point. Then reversed the direction and moved ten feet, maybe yards, across the terrain?"

Caleb's brow furrowed, his exhaustion momentarily forgotten as a spark of hope flickered. "So... you're saying we're starting in the wrong place, working from the wrong end?"

"Exactly." Joanna's gaze fixed on him like a predator sizing up her prey. "If we took the reading at the rock first, then moved away from it instead of toward it, we might be looking for treasure in the wrong patch."

Caleb exhaled sharply, the weight on his chest lifting just a fraction. "Then tonight… we need to get up here in the dark and take a new compass reading?"

"No." Joanna shook her head, a small grin teasing her lips despite the cold bite of the afternoon. "Too risky. The climb's tough enough in daylight. I can shift the readings we took last night over to the front of the rock, safer from down below. I just need the topo map, that's back in the car. You coming?"

Caleb nodded, the fire rekindled behind his eyes, the thrill of the hunt replacing the exhaustion. They moved back down the hill, shadows stretching long as the sun dipped, the night promising a new path, one they'd follow with star-crossed hope and a stubborn hunger for what lay buried beneath the dirt and secrets.

As Caleb followed Joanna back down the steep, pine-shadowed hill, he tried to make sense of what she'd just said. Numbers and bearings floated through his brain like fireflies in fog, brief flashes of logic that fizzled out before they could land anywhere useful. He was good with a rifle, great with a plan, and hell in a fight, but when it came to trigonometry and celestial alignments? That was Joanna's wheelhouse. Always had been. He trusted her instincts, even if he didn't understand the math. Besides, the damn hill was steep enough without dragging a mental chalkboard up and down it.

By the time they reached the edge of the makeshift campsite again, the sun had begun its slow dive behind the line of trees. Shadows were lengthening, crawling like old ghosts across the clearing, but the fridge in Joanna's Land Cruiser still purred away quietly, and inside it was salvation in a can.

"A cold beer went down real nice," Caleb muttered, wiping the sweat off the back of his neck as the first sip cooled his insides like river water. Joanna sat cross-legged with the topographical map splayed out in front of her like a sacred text, the plastic compass in her hand spinning slightly before she locked it into place with the precision of a surgeon.

"Two-fifty-two degrees west," she said, more to herself than to him. Her finger traced a fine line on the map. "So we go from the centre of the rock, ten yards by seventy-eight degrees east." She looked up at him, her eyes shining with the kind of glee a kid has when they've just found out where the presents are hidden before Christmas.

"That's exactly where the treasure is buried," she said with a giggle, the sound light and eerie against the deepening quiet of the woods.

Caleb couldn't help it. He grinned, the fatigue sloughing off his shoulders like dead skin. Hope was a hell of a drug.

They downed the rest of their beers, set the empty cans beside the fire pit, and with the compass, the map, and a renewed sense of purpose, they started up the hill again. The incline didn't seem as steep this time. The wind had stilled. Somewhere in the trees, a kookaburra cackled like it knew something they didn't.

They weren't just chasing gold now. They were chasing the promise of being right. Of finding something real in the middle of myth.

That was exactly where the gold was buried, right there beneath the twisted roots of a skeletal tree, in soil so soft it crumbled like stale cake. Maybe 400mm deep. Eighteen inches, give or take. Caleb could have scratched through it with his bare hands if he'd been desperate enough. And in that shallow grave, lined up like obedient soldiers waiting for orders, were seven gold ingots. Each about 300mm long, maybe 80 wide and 50 deep. Heavy bastards, too, each one weighing close to twelve kilos, which in the old American way Caleb understood better, came out to around twenty-five pounds apiece. Enough to kill a man if you dropped one on his foot.

But it wasn't the weight that stunned them. It was the reality. The finality of it. The way the bars gleamed dully, like something out of a dream that had gotten too close to the waking world and hadn't quite figured out how to hide its magic.

Joanna knelt beside them, her breath short and visible in the cold air. Her eyes were locked on the gold, not moving, not blinking, as if afraid it might vanish if she looked away. "I can't believe it," she whispered. "I actually can't believe it."

But Caleb believed. He didn't need charts or star maps or calculations, he had belief written across his face in sweat and soil. His knees hurt. His back ached. But all he could do was stare and feel that deep, wild spark that only ever comes once in a lifetime. The kind of spark that makes sane people do stupid things. Dangerous things.

They sat like that for what might have been five minutes or five hours, the forest around them so quiet it seemed to be holding its breath.

Then Joanna's voice, sharp and alive with sudden fear, broke the spell.

"Caleb! What if someone, anyone, a ranger or just... someone, comes across us now?"

Her voice cut through the calm like a blade. Caleb blinked, slowly turning his head toward her, as though the gears of his brain were grinding back into motion. It took him thirty seconds to process it, thirty seconds too long.

Then the penny dropped.

"Shit," he said. "You're right." And just like that, the soldier in him came back. The Marine. The man who knew what it meant to keep something hidden that wasn't supposed to be found.

He dropped to his knees and began placing the bars back into the earth like sacred relics. Joanna joined him, both of them moving fast but trying not to look like they were panicking, even though they absolutely were.

Caleb kept glancing over his shoulder, scanning the tree line, every crunch of leaves in the distance now a possible footstep, every breeze a whisper of danger. Joanna, too, was beginning to feel it, the hair rising on her neck, that ancient instinct that tells you you're being watched even when you're not. Yet.

When the last bar was covered, and the dirt smoothed over, they knelt back on their heels and surveyed the site. Caleb narrowed his eyes. Something about the way the soil sat didn't look right.

"We need to mess it up a little more," he muttered. "Make it look older, like it hasn't been touched."

Joanna nodded, and for the next few minutes, they scuffed and scattered leaves, placed a few sticks just so, even dragged a fallen branch across part of the clearing.

When they finally stepped back, it looked... natural. Or as natural as it could. But still, Caleb didn't trust it. The paranoia was setting in, thick and heavy, like a second skin. Every rustle in the underbrush was a boot step, every creak of a tree limb the sound of someone watching from the shadows.

"We've gotta go," he said tightly. "Now. Back to camp. Figure out the rest from there."

Joanna put a hand on his arm. "It'll be fine for a few hours. Nobody knows we're here."

Caleb nodded, but the look in his eyes said otherwise. He didn't believe that, not really. Not anymore. Because now they weren't just campers in the woods.

Now they were keepers of a secret someone might kill to uncover.

It was now painfully, thrillingly obvious to both of them: they had never really expected to find the gold.

Sure, they'd come all this way, trekking through hostile terrain and following a compass bearing that relied more on hope than certainty. They'd studied the map, they'd traced the lines under lamplight like fortune tellers reading fate in the creases of an old palm, but all along, somewhere deep inside, neither of them had truly believed they'd strike the motherlode. And now here it was. Real. Cold. Heavy. Tangible in a way that felt surreal.

It was like buying a Lotto ticket. You do it because maybe. Because dreaming is free. But you never actually expect to win. And when you do, if you do, it doesn't feel like joy. Not at first. It feels like something bigger. More dangerous. Because now you've crossed the line. Now the world knows you're lucky, and luck always comes with a price.

Their immediate problem was as real as the gold bars buried beneath that brittle patch of shale. How in the hell were they going to get the stuff down the hill and into the car without drawing attention?

The plan, such as it was, came together quickly and under pressure.

"We'll each carry one bar per trip," Caleb said, wiping the sweat from his face with a sleeve that was already soaked through. "They're twenty-five pounds each. We could carry two, maybe even three, but that's asking for trouble. People notice strain. People notice odd behavior. And people, Jo, people ask questions."

They agreed.

One bar each. Quiet trips. Downhill. It wouldn't be easy, but it would be manageable. At least gravity was on their side. And if anyone happened to cross their path on the trail, their packs wouldn't give them away. They'd just look like a couple of weekend hikers, hauling tents or sleeping mats. Maybe a six-pack if someone was feeling optimistic.

But the gold in the car, that was a whole different nightmare.

"What if someone comes up the track while we're still ferrying the rest down?" Joanna asked. "What if they see the car? Ransack it, take it? Hell, just find it?"

It was a valid point. A terrifying one.

So they adjusted the plan. The first run would be a team effort. One bar each. Get it down, stash it in the car. The floor of the backseat would work. They'd peel back the carpet liner, lay the bars flat, cover them with whatever they had, clothing, spare blankets, a half-deflated sleeping bag. Make it look messy in a way that suggested disorganization, not hidden treasure.

After that, Caleb would take over the ferrying.

Joanna would stay behind. Guard the car. Keep the engine cold and the windows dusty. Just another vehicle in the bush, nothing more. But she wouldn't be lounging.

She'd be armed.

Her US Marine-issue Colt .45 automatic sat snug and sure in her thigh holster, the matte black steel of it gleaming faintly in the filtered light beneath the canopy. There was no bluff with that weapon, no threat. Just certainty. If someone got too curious, if someone got too close, Joanna would not hesitate.

Caleb looked at her and gave a short nod, no words needed. She was more than capable. He trusted her. But even so, as he turned and began the slow, careful journey up the hill to retrieve the second bar, he couldn't shake the feeling that they'd just stepped into a new game. A darker one.

Because finding gold wasn't the end of the story.

It was three o'clock in the afternoon, and the shadows were already beginning to lengthen across the ridgeline. Joanna stood with her hands on her hips, squinting at the sinking sun. "It's too late to start," she said flatly. "You know how long it took us to get up there. Two hours each way, Caleb."

But Caleb wasn't having it. His eyes were set, jaw clenched with that quiet stubbornness she'd learned not to argue with unless she had to. "We can do one trip now. I'll take two bars. One in each side of the pack. You take one."

"That still leaves four bars."

"Which I'll carry down tomorrow. Two trips, tops. We can have all of it out before noon."

And so they did. The sun was dipping below the hills when they returned, legs aching, backs screaming, but hearts pounding with adrenaline. It was past seven and pitch dark by the time they stowed the three gold bars in the floor well behind the front seats of Joanna's four-wheel drive, covering them with a disheveled pile of spare clothing and a picnic rug.

They didn't bother cooking dinner. Not out of fatigue, though they were exhausted, but because of the thrill. The kind that settled in your gut like lightning in a bottle.

Caleb couldn't take his eyes off the gold bar he'd washed in a pot of clean water. It gleamed now, and on its underside, a series of sharp, blocky characters caught the lantern light:

N S W G 99.9

"What do you reckon that means?" he asked, turning it in his hands.

Joanna studied it but shook her head. "No idea. Can't Google it out here."

There was no phone signal, no data, no help from the digital world. Just two people and three bars of pure, nearly one-hundred-percent gold.

The next morning, Caleb set off early and returned by ten with two more bars, drenched in sweat but grinning. Joanna had steak and beans waiting on the portable BBQ. They ate without speaking much, just shared glances that said this is real.

Then he went back for the final two bars.

But when he reached the narrow, scrub-lined section of the four-wheel drive track that cut through the hill's lower slope, he froze. His body reacted before his mind caught up, he crouched low and stilled his breath.

Thirty metres off the track: horse dung.

Fresh.

It hadn't been there earlier that morning. He was certain. The position matched almost exactly the route he'd taken. The ground confirmed it, hoof prints. Shod. At least two horses. New.

He waited for three minutes, ears straining, hearing only the high call of lorikeets and the distant rustle of dry leaves. No hoofbeats. No human voices.

Still, the cold sweat broke over him. Someone had passed by while he'd been up the mountain. With horses. Shod horses. This was no recreational ride, this was official.

He resumed his ascent, heart pounding now not from exertion, but from something older, deeper. The kind of primal fear that whispered, You're not alone anymore.

Back at the campsite, it was around three when Joanna heard the engine. A low diesel growl.

She stepped out, heart jolting.

A white Toyota LandCruiser F78, towing a two-horse float, trundled along the rough trail and passed within ten metres of their tent. On the door of the vehicle, bold black letters read:

RANGER

NSW FORESTRY beneath a government crest.

The two occupants inside wore khaki and broad-brimmed hats. They smiled and waved casually as they passed, like locals greeting weekenders. Joanna returned the wave stiffly, a practiced smile on her lips. But inside, everything went cold.

NSWG.

She turned toward the car and looked at the gold bars buried beneath their belongings.

"New South Wales Government," she said aloud, barely a whisper.

That night, over the crackle of a modest fire, they sat and stared into the flames with their drinks untouched.

No matter how they spun it, whether in hushed tones or speculative reasoning, it all came back to the same thing. The gold was marked. Stamped. Belonging to the government. Found was not the same as owned. And they both knew it.

An honest Australian citizen would take the gold straight to the authorities. Fill out forms. Cooperate. Hand over the treasure and walk away with nothing but a thank-you.

But they weren't Australians. Not technically. And even that thin thread of moral ambiguity offered no comfort. Because now they had a different problem, they had the gold, and the gold had history.

They didn't know who had put it there.

They didn't know who might still be looking for it.

And worst of all… they didn't know what to do next.

Gold

The next day broke warm and bright, like the world had no clue it was now playing host to stolen treasure. Caleb and Joanna pulled up outside her modest brick townhouse just before noon, the shadows of the building stretching long across the driveway like dark fingers pointing toward guilt. The gold, nearly a hundred kilos of it, lay quiet in the back of the car, wrapped in duffle bags and swaddled like sleeping children. It shimmered beneath the blankets, heavy with the weight of centuries and consequences.

They moved it carefully, reverently even, from the boot to the garage, then through the internal door and into the cool sanctuary of Joanna's home. Not a curtain twitched. Not a single neighbor poked their head out to offer a nosy greeting. And thank God for that, because in that moment, the pair of them were nothing short of criminals, smiling, tired, elated criminals.

Inside, Caleb took each bar of gold, thick, cold, dense with history, and placed it on the digital bathroom scale in his ensuite. He bent to record the numbers with a shaking hand, like some obsessive record-keeper in a lunatic asylum. Ninety-six kilograms. A figure with the gravity of a tombstone. At roughly $2,000 an ounce, that came to just north of six-point-seven million U.S. dollars.

Joanna's share was a little over one and a half million. Caleb's the same. His parents, back in Kansas or Topeka or wherever the hell they called home, were down for the rest, a cool three million, give or take. But as the numbers were being written down, the air between them grew colder. Not the kind of cold that comes from air conditioning or cracked windows. The kind that crawls up your spine when your soul starts to suspect you might have gone too far.

Joanna broke the silence first.

"Caleb," she said, in a voice caught between a laugh and a low-level panic, "tell me, how exactly do you plan to turn these gold ingots, stamped with the name of their owner, no less, into spendable cash? And then, how do I get my million and a half out of Australia and back to the U.S.? Do you even have a plan? At all?"

She smiled when she said it, but there was a tightness around her eyes, a shadow behind her levity that suggested she already knew the answer.

Caleb opened a beer, his second, or was it his third?, and let out a breath that came from somewhere low and hollow in his gut. "Honestly? I didn't think that far ahead. I just… I wanted to find it, Jo. That's all. And I didn't even really think we would, you know? I mean… did you?"

Joanna leaned against the kitchen counter and crossed her arms, her eyes scanning the gleam of gold like it was some relic from another world. A cursed one.

"No," she said softly. "No way did I think we'd actually find it. But that's not why I came. When you called, God, when you said you were coming here, chasing some half-baked legend, I didn't care if we came back with nothing. I just… I wanted the adventure. With you."

He looked at her then, really looked at her, but the moment didn't settle. It twitched and moved, like something living under the floorboards.

"So," he asked, his voice thick with beer and wonder, "what do you think the Australian government would give us as a reward? For finding it?"

Joanna laughed, sharp, almost mean. "Two words, Caleb. Fuck all."

He grinned, but the grin didn't reach his eyes.

"I mean, what do you think would happen if we got caught?" she added, the question hanging there like a noose.

"We really do need a plan," Caleb said, his voice dropping. "I mean, there's no way in hell I'm handing this back. Not without knowing who it belongs to. It could be a museum's stash. Or an insurance company's problem. How do we even know it's still on the books?"

Joanna nodded, but it was empty agreement. She was still staring at the gold, and something in her was unraveling just a little.

"Good point," she said at last. "If it was insured, someone got paid. So it's… like, victimless, right?" She tried to laugh, but it came out like a cough.

"We've got four weeks before I head back," Caleb muttered, picking up one of the bars and turning it in his hands. The engraved letters on the underside seemed to sneer up at him: N.S.W.G. The mark of the New South Wales Government. A tattoo on a corpse.

"First thing we do," he said, "is figure out how to get rid of that."

"Right," Joanna replied. "Those letters make it unsellable. It screams stolen. Any ideas?"

Caleb's eyes narrowed. "Yeah. But once we tamper with it, we're crossing a line we can't uncross."

Joanna's laugh this time was bitter, almost barking. "Jesus, Caleb, you don't think we're already thieves? Really? Wake up! We've crossed that line with both feet. Hell, we danced over it."

She stepped forward now, closer, her voice low and hard. "We either commit, or we turn it in. No halfway. No bullshit. Yes or no. Because I vote we keep it. Fuck it. We've come this far."

Caleb didn't say anything, but the bar of gold in his hand felt heavier than ever. Not with weight. With choice.

It was settled, though not with the ease of a handshake or the ring of finality, more like the unspoken nod exchanged by two people peering over the edge of a cliff and agreeing to jump together. Caleb's idea was simple, even ingenious in its bluntness: obliterate the stamped letters from the gold bars by melting the metal with an oxy-acetylene gas torch. No grand plan, no chemistry degree required, just fire, blue and hungry, and time.

The gas welding kit was easy enough to acquire. Fyshwick, with its maze of industrial shops and grey concrete blocks, provided the perfect cover for quiet transactions. No one asked questions in Fyshwick, not about torches, not about intentions. You paid your cash, you walked out with your gear, and that was the end of the conversation.

Caleb took to the task like a man discovering a hidden talent. In the shadowed cocoon of Joanna's garage, where silence pressed against the walls like a blanket of snow, he practiced until the motion became instinct. Adjusting the flame until it burned that perfect shade of almost-pure blue, just a kiss of yellow at the tip, he learned to dance the torch across the gold's surface with a craftsman's precision.

The result was crude, but functional. The offending letters, someone's name, someone who may or may not have died with the secret of that gold still wedged in their cold, blue lips, were gone. In their place, a soft depression remained, like the hollow in a frog-brick. Caleb had been careful, almost reverent, not to touch the purity mark: 99.9 still gleamed on the underside of each bar, untouched and proud.

Joanna watched from the doorway, arms crossed, her posture shifting slowly from curiosity to anxiety.

"What are we going to do with all this gear?" she asked. Her voice sounded too sharp, like it had been filed down to a point.

Caleb turned, wiping sweat from his brow with the back of his hand. "What gear? You mean the bottles, the torch?"

"And the detector," she added. "We can't leave this shit in the garage. If the embassy sends another staff member to stay here, and they find any of this…" She didn't finish the sentence. She didn't need to. The image was there, unspoken: men in suits, latex gloves, evidence bags.

Caleb nodded slowly, as if the reality was only now beginning to settle into his bones. "You're right. You're absolutely right. This stuff, any of it, could point straight back at us. It's evidence. Proof."

"But," he added, raising a finger, "we'll need the detector. There are other targets on that map. We're not done yet."

Joanna stepped forward then, the light catching in her eyes. Her voice was quiet but firm, each word punctuated by years of common sense clawing its way to the surface. "I don't think we should even think about the other targets, not yet. Not until we've sorted this out. All of it."

There was a silence between them, long, thoughtful, the kind that made the garage feel a little colder.

She broke it with a sigh. "I'll put an ad on Facebook, Canberra buy-swap-sell page. We'll flog the gas gear, the detector too. We can always buy more if we need to later."

Her lips curled into the faintest smile. "Fuck the expense, right?"

And just like that, they were no longer treasure hunters on a high. They were co-conspirators, cleaning up the scene, erasing the fingerprints. The stakes had grown fangs. But at least now, at long last, they were beginning to take the gold, and what it meant, seriously.

The gas gear went fast, no questions asked. Some guy from Queanbeyan turned up with a tray-back ute, handed over the cash, and disappeared like a ghost in the smoke. But the gold detector? That was another story.

They had listed it at nearly a thousand dollars below what they'd paid, practically a bargain, but the listing sat online like a rusting bike chained to a lamp post. Only one real bite, and he came sniffing around just after midday, a Thursday that felt too quiet, too still.

He arrived on foot, wearing steel-capped boots caked in red dust, a battered felt hat, and a face that had seen too many summers without sunscreen. Fifty-ish, maybe older. The kind of man who smelled of dry sweat and metal filings. He barely glanced at Joanna when she opened the door, but his eyes lingered on the detector like it was an old flame.

Nine thousand five hundred was the asking price, firm. But instead of cash, the man asked, "Would you take the equivalent… in gold?"

That made the air go still.

He said it like a joke. But it wasn't one.

Caleb, playing it cool, asked, "Where do you sell your gold?"

That did it. Something changed in the guy's posture, like someone had twisted a key in his spine. He looked from Caleb to Joanna and back again, taking in their tidy appearance, the clean hands, the neatly combed hair. His eyes lingered on the detector, spotless, barely a scratch, like it had never seen a day's work in the bush. The man's expression hardened. Suspicion bloomed like a bruise.

"You two cops?" he asked flatly.

Caleb's gut clenched. He'd seen that look before, usually right before someone slammed a door or bolted out the back.

"We're not police," he said quickly. "We're with the U.S. diplomatic corps, stationed at the embassy."

He reached into his pocket and produced his U.S. Marine ID. Joanna followed, doing the same. It was a bluff, but a good one, and it worked. The man relaxed almost immediately, his laugh low and scratchy.

"Diplomats, huh? Well, shit. That explains a few things."

Caleb nodded, easing back into the conversation. "We found a little gold. Just enough to raise questions. But as diplomats, we're not allowed to earn income here. Complicated treaties, tax implications, all that nonsense. So, we're stuck. Can't sell. Can't keep."

The man, who now introduced himself as Alex Gregory, chuckled, this time with genuine amusement. "Now that's a bugger of a situation."

He scratched his chin. "I don't work for no one. Haven't in years. Just me and the land. I find a bit, sell a bit, live off what the ground gives. And yeah, I reckon it's pretty rank that you can't even offload a bit of colour without it becoming a bloody international incident."

Joanna, now stepping into the performance, added with a touch of bitterness, "We can't even take it home with us. Export laws. We'd be breaking international trade regulations just for carrying a couple of nuggets through airport security. The whole thing's been a waste of time and a hell of a lot of money."

Alex leaned forward, his eyes gleaming just a little. The predator beneath the dusty exterior was starting to sniff an opportunity.

"Well," he said slowly, "if you ever did come across any gold, nuggets, flakes, whatever, I might be able to help. I can buy it. Cash. No receipts. No records. Just mates doing mates a favour."

He raised a calloused hand. "The price would be about twenty percent below the day's official buying rate. Not the selling rate, mind you. That's always higher. But I'm fair, and I pay in full."

Joanna tilted her head. "How much gold could you buy?"

Alex grinned like a wolf at a lamb. "How much you got?"

There was a pause. The moment stretched just long enough to make everyone aware of what had not been said.

Then Caleb stepped in, voice calm but urgent, cutting through the tension like a scalpel. "How about we all get together later? Dinner. Your choice of place. Somewhere quiet. We'll talk more, maybe over a couple of drinks."

Alex's grin didn't falter. If anything, it widened. "Sure. Why the hell not?"

As he left, they both watched him go. The silence afterward was not comforting, it pressed on the walls like a storm front gathering over the hills.

Caleb didn't say it aloud, but he was thinking the same thing Joanna was: they'd just taken the next step deeper into the dark.

They met at a place that Alex called a restaurant, but Caleb would have bet his left foot it had started life as a pub, low lighting, varnished wood tables, and the smell of hot oil and old beer soaked into the bones of the place. Officially it was a bistro, tucked into the corner of Green Square in Kingston, a spot more known for wine bars and boutique pretensions than backdoor deals.

They'd spent the afternoon after Alex left in a state of simmering deliberation. The gold detector had passed inspection; Alex had said he'd come by to collect it the next day,

Max Barrington

assuming they were really done with digging up half the territory.

"Let's hit him with it," Joanna had said as she leaned back on the couch, her eyes narrowed in that calculating way she had when she was figuring odds. "See how he reacts to four hundred ounces."

"Not at twenty percent," Caleb had muttered. "That's daylight robbery."

Now, at the bistro, their steaks were bleeding onto their plates and the schooners of beer were sweating in their hands. Alex had taken to telling them his life story, rambling in that boisterous, half-boozed, confessional way men sometimes do when they sense money nearby but aren't sure how heavy the bag will be when it lands.

It had started with the Navy, he'd enlisted at sixteen, discharged dishonourably at seventeen. He said it with a grin, like it was a punchline. He'd gone from plasterer's labourer to fixer, and then, somewhere in the blur of his early twenties, slipped into the real estate game. "Found my calling, mate," he'd said, stabbing his fork into a chunk of rump steak. "The suits, the wheels, the ladies, it was bloody magic."

By the time Caleb came back from the bar carrying three fresh schooners, Alex was halfway through a story about selling a haunted house to a Pentecostal couple.

He slapped the beers on the table, foam rising. "All right, enough ghost stories."

Alex took a long gulp. "Ghosts are real, mate. Just depends what you're afraid of."

Caleb leaned in, voice low and serious now. "Seriously speaking, Alex... Could you handle one hundred ounces of gold?"

Alex didn't miss a beat. "Piece of piss, mate. That's just another Tuesday."

Joanna leaned forward, her tone deceptively light. "How about four hundred?"

That stopped him.

He set down his schooner slowly, carefully. A flicker of something unreadable passed over his eyes. "You two got a full gold bar or something?"

There was a beat. Caleb met Joanna's eyes. A decision passed between them, wordless, swift.

"Yes," Caleb said. "One bar."

Alex's gaze sharpened, laser-like. "Any stampings? Indent names?"

"Just '99.9'," Caleb replied. He felt a ripple of tension in his chest and hoped it didn't show in his voice. "That's all."

Alex nodded slowly. "All right. But not at twenty percent, right?"

Caleb's smile was thin. "Not even close."

"For that kind of weight," Alex said, scratching at the scruff along his jawline, "I can probably swing ten percent. But I'll need a quality check. I've got a guy."

Caleb leaned forward slightly, lowering his voice. "Will it be a cash payment?"

Alex chuckled, the sound rough as gravel. "At that kind of number? You're pushing eight hundred grand, easy. I might have to go eleven percent for that much."

Caleb didn't blink. "How about ten point five? Split the middle."

Alex tapped his schooner thoughtfully against the edge of the table, foam bubbling near the rim. "Let me have a hunt around tomorrow," he said. "See what I can do. But don't hold your breath, right?"

They stood in the carpark beneath flickering fluorescent light. Alex gave them both a two-fingered salute and turned back toward the shadows of his ute. His footsteps echoed off the asphalt.

As they watched him vanish into the night, Joanna turned and said, "We're either about to make the easiest money of our lives… or we just invited the devil to dinner."

Caleb didn't answer. But the weight in his chest hadn't lifted, not one bit.

Back at the townhouse, the air was thick with a kind of restless satisfaction. They'd done it. Found the gold. The weight of it wasn't just physical, it was the weight of a secret that could crush them if they slipped. Joanna paced the small living room, biting her lip, her mind churning. Then, like a shadow creeping into a sunlit room, the question came.

"How are you going to get the money back to the States?" Joanna's voice was low but urgent. "You know the rules, anything over ten grand Aussie has to be declared. You can't just drip-feed nine-thousand-dollar chunks across the ocean. They'd catch on. They'd shut you down."

Caleb's face went slack, a dull sort of defeat setting into his eyes. "I never even thought about that part," he said, voice cracked with the weight of it. "We're fucked, Joanna. Sitting on a mountain of gold, and we can't do a damn thing with it."

She stopped pacing, turned to him, her eyes sharp despite the worry. "Don't panic. Plenty of time to figure it out. You think I'm leaving my share behind? Hell no."

He sank into the old armchair, rubbing his hands over his face like he was trying to erase the frustration etched deep inside. "I was so focused on finding the gold, the real chase, I never planned beyond that. I gave myself decent odds I wouldn't find it at all. But here we are. And, damn it, I'm glad it was you out there with me. The thrill of the hunt, and your company, it's what kept me going."

Joanna softened, a ghost of a smile curling her lips. "Plans change. We'll figure out the cash part. We have time. And we're not turning back now." The weight of their secret, heavy as gold bars, pressed down on them, but it also bound them, two souls tangled in a dangerous game where every step could be their last.

The next morning dawned pale and overcast, the kind of morning that pressed down on you like a weight, thick with the unspoken tension of secrets yet to surface. Joanna sat at the kitchen table, the faint hum of the city just beyond the window, and dialled the number she'd been holding onto, a lifeline to someone inside the embassy who might help them navigate the murky waters they'd plunged into.

"Ben," she said quietly, "I need you to run a check on a guy named Alex Gregory. I don't have much, just his name, that he was in the Royal Australian Navy once, and he ran a real estate business in Canberra. I'm sending you some photos I took at the tavern last night."

There was a pause on the other end, a soft sigh. "Not much to go on, Joanna," Ben said, his voice low and cautious. "But I've got a photo wizard kicking in now, running a face recognition scan. Any idea how old this guy is?"

"Fifties, maybe," she replied, her eyes scanning the street outside as if Alex might be walking by any moment.

"Right. Well, looks like our 'naughty boy' is already on the radar. The wizard's found him, means he's known to the cops. I'll dig deeper, get everything I can, and shoot it over to your email.

Make sure you delete it once you've seen it, yeah? We don't want this floating around."

"Got it. Thanks, Ben. Talk soon."

She hung up and sat back, the weight of uncertainty settling heavier. The hunt was no longer just about gold or greed, it was about trust, danger, and just how deep they were willing to go into the shadows.

One hour later, Joanna sat staring at the screen, the words crawling over her like a creeping chill in the bones. The police report on Alex Robert Gregory unfolded like a sinister dossier, each line a brick in a wall they hadn't wanted to build around him.

Alex Robert Gregory
DOB: 23/02/1964

1975, A.C.T Children's Court: placed on good behaviour bond for shoplifting.

Jan 1981, HMAS Cerberus, Victoria: Military Court. Guilty of stealing personal items from lockers. Three months imprisonment. Dishonourable discharge.

1984, A.C.T Court of Petty Sessions: charged with attempted fraud against employer, 24-month suspended sentence.

1990, A.C.T Supreme Court, Australian Taxation Office vs. Gregory: sentenced to 3 years imprisonment for attempted defrauding of Commonwealth funds, sentence suspended.

2000, A.C.T Law Courts: wholly suspended from holding a licence to deal in real estate within the Australian Capital Territory.

Joanna slid the report across to Caleb with a sardonic smile, "Perfect."

Caleb shook his head, the slow, incredulous kind of shake that says, What have we almost walked into? "Wow. To think we were actually going to do business with this guy. Well done, Joanna."

She shrugged. "What are you saying, Caleb? This guy is perfect for us. You wanted a goody-two-shoes who might chicken out and rat us out? No. We know all about him now, and once he knows we know, he'll be straight with us. Trust me."

Caleb laughed, a dry sound. "I keep forgetting that what we're about to do is illegal. We should ask Alex if he has any ideas about how to get the money back to the States. Bet he'll freak when he finds out we've got seven gold bars. He's thinking one, maybe two."

"Exactly. We tell him the truth and ask for his opinion. What do we have to lose?"

They agreed: at today's lunch meeting at the Leagues Club, they would tell Alex everything, except for the gold map. That secret was staying buried for now.

Caleb fired off a cheeky email to his parents, using coded language he hoped they'd grasp:

Hi you pair, trust all is well.
Looked for your Godson last week and found him without any problems. He wants to come and live with you in San Francisco so I am trying to work out the details to get him over there.
Missing the saloon, Joanna sends her love. Talk soon.
Caleb.

Joanna read it and burst out laughing. "Very clever. Quite brilliant, actually. I'm sure they'll get the gist."

Later, over lunch, Alex confirmed he could push the deal at ten and a half percent, but just barely.

Caleb leaned in, lowering his voice. "Alex, we've got seven ingots. Each one weighs around twelve kilos."

The words seemed to hit Alex like a cold wave. His face went slack.

"We also know your full criminal history, Alex. Just so you feel relaxed around us," Caleb said, smirking. "Straight to the point, we need your help."

"Seven gold bars?" Alex echoed, blinking. "Wow. This is a big deal now. Maybe too big. But… maybe a little at a time?"

Alex's mind was spinning. "This is big dollars. Millions, maybe. What kind of help do you need, Joanna?"

Alex didn't even flinch at the mention of his record. He wasn't worried, he was stunned.

Caleb knew honesty was the only way to keep this fragile alliance intact. They couldn't hide anything but the map.

He told Alex everything, the coordinates for the gold from a man in San Francisco, the bushranger robbery from over 150 years ago, how he'd melted the letters NSWG from each ingot.

He confessed their biggest worry: no clue how to get the money back to the U.S. from selling the gold.

Alex sat there, eyes wide, not quite believing what they'd just dropped on him. It was like a movie, too good, too crazy, too surreal to be real. But here they were, standing in the middle of it, hoping the story would end well.

They had just polished off lunch and migrated to the lounge, a dim, cozy refuge where the muffled clinks of glasses and the faint hum of distant chatter faded into the background. The kind of place where secrets felt safer, wrapped in shadows and whispered voices. Here, Caleb and Joanna laid it all out for Alex: the gold, the weight of it, the impossible task of getting it out.

Alex listened with that wary, half-cynical look of a man who's seen enough trouble to know when to jump in and when to run. When the last word fell from their lips, he nodded slowly, the wheels turning behind his eyes. He was eager to help, sure, but his voice carried the rough edge of hard-earned caution.

"No way you're sneaking that kind of gold out without paying a heavy toll. And I'm talking riskier than you want to imagine." His gaze flickered, eyes darting like a man checking the exits in a room he doesn't trust. "But I've got a plan. Not the slick, fast kind. More like a slow burn, drawn out, patient. Might take a while."

He hesitated, like a gambler counting chips before the big bet. "Gimme a couple days. I need to check some things, run my fingers over the map, and talk to some ghosts I know. Then I'll lay it all out."

Caleb's mind was still wrapped in the golden tangle when Joanna, ever the one to pull him back from the edge, suggested a change of scenery. "Let's hit the coast for a couple nights. Batemans Bay, fresh air, salt in your lungs. Forget the gold for a while."

The idea caught like wildfire. She packed her surfboard, that weather-beaten plank with stories etched in every scratch, and spent a whole sun-soaked day teaching Caleb to ride the restless waves. He tumbled and flailed, crashing into white foam and salt spray, but by sunset, there was something fierce and stubborn growing in his stance.

Evenings slipped into nights filled with music and laughter at the Catalina Golf Club, a place alive with flashing lights and live bands humming deep into the darkness. The motel was close enough to walk, a short stumble through quiet streets wrapped in the soft glow of street lamps.

Saturday morning cracked open slow and lazy when the phone finally rang, cutting through the calm like a sharp blade. Almost four days had slipped by without word from Alex, and the silence had begun to gnaw at them, was he still in, or had the whole thing fallen apart?

When Alex's voice came through, it carried a tired but steady warmth. "Stay put," he said, a hint of a smile you could almost hear. "I'm coming down. Could use a break myself."

So the three of them spent the week cradled by the coast, caught in the rhythm of waves and quiet moments between them. And just like Joanna had hoped, something started to bloom, soft and unforced, like moss growing over old stones. Love. Something tentative and sweet, settling in the spaces between the gold bars and whispered plans.

Caleb, once so certain his future lay back in the States, found himself thinking differently now. He was already plotting to stay. To make Australia home, no matter what Alex's plan might turn out to be.

The afternoon sun was fading slowly when Alex rolled up to the Catalina Club, not alone but with his wife, Carol. They moved together through the door, the kind of quiet partnership born of shared battles and secrets spoken in low tones. Joanna and Caleb stood to greet them, and soon the four were settled in the club's dim, smoky lounge, beers sweating cold in their hands, potato chips crackling softly between sips and murmurs.

Alex leaned back, a calm sort of confidence in his eyes, and said something that caught Caleb off guard. "There are no secrets between Carol and me, in respect to you buying" he said, voice steady. "She knows everything about this, the whole business."

"Buying? Buying what?" Caleb's voice cut sharp through the low hum.

"Real estate," Alex replied simply, as if that explained it all.

He began to unravel the plan with a slow precision, as if painting a picture stroke by deliberate stroke. "First thing, US citizens can buy property in Australia, no restrictions beyond the usual. Second, here's the kicker: the exchange isn't in dollars or bank credits. It's in gold. Real gold." He nodded, watching their faces carefully. "Cash deals in Australian real estate? That's just a figure of speech. What it really means is no bank finance is involved. All transactions are bank transfers, but this one? It's gold bullion instead of money."

Alex paused, letting the idea settle in their minds before hitting the next point. "And here's the best part, it'll cost you about seven and a half percent of your gold's value. That's the fee."

Joanna and Caleb exchanged glances, skepticism lurking in the corners of their eyes, but Alex raised his hand, stopping them before they could interrupt. "Hear me out. Let me finish."

He leaned forward, voice dropping to a conspiratorial whisper as he laid out the details. "You find a property or properties, right? Then you nominate to exchange your gold bullion for the property instead of bank funds. To settle, you deposit the gold with the vendor's gold merchant or agent. They credit the vendor's gold bullion account. Simple as that."

Caleb's brow furrowed. "And once the property's in our name?"

"Then you sell it for whatever price you want," Alex said, his tone serious. "But as foreigners, you'll be taxed at sixty percent on any profit from the sale. The sale proceeds go into your Australian bank account. No questions asked. From there, you're free to transfer money internationally, legally, within limits, of course."

Alex took a long swallow from his schooner, eyes scanning the room before Joanna pressed the obvious question.

"So where does the seven and a half percent fit in?"

Joanna beat Caleb to it, the two leaning in.

"Five percent goes to me," Alex said flatly, "and two and a half percent is an incentive for the property vendor, a discount on the gold bullion. So if you buy a property for two million dollars, the vendor gets an extra fifty thousand in bullion value. Easy."

Caleb chuckled, voice dripping sarcasm. "And you pick up a hundred grand?"

Alex nodded, a slow grin spreading across his face. "Real estate commission. Carol's a licensed agent. We'll handle everything for you."

"But won't the gold merchant get suspicious when we deposit all that gold?" Joanna asked, her tone cautious.

Alex shrugged, as if shrugging off suspicion itself. "Here's the thing, if you, an individual, try to deposit gold bullion, yeah, the questions come fast and hard. But if Carol's company, the real estate firm, submits the gold as a deposit against the property, it's routine. They just assay it, certify it, and credit the vendor's account. Since it's the real estate agency handling it, there's far less chance of anyone digging into where the gold came from. I'm guessing, sure, since we haven't done it before, but that's how it looks."

The plan was starting to settle into something real, something they could almost reach out and touch. Caleb's mind raced, already spinning possible ways to break the news to his parents, it was going to be longer than a month before any money made its way to them.

Finally, they told Alex and Carol they needed some time, to talk, to think it all over. The gold was no longer just a wild story. It was a game now, and every piece mattered.

Joanna's mind was already racing miles ahead of Caleb's, weaving possibilities and plotting moves like a grandmaster setting up for a checkmate. Later that evening, back in their cramped motel room, the hum of the night seeping through cracked windows, Joanna booted up her laptop. The pale glow of the screen painted her face in ghostly light as she scoured Google Maps, hunting for answers hidden in pixels and lines.

"Why can't we just buy the property those two targets are sitting on?" she asked Caleb, her voice low but steady, like she'd just unlocked a secret no one else had. "Then we can hunt for treasure on our own land. Whatever we find, that's ours." She pulled up the property boundaries on the map, the faint outlines tracing a sprawling patch of land, somewhere between four and six thousand acres. A kingdom of secrets, waiting to be uncovered.

Switching to satellite view, she zoomed in around the homestead. "Hard to tell much about the house or how old it is." The aerial view was grainy, shrouded in trees and time. Not satisfied, she shifted to Google Earth and activated the 'time machine' feature, rewinding the years. The house stood its ground stubbornly, refusing to vanish or change shape, proof it had been there for a long time. "That place must be pretty damn old," she murmured. "Maybe we should get Carol to check it out for us."

Caleb nodded, and together they wrote down the address, the seed planted firmly in their minds. The next night, at dinner, Joanna laid the idea out carefully.

"Why would you want to buy a house out in woop-woop?" Carol asked, genuinely bewildered.

Joanna smiled, weaving a little white lie like a charm. "I love country life. My folks have a ranch back in Midland, Texas. I miss that." It wasn't exactly a ranch, but Carol didn't need to know that.

"We talked about it last night. We're thinking of applying for permanent resident status and making it our forever home."

Carol took the address, tapping it into her phone with practiced ease. "I'll check it out, figure an estimated valuation, and we can work out a figure to offer. Everything's for sale, dear, at the right price. You guys have a lot of bargaining power."

Alex said almost nothing, but Joanna caught the flicker of suspicion in his eyes. He didn't like that they wanted a place out in the middle of nowhere. Something about it unsettled him, but he kept quiet.

After dinner, Caleb and Joanna said their goodbyes to the Gregorys, thanking them for their help and promising to keep in touch. "Glad to be doing business with you," they said, trying to sound confident, steady.

Later that night, back in their room, Joanna's voice was barely above a whisper. "I don't trust Alex," she said, eyes shadowed with doubt. "I could see his brain working overtime the moment I mentioned buying that property."

Caleb said nothing at first, but after a pause, he spoke quietly. "I think I'll make a quick trip back home to tell my parents what's going on. Just for a couple of weeks. After you get back to work next week."

Joanna nodded, feeling the weight of the moment. For now, though, the holiday stretched ahead like a thin, fragile thread, a moment of calm before the storm.

"A ranch!" Caleb's mother exclaimed, the word rolling off her tongue like something out of a dream she hadn't dared whisper before. "Well, that sounds mighty fine." They sat together in the dim back room of the saloon, the dusty air thick with the scent of old wood and spilled whiskey, while Caleb unfolded the entire tale, how he'd followed the crude, hand-drawn map like some modern-day prospector and actually found the gold on their very first try.

His parents had been thrilled to see him back home, safe and sound in San Francisco, but the harder part, the part nobody could fix with a shovel, was getting that gold out of Australia. Caleb spoke with a kind of weary certainty, explaining how tightly the country had sealed its borders around their treasure, every loophole guarded by red tape and watchful eyes. "They've got it all covered," he said, "but hopefully, the plan I told you about will work. The catch is, you have to hold onto any property you buy for at least two years before selling, or the penalties come crashing down like a hammer."

His father, Wesley, rubbed his weathered hands together and shook his head. "Without you here for two years, Caleb, we wouldn't even be standing in this saloon. It's just too damn hard to keep the place going without your help. We're getting too old for all this hard work."

Adina, his mother, glanced around the worn room, the tired glint in her eyes softening for a moment. "Maybe we should start thinking about selling the saloon... and moving to that ranch in Australia. To live with you."

Caleb blinked, caught off guard but intrigued. "Mom! That might actually be the perfect idea. It'd sure make life easier for all of us. But... would you really sell the saloon? I thought you both loved it."

Wesley sighed, a slow, heavy sound like a storm brewing on the horizon. "We did love it, once. But not all the work that comes with it. After all this time, it still isn't really making the kind of money we'd hoped for. It's costing us big Adina! It's more of a liability than an asset."

Adina nodded, biting her lip thoughtfully. "You know, maybe we really ought to think about this seriously, about becoming permanent residents in Australia."

Caleb's eyes lit with a flicker of hope. Joanna had already done the homework, digging into the residency options like a prospector sifting through dirt for nuggets of gold. He helped his parents fill out the application forms online, documents flying across continents and time zones as they were sent off to Joanna at the embassy in Canberra.

"Nothing ventured, nothing gained," Adina murmured, a faint smile tugging at the corners of her mouth as she glanced at her husband.

In that moment, beneath the flickering light of the saloon's old bulbs, the impossible seemed just a little bit closer to reality.

Caleb had returned to Canberra with a restless mind, the weight of a thousand miles still pressing down on his shoulders. The news Joanna carried about the sprawling acreage they longed to own felt like a whisper from a distant, haunted past. The place was called Kimbarry, a name that lingered in the air like a ghost's sigh.

Nestled between the tiny, almost forgotten hamlets of Reids Flat and Bigga, Kimbarry sat isolated and silent. The nearest town of any consequence was Cowra, a gruelling hour and a half drive to the northwest. Forty kilometres of that journey was a rough dirt road, where dust hung thick like a choking fog and the wild, dry earth seemed to clutch at your tires with unseen fingers.

The property sprawled across seven hundred and fifty acres, a wild patch of land marked by rugged hills and wind-swept pastures. At its heart stood the homestead, a sprawling, rambling beast of a building with a history carved deep into its weathered stone walls. It began life in 1853 as a Cobb and Co staging point, a dusty haven for horse-drawn coaches and weary travellers, before transforming into an inn where secrets, rumours, and stories bled into the timber floors like spilled wine.

The stones themselves were quarried from Glenella, near Bigga, cold and hard as the years that had passed. In 1921, the property had been claimed by Brendon Barrington Hewson, known simply as Barry, a man who poured blood and sweat into renovating the place, turning it into a family home for his wife, Kimberly, and their four sons. The homestead was no longer just shelter, it was a fortress of memory, etched with laughter and loss.

That loss came like a storm. On September 3, 1939, when Prime Minister Robert Menzies announced Australia's entry into the Second World War, the Hewson family was shattered. By 1942, all four sons were serving overseas in the infantry, young men swallowed whole by the endless hunger of war. None returned. Kimbarry became a monument to absence and grief.

In 1960, the estate passed quietly to Barry's nephew, who held onto it like a secret too heavy to bear. Since 2010, no one had lived there, the silence stretching thick like spider webs across empty rooms. Yet the land lived on, leased out to graziers who coaxed life from the sprawling acres, riding the weather and seasons with dogged patience.

 Max Barrington

To Donal Hewson, the current owner, the offer to buy Kimbarry was a lifeline thrown into a storm. Other investments were sinking, haemorrhaging value, and the promise of a cash injection, gold bullion, no less, arrived just in time to steady the boat. The asking price was a staggering six and a half million dollars, but Carol Gregory, sharp and unyielding, carved it down to a neat five million, a figure that suited everyone.

There was one catch: the grazing leases would remain in place until their term expired, the new owners stepping into the shoes of the old ones. It was a condition Donal accepted without hesitation, relief thick in his voice.

A contract had been drafted, waiting on Joanna and Caleb's signatures, a fragile promise hanging on the edge of their inspection, their judgment. The land, the house, the history, it was all theirs to claim or abandon.

Caleb's nerves were stretched thin as the weekend approached, the clock ticking down to Joanna's five-day leave. Their plan was clear: inspect Kimbarry in person, see the sprawling property with their own eyes, breathe in the dust and the history. They'd booked a room at the Federal Hotel in Bigga for Friday and Saturday nights, Bigga, that tiny speck of a town about fifteen minutes from Kimbarry, where the air smelled faintly of woodsmoke and old secrets.

On Friday afternoon, a small but crucial piece of the puzzle arrived: the keys to Kimbarry. Carol had received them in the mail and wasted no time calling Caleb, asking him to swing by her office to collect them. Then, with a tone that carried just a hint of excitement, she suggested something Caleb hadn't quite expected, why not have her and Alex come along for the weekend? "It could be fun," she said breezily, as if it were no big deal.

Caleb hesitated. The idea of sharing this private mission grated against his instincts, yet he didn't want to stir up any tension. So he agreed, forcing a smile into his voice, "Sounds like a great idea." He even promised to book another room at the pub for Carol and Alex for the two nights, trying to keep things smooth.

Carol's enthusiasm bubbled over. "I'll bring the keys with me tonight, saves you a trip," she said. "We'll see you at Bigga."

But Caleb's heart wasn't in it. He didn't want company when he and Joanna finally walked the grounds of Kimbarry. There were other treasures on the map he wanted to explore, quiet places he wanted to examine without prying eyes. Yet he swallowed his misgivings. The dance of diplomacy was delicate, he had to keep Carol and Alex close, at least until the property deal was done. The other sites would have to wait. There was always time.

Friday's drive to Bigga was its own kind of madness, Friday night traffic thick and unforgiving, cars and trucks bumper to bumper. Relief washed over Caleb once they turned off the highway just past Yass. The road narrowed, the chatter of the highway fading into silence, the countryside stretching wide and empty around them.

Joanna, meanwhile, hadn't been troubled by the plan to meet up with Carol and Alex. She liked Carol, bright, funny, easy company. And the prospect of a weekend with friends added a lightness to the trip, a welcome contrast to the tension Caleb tried to hide.

The hotel was a relic from another time, its weathered façade and creaking sign whispered stories of decades long past. Inside, the upstairs rooms were no different. They were cloaked in a thick patina of nostalgia: faded wallpaper peeling slightly at the edges, the scent of old wood and forgotten memories hanging heavy in the air. But despite the age, the rooms were surprisingly clean, the beds made neatly, the sheets crisp. At each end of the narrow hallway, bathrooms stood ready, their tiled floors shining faintly under the dim overhead lights, promising at least some measure of comfort in this rustic outpost.

Downstairs, the two bars beckoned with low wooden beams and worn leather stools. One of the bars boasted a lounge-dining area where shadows clung to corners like secrets. The rough-hewn timber and cracked paint spoke of years spent soaking up laughter, arguments, and the clinking of glasses. Caleb and Joanna were on their second round when the door swung open and Alex and Carol walked in, just as the clock struck seven, the usual time for the evening's first meal. After warm greetings and the necessary replenishment of drinks, the four of them moved to the dining room, where Carol wasted no time laying out the details of the deal.

Her voice was steady, practiced, but there was an edge to it that Caleb couldn't quite place.

"My company will accept a deposit from you, ninety-five percent of the asking price, five million dollars, in gold bullion," she explained carefully, like a banker quoting terms. "This deposit will be held in trust by ACT Bullion Managers. They'll assay the gold, certify it. Once that's done, any excess value over ninety-five percent, say, if five gold bars weigh a little more or assay higher than expected, will be returned to you in cash at settlement. The bullion stays in trust until settlement day, when it will be transferred to the vendor."

She paused, gauging their faces before continuing, "My commission, five percent, will be deducted from the balance of the house payment you make on settlement day. Plus, there's the other five percent you'll owe us for the launder."

Caleb's brow furrowed. "What other five percent?"

Before Carol could answer, Alex jumped in, sharp and quick like a snake striking. "The five percent I mentioned, the cost to convert the gold to money. Originally it was ten percent, but since we're already taking five percent as commission on the house sale, I dropped the laundering fee to five percent too. Fair's fair."

Caleb swallowed hard, the scent of a con curling in the back of his mind like smoke. Something didn't sit right with all this talk of percentages and laundering, but he pushed it aside, for now. They were already miles ahead of where they had been, and sometimes, to win the game, you had to play their rules. Still, he'd keep a careful eye on Alex. In this game, trust was a currency far rarer than gold.

The homestead was far grander than Caleb and Joanna had imagined, its scale almost overwhelming in the late afternoon light. They stepped through a formal entry, a wide vestibule where timeworn timber armchairs circled the room like sentinels guarding old stories. To one side, a set of double doors opened into the lounge, spacious, with high ceilings and dust motes dancing in the shafts of sun slicing through stained glass windows. On the other side, a single door led to an office, the kind of place where secrets and plans had been whispered over decades.

Behind the vestibule, a narrow corridor led to six bedrooms, their worn floorboards creaking beneath their feet. At the rear, a modest restroom waited, functional but faded. Beyond the lounge, the kitchen and dining room beckoned, cavernous and full of potential, though stained by years of neglect. Near the rear entry sat a laundry and a jumble of utility rooms, remnants of a household once lively, now quietly fading.

The house was rough, the years had not been kind. Since Donal Hewson had taken ownership, it had mostly been empty, a place visited sporadically between his frequent overseas travels. He preferred the concrete and noise of his Sydney apartment, leaving the homestead to weather the seasons alone.

Yet Joanna and Caleb saw something else, possibility, a future stretching out like the vast acreage surrounding the old stone walls. It was perfect for them, a place to share with Caleb's parents, a new chapter waiting to be written.

Alex, ever blunt, frowned. "Why would anyone want to live in this place, so far out here?" His tone was serious, a chill wind cutting through the excitement.

Carol shifted uncomfortably beside him.

Joanna smiled, undeterred. "Not everyone's cup of tea, I know," she said softly. "But just wait until you see it a year from now, I promise you'll be amazed."

Alex shrugged, unconvinced. "To each his own, my dear. But it's still out here in the bush, no matter what."

Later, they piled into Joanna's Jeep and set off down dirt tracks that wound like veins through the sprawling property. Agistment stock grazed lazily across the fields, their presence a quiet hum of life on the land. The country looked good, weathered but fertile, the kind of place that whispered opportunity in the wind.

Alex commented on the agistment as a solid passive income, a reminder to Caleb that there was more to do before the dream could fully take shape. His parents' permanent residency had been approved, a green light to a new beginning, and the old saloon was now listed for sale back home, the final step before the move to Australia could begin in earnest.

Caleb glanced at the rolling fields, the homestead fading into the golden dusk. A new life was waiting here. They just had to reach out and claim it.

Back at the old Federal Hotel in Bigga, the evening was thick with the warm hum of celebration. The locals, rugged and weather-beaten, had gathered like moths to a flame, welcoming Caleb and Joanna with easy smiles and the kind of hospitality born from years of solitude and shared hardship. The air inside the rustic bar was thick with laughter, the clink of glasses, and the low murmur of stories swapping hands like currency.

Among the new faces was an elderly man, weathered and bent like the gnarled branches of a drought-stricken gum tree. He introduced himself as Kerry, a name that seemed stitched from the very soil of the place. He chuckled when he told them they would soon be his new landlords.

"I live in one of those two workers' cottages, about three clicks from the homestead," he said, his voice a gravelly whisper. "Used to be the overseer here, that was the job title. The cottage was part of the pay packet." His eyes twinkled with mischief as he continued. "The job's long gone now, but no one's ever told me I've got to move out. Hope no one tells you either."

Caleb and Joanna shared a laugh, the kind that loosens the tight bands of worry around their chests. Joanna shook his hand warmly, "I'm Joanna, and this is Caleb. We'll be sure to come by once we're settled."

Kerry nodded, a knowing grin tugging at his lips. "Looking forward to it. But mind you, best pay a visit to the squatters in the other cottage. Could be interesting." And with that, he let the thought hang in the air like a shadow.

The settlement on Kimbarry had gone smoother than either of them dared hope. The gold, those heavy ingots, had been counted, weighed, and exchanged with precision. In fact, there was a tidy sum left over, nearly two hundred and forty thousand dollars in change from five bars.

Alex had casually asked Caleb if there was a safe place for the remaining gold, and Caleb had simply told him, "Joanna took it to the embassy for safekeeping."

Inside, Caleb's mind snarled with suspicion. Fuck you, he thought sharply. The trust wasn't there, not with Alex. Not yet. The gleam of gold was bright, but the shadows lurking around it were darker still.

They hadn't wasted a single moment. Before the dust of the settlement had even settled, a local builder had arrived, boots crunching on the gravel, clipboard in hand. He led Caleb and Joanna through the vast, weathered homestead room by room, eyes sharp, fingers tracing cracks in the plaster, worn floorboards, and faded wallpaper peeling like dead skin. Together, they drew up a scope of works that would breathe new life into the old bones of the house, renovations, repairs, painting throughout, everything the house desperately needed to shake off decades of neglect.

The list grew longer with each passing hour. Roof repairs, window restorations, plumbing upgrades, electrical rewiring, and fresh coats of paint to chase away the musty, forgotten air of emptiness that had settled over the place. The numbers climbed quickly, and when the estimate came in, it was a cold splash of reality, over two hundred thousand dollars.

But Caleb and Joanna had a plan. They covered the entire cost with the change leftover from the settlement funds, the gold that had been counted and exchanged with such careful precision. It was money that would transform 'Kimbarry' from a haunted relic into a home, ready for new stories, new lives, and new beginnings.

The sale of The Twilight Star saloon had been surprisingly swift, almost like a sudden gust scattering dust on a long-forgotten trail. Wesley and Adina found themselves caught off guard by how quickly everything had unfolded. One moment they were holding the keys to their beloved, yet burdensome, saloon, and the next, they were boarding Qantas flight QF74 bound for Sydney. Fifteen hours in the air, crossing half the world, and leaving behind decades of memories wrapped in oak and whiskey.

Caleb and Joanna had made a decision: no tedious domestic flights from Sydney to Canberra for Wesley and Adina. Instead, they would pick them up at the airport and drive straight out to Bigga, a quiet dot on the map nestled almost halfway between Canberra and Sydney, but stretching out towards the rugged west.

The reunion was raw and bittersweet. Caleb's parents stepping off the plane, their faces a mix of exhaustion and cautious excitement, and Caleb greeting them with a fierce hug that spoke of relief and the unspoken fears of change. For Joanna, it was a first meeting with Wesley and Adina, a delicate dance of introductions and shy smiles under the muted fluorescent lights of the Sydney airport.

Joanna's Jeep was packed tight with luggage, essentials, and a quiet excitement that hummed beneath the surface. The drive to Bigga was swift but felt like crossing a threshold into a new chapter. By the time they arrived, the old homestead stood patiently beneath a sprawling sky, its weathered stone walls promising shelter and stories yet to be told.

Joanna had already stocked the house with enough food and drink to last them through the first few days of this new beginning. She had transformed one of the huge bedrooms, complete with its own ensuite, at the far end of the long corridor into a welcoming sanctuary for Wesley and Adina. Their room felt like a private haven, while Caleb and Joanna's own quarters lay at the opposite end of the house, separated by what felt like miles of creaking floorboards and the silent watch of the old homestead.

When Monday crept in like a thief, cold and unwelcome, it stole Joanna away.

Duty called her back to Canberra and the tidy, clinical corridors of the U.S. Embassy, back to the place where reality still held dominion over dreams. She was close to the end, just two months shy of finishing her service in the United States Marine Corps. But instead of returning to America for her discharge, she was trying to arrange it from Australia, wrestling with bureaucracy that moved slower than an old tortoise in molasses. No word had come yet, and until it did, she was stuck playing the part of diplomat by day and dreamer by night.

Caleb watched her go with a knot in his stomach he couldn't untie. The house felt bigger when she was gone, more echo than home.

That morning, he and Wesley packed their gear and headed out, chasing whispers from the map like two treasure hunters on the trail of half-buried myths. They were heading to the marked sites, where the gold targets winked on paper like promises made under candlelight. The land around them was eerily familiar, its rugged skin not unlike the place they'd stumbled across the seven gold bars. Same harsh terrain. Same quiet hum of something ancient and waiting.

But it was no good trying to take a compass reading under a wool-blanket sky. Without the Southern Cross overhead, Australia's celestial north star, they might as well be walking in circles. So they waited, watching the heavens and hoping for the weather to cooperate.

That night, the sky cleared like a stage curtain rising on Act Two.

They piled into the ancient Land Rover, a boxy, wheezing beast Caleb had salvaged from one of the forgotten sheds scattered across the property like ghost towns. It had taken him two full days to get it running, scavenging parts from a wrecking yard in Goulburn, a hundred klicks away. But now it roared to life with the stubborn resolve of something that had known better days but wasn't ready to die yet.

The vehicle got them partway up the hill before coughing in surrender, its engine chugging out a final breath. The rest of the journey was on foot. Four hundred meters of rocky climb brought them to the high outcrop etched into the map like a landmark from a dream.

Armed with compass, map, and the Southern Cross itself gleaming above like an ancient watchman, Caleb tried to align the angles. North star to stone. Heaven to earth.

But something was wrong.

The stars, those goddamn stars, looked all wrong, skewed somehow, like a jigsaw puzzle forced together by the hand of a child. He couldn't get the compass to cooperate. The line between the northernmost and southernmost points refused to make sense. It was like trying to navigate a house of mirrors with a broken flashlight.

He stared, squinting, breathing in frustration, checking and rechecking until his brain throbbed. No matter what he did, it didn't feel right. The terrain was close, familiar even, but maybe not exactly the place marked on the map. Maybe they were off.

Maybe the map itself was wrong. Maybe the stars had changed while no one was looking.

After what felt like hours, he gave up. He tucked the compass and map back into his coat and said nothing as they descended in the darkness, the sky above them indifferent and infinite.

Back at the house, Caleb laid the tools out neatly on the old timber desk in the office, like a priest setting down relics at the altar. He would wait for the weekend. Wait for Joanna. Somehow, she made things click. She saw patterns where he saw puzzles.

Until then, the stars could keep their secrets.

While the week drifted by, slow and drowsy like a river through the paddocks, Caleb and his parents immersed themselves in the curious task of settling into the old homestead. It was more than just a house, it was a relic, a time capsule from a century gone, whispering stories from every creak of the floorboards and echo of footsteps down its long hallways.

The place was massive. Not just big, but sprawling, with an almost unnerving complexity. Odd little rooms branched off hallways like forgotten tributaries, narrow spaces that felt more like storage vaults or servants' quarters, although no one could be sure. Joanna had joked about them being hidey-holes for ghosts of farmhands past, but now she was gone, and her laughter didn't echo here anymore.

The main section of the house, the heart of the place, was a hulking, cold beauty built from basalt stone blocks, quarried, no doubt, from the local countryside back in 1853. The craftsmanship was undeniable, and the ceilings soared to three-point-six metres, twelve feet in the old measure. That towering space had been a clever bit of bush engineering back in the day, a natural way to trap the heat above in summer and keep the fire's warmth lingering in the bitter Southern Tablelands winters.

But what puzzled both Caleb and Wesley was the roof.

With a pitch that soared at least another three metres above the ceiling, the space beneath it seemed cavernous, like a hidden world suspended above them. Yet, no matter how thoroughly they searched, no access panel could be found. No ladder, no trapdoor, no dusty corner where some carpenter had left a hidden clue. It was a sealed cathedral of timber and shadow. Strange, Caleb thought. Uncommon, even for a house this old. He couldn't shake the feeling that there was something up there.

The newer sections of the house, the bedroom wings, flanked the original stone core like outstretched arms. These additions were practical, tacked on over the years with more modern materials. Their ceilings were lower, 2.7 metres, or nine feet if you asked someone who remembered when petrol was sold by the gallon. Unlike the central chamber, these wings had easy access panels into the roof space, typical and unremarkable. Still, even those rafters seemed to creak with history.

Wesley, for his part, was delighted by the whole thing. He poked and prodded the architecture with a boyish enthusiasm Caleb hadn't seen in years. Adina, on the other hand, was methodical, cataloguing, cleaning, organizing. She treated the house like a patient needing careful diagnosis.

By Thursday, they'd uncovered an old root cellar behind what appeared to be an unused pantry and found a rusted, padlocked cabinet in one of the storerooms that Caleb had made a mental note to investigate further. The house seemed to be breathing around them, stretching, adjusting to its new inhabitants, revealing secrets slowly, like an old man remembering stories he hadn't told in decades.

And above it all, somewhere in the vaulted, sealed void of the high roof, something waited.

Caleb found himself glancing upward a lot, especially at night, when the wind sighed through the eaves and made the timber creak like footsteps pacing above. He told himself it was just the house settling.

He didn't believe it.

The property, it turned out, was more than just an old homestead resting in a sea of paddocks, it was a living monument to a bygone era of hard sweat and hardier men. And it carried the bones of that history like a badge of honour.

To the west of the house, set low in the gently rising land, stood a vast shearing shed, eight stands wide, with a raked tin roof that groaned when the wind kicked up from the hills. Weathered timber and rusted iron clung together in defiance of time. The scent of lanolin still lingered faintly in the boards, a ghost of the thousands of sheep once dragged across its floor. It wasn't just a shed; it was a cathedral of the wool industry, silent now, but heavy with the echoes of bleating sheep and the buzz of clippers.

Beside it, in an equally aged but surprisingly sound structure, stood the shearers' quarters. Twelve small rooms lined a breezeway like cells in a monastic outpost, simple, spartan, and undeniably Australian. A mess room with long benches and battered enamel teapots stood at the heart of the building, its adjoining kitchen bearing an old cast iron stove and wood-fired copper for boiling water. A separate storeroom, laundry, and an ablution block stood nearby, the latter complete with three long-drop toilets set back a respectful ten metres. The smell still lingered, faint but unmistakable, even after all these years.

Off one corner of the shearing shed was a smaller lean-to that housed a once-thrumming Lister diesel engine, its paint flaking, but its bones still solid. It had powered the entire operation, clippers, grinders, and whatever else the shearers needed when the sheds were full and the wool was flying. A more recent addition, a 240-volt electric motor, sat beside it like a young apprentice waiting for the master to finally give out. Caleb hadn't tested either machine yet, but he had a suspicion the old Lister would cough back to life with enough coaxing.

All around the property, in what might once have passed for a loose semi-circle, stood other sheds, leaning, grumbling structures whose purposes had long since drifted into myth. There had been stables once, judging by the worn timber rails and scattered horseshoe nails. A run-down kennel with a dozen rusted feed bowls spoke of working dogs long gone. A henhouse sagged at one end, chook wire flapping loose in the breeze. And others, sheds for storage, saddlery, fuel, each one a mystery waiting to be solved.

To the Ahrens family, it was like stepping onto another planet.

Sheep? Caleb had never even seen one up close that wasn't behind a fence or on a plate. Wesley kept scratching his head and muttering about sheep-dipping and dagging and how the hell any of it worked. Adina took one look at the quarters and said she wouldn't mind giving them a good clean and maybe turning them into guest accommodation, "once we learn what in God's name used to happen here."

But despite the unfamiliarity, there was a growing sense of curiosity in the family, a readiness to learn, to uncover. Caleb especially felt it stirring deep in his bones. This wasn't just land. It was a story written in dirt and timber, in sheep's wool and rust. And now it was theirs.

He knew one thing for sure.

They might be out of their depth, but they were in exactly the right place.

The day before Joanna was due back, the skies over Bigga were a vast sheet of soft blue, unmarred by cloud, the kind of day that whispered of possibility and half-forgotten dreams. Caleb had decided to take his parents on a leisurely exploration through the rolling paddocks, tracing dusty fencelines and reminiscing aloud about the mysterious gold map and its elusive promise.

They were nearing what Caleb believed to be the area marked on the map when Adina glanced out across the scrub-dotted rise and shook her head. "It doesn't feel right," she murmured. Wesley, seated beside her in the back of the old Land Rover, agreed. "Too flat. Too open. The place on the map felt... tighter. Hemmed in."

The doubt wormed its way into Caleb's mind like a cold breath on the back of his neck. He slowed the vehicle, frowning at the landscape, then changed course. Just ahead, nestled under the arms of some ghostly old gum trees, was one of the two workers' cottages noted on the property plan. It had that forgotten, slouched look, a dwelling barely holding itself up, like an old boxer still standing out of habit.

"I reckon that might be Kerry's place," Caleb muttered. "Remember him? The old fella we met when we first looked at the property."

They drove up slowly, wheels crunching over dry gravel and sunbaked weeds. The cottage, if you could still call it that, looked like it had lost its will to be lived in. Walls leaned where they shouldn't. Windows were patched with cardboard and tarp. Rubbish was scattered around in heaps, rusted tins, old furniture, plastic bottles, and mounds of something else too far gone to identify.

Then the dogs came.

Two of them, filthy and snarling, shot out from under the house like demons loosed from the shadows. They circled the vehicle, barking with a mix of madness and malice, teeth bared and hackles raised. Caleb had started to open the door, but froze mid-motion. These weren't farm dogs. These were something else, half-wild, and fully unhinged.

A moment later, the front door slammed open.

A man emerged, hulking, barefoot, his clothes filthy and torn. His beard was a bush of tangled grey, his eyes bloodshot and twitching. He stank even from a distance, a foul chemical odour carried on the air like a curse.

"What do youse pricks want?" he barked, advancing toward the Land Rover with a staggering gait, fists clenched at his sides.

Caught off-guard by the raw hostility, Caleb lifted his hands slightly in a peaceful gesture. "Just looking around," he said evenly. It was true enough.

The man sneered. "Well, d'ya know youse are on private property? Yeah, ya do, don't ya. So fuck off, and don't fucking come back!"

Caleb bit his tongue, not because he was afraid, far from it, but because his parents were sitting right behind him. He turned the vehicle around slowly, the dogs snapping at the tyres as he pulled away, his foot light on the accelerator.

"That was unpleasant," Adina muttered, wiping at her nose. "What is that smell?"

Caleb rolled up the window. The stench had seeped inside, a reeking chemical fug that made his stomach turn. But he knew it all too well. Meth. Or at least, the ingredients used to make it. An old cottage, piles of rubbish, aggressive dogs, a paranoid, erratic inhabitant, and that stench.

He didn't say anything for a moment, just narrowed his eyes as he watched the cottage fade behind them in the rear-view mirror.

"Looks like a job for later," he said at last, his voice cold and calm. He'd been inside meth labs before, back when he was conducting raids as part of the Marine Recon Unit. They were always dangerous, always unpredictable. But they were also familiar. "Could be interesting," he added under his breath.

Back at the homestead, the mood was lighter. Joanna had arrived home for her four-day break and was already waiting on the veranda, a bottle of wine in one hand, her boots kicked off and a smile tugging at her lips.

"Welcome home," she called out, raising the bottle.

Caleb stepped out of the car, the memory of the cottage still lurking behind his eyes like a bruise.

"Good timing," he said. "I think we've got ourselves a situation."

They were all heading to Canberra the next day, a trip that had been planned for weeks. Wesley's new Toyota LandCruiser was finally ready for collection, a shiny, white beast of a machine he'd ordered with every optional extra the salesman could throw at him. The plan was simple: collect the vehicle, do a bit of shopping, attend an embassy function that evening, and return to Kimbarry first thing the following morning. They had booked two adjoining rooms at the Crowne Plaza, a place of polished floors, quiet luxury, and feather-soft duvets, a welcome change from the rough, unpredictable edges of the homestead.

As they arrived in Canberra that bright Saturday morning, Caleb leaned forward in the back seat and spoke low to Joanna.

"Before we head to Fyshwick, can we stop at the embassy? There's a package in your bag. Delivered last week."

Joanna shot him a look, not suspicious exactly, but sharp. She'd been briefed enough times in her diplomatic role to know when something smelled off, and Caleb wasn't one to make careless requests. Still, she nodded without a word and swung the car down Constitution Avenue toward the embassy. Inside, she returned with a slim, tightly wrapped parcel, a small, dense object she handed to Caleb without comment as she slid behind the wheel again.

"Thanks," he said, slipping it into his satchel.

From there, they continued on to Fyshwick. The Canberra Toyota dealership gleamed under the mid-morning sun, a hive of motion and metallic reflections. Wesley lit up like a boy on Christmas morning when he spotted the LandCruiser waiting for him in the delivery bay. The paperwork was swift, the handover efficient. Soon they were cruising in tandem across town to the Woden Shopping Centre.

Caleb wandered the aisles of a local gun and outdoors shop, casually picking up a box of CCI Subsonic Stingers, .22 calibre, 32-grain hollow points. They were quiet and deadly accurate, ideal for his purposes, whatever they might be. He said nothing to the others about it, and nobody asked.

Dinner that night was a relaxed affair, laughter echoing off the glass walls of the Crowne's restaurant, their table strewn with wine glasses and half-finished desserts. Later, from the quiet of their rooms high above the city, they could look down on Lake Burley Griffin and the slow, deliberate pulse of Canberra's nightlights.

Sunday came with the usual hotel breakfast buffet and a long, easy drive back toward Kimbarry. Wesley took to the LandCruiser like a duck to water, though now and then he still found himself drifting toward the right-hand side of the road, his instincts from overseas not yet entirely overwritten.

That evening, as twilight bled slowly over the hills and the golden paddocks took on the hue of burnt umber, they drove past the second site Caleb had marked on the map. It was just as elusive as the first. Joanna, armed with a compass and a practised eye, climbed a low ridge and scanned the area, then shook her head.

"Too exposed," she said. "Doesn't fit the notes."

They stood for a few moments, watching the last light drain from the land. Nobody spoke. The air was cool, filled with the scent of dry grass and eucalyptus.

Eventually, it was Wesley who voiced what they were all thinking. "We've done enough for today. Let's try again later. We've got time."

Caleb nodded. "Yeah. It'll wait."

He didn't say it aloud, but he could feel something building, a current beneath the surface. The meth-stinking cottage, the package from the embassy, the ammunition, the maps, each piece slotting into a puzzle that hadn't yet shown its final picture.

But it would. And soon.

Waking before the sun had so much as stretched across the eastern paddocks, Caleb slipped from beneath the bedcovers and padded quietly through the house. The others were still sleeping, wrapped in the comfort of hotel fatigue and country silence. The creak of old floorboards beneath his bare feet was the only sound as he made his way toward the office, the early morning chill clinging to his skin like a second breath.

Joanna's car was parked just outside the homestead. He retrieved the diplomatic bag from the back seat, the weight of it familiar in his hand, and brought it inside. The office door clicked softly behind him as he entered and flicked on the lamp, just a pool of amber light spilling across the polished timber desk.

He placed the bag on the desk, unzipped it, and pulled free a parcel wrapped tightly in black plastic and sealed with heat-shrunk tape. It was no bigger than a thick novel. He worked the tape free with a utility knife, carefully peeling it back to reveal the contents. Inside lay his old friend, the Smith & Wesson M&P .22LR Compact, its matte-black slide catching the light like a whisper. Nestled beside it was the screw-on suppressor and, neatly boxed, the CCI subsonic ammunition he'd picked up in Woden.

He was about to stash it when his gaze flicked to the far side of the desk, something was wrong.

The map was gone.

The orienteering compass still sat where he'd left it, a trusted instrument from Joanna's collection, its bezel glinting faintly in the light. But the map, the one with his pencilled notes and GPS overlays, wasn't there. He stood still for a moment, letting the thought settle, weighing the implications. Had someone moved it? Or had someone taken it?

He said nothing aloud, but his gut churned. Someone had been in here. And not just anyone, someone who knew what they were looking for.

He refocused, slipping the pistol into the bottom drawer on the left-hand side of the desk. It fit snugly, as though the drawer had been built for it. He placed the ammunition beside it, lining up the box as neatly as a soldier laying down kit for inspection.

This weapon, small and elegant in its brutality, had been his go-to during covert ops in the Marines Recon. Among black ops units, government, foreign service, contractors, it had become a favourite. The M&P Compact was unassuming, deadly, and reliable. Ten rounds per magazine. Subsonic hollow-points that were whisper-quiet when paired with the suppressor. Little to no recoil. Near-zero muzzle flash. And when it hit, when those 32-grain hollow-point projectiles made contact, they exploded inward, creating catastrophic damage without an exit wound. Silent. Swift. Final.

He closed the drawer slowly, almost reverently. Locked it.

Then he sat, staring at the compass for a moment longer than necessary.

Somebody knew something. And if they'd seen the map, really seen it, then things were about to get complicated.

Damn complicated.

Caleb took the binoculars from the hook beside the door, their black strap smooth and worn from long use, and slung them around his neck like a priest might don a crucifix. There was a kind of ritual to it, this morning thing. He'd been dreaming again, something gray and hot and whispering, and though he couldn't recall the details now that sunlight had cracked the edge of his mind like a crowbar, it had left him with that same old buzzing under his skin. The kind of buzz you don't shake off with coffee.

He slid behind the wheel of the old Land Rover, its seat springs creaking under him like a warning groan from something buried too long. The engine coughed, hesitated, then rumbled to life. He guided the vehicle through the dew-slicked paddock behind the house at Kimbarry, dew sparkling like diamonds in the early light, the air damp and full of earthy smells. The track he turned onto wasn't one he'd traveled before, at least, not in this vehicle, not alone. But he had a hunch, and hunches were a thing he'd learned to trust in the Corps, back when trusting your gut meant maybe you lived long enough to call home.

The track ran narrow and rough, the kind of path you'd miss if you weren't looking for it, weaving like a lazy brown snake through scrub and gum trees. Caleb figured it ran somewhere near the back of the old worker's cottage, the one he'd visited last week with his folks. The one that had made the hairs on the back of his neck stiffen with that sour, metallic tang of wrongness. There'd been something off about it. The look of it. The smell. The two dogs that lived underneath the house like trolls guarding a bridge, their eyes glassy and too still. He'd had his suspicions then, meth, maybe. Or worse.

This morning, his plan was simple: swing in from the rear, keep his distance, and take a look without kicking up the dirt. No dogs barking. No shadows shifting behind the curtains. Just eyes on target.

The track hugged the base of a wooded incline, a natural barrier between the homestead and the cottage. Trees loomed on either side, leaning in close like gossips with secrets. As he rounded a bend where the track twisted tighter and began to climb, something caught his eye, a flash, a bright glint of light from up on the ridge to his right. It came and went so fast he almost thought it had been in his head. But no. He knew that kind of light. Sun bouncing off glass or steel. He hit the brakes, the Land Rover rocking to a halt on its ancient shocks.

Caleb stared up at the ridge, eyes narrowed, but the trees held their secrets tight. He backed the vehicle up slowly, the tires whispering over gravel and dirt, and paused again. There.

Flash.

This time, it was unmistakable. His pulse kicked up a notch.

He killed the engine and stepped out, closing the door with a gentle click instead of a slam. The silence that followed was dense and humming. He pulled the binoculars to his eyes and scanned the trees, but the glint was gone again, like a magician's coin. Only the hill stared back at him, unmoved.

He began to walk.

The ground rose beneath him, the incline steeper than it had looked from the track. Brambles tugged at his jeans and gum leaves crackled underfoot. A kookaburra laughed somewhere off to his left, but there was no humour in it. Just a sound like a door opening in the dark.

Then he saw them, faint, but there. Tyre tracks. Fresh enough that the crushed leaves hadn't started to curl back upright yet. Something heavy had come through here, something four-wheeled and probably unwelcome.

His lips pressed into a thin line.

Who the hell was up here? This was his land. His family's land. And that wasn't just a matter of ownership on paper. It meant something.

He followed the tracks, moving quietly now, every instinct alert and electric. There was a story unfolding here, he could feel it, some hidden chapter scratched into the dirt and waiting to be read.

Caleb stopped short, crouching low behind a squat, weathered rock half-sunken in the hillside like the skull of something ancient and buried. Just beyond it, parked in a patch of dead grass as if dropped there by some giant's careless hand, sat a white Toyota LandCruiser. It looked like it had been there a while, its flanks dusted with pollen, bird droppings marking the roof, a faint veil of grime across the windscreen, but the crushed grass around it told a different story. It hadn't died here. It had arrived. Recently.

He didn't get any closer than ten meters. Not yet. Not until he knew more.

The LandCruiser had New South Wales plates, sharp and clean and ordinary, but it was the kind of ordinary that made Caleb's gut do a slow, tight twist. The kind of ordinary you didn't want to find miles from a sealed road, on private land, with no prior notice and no reason. People didn't just turn up here.

He pulled his phone out, careful not to let the sun catch the screen, and opened the Notes app. His fingers were steady as he tapped in the plate number. The digital letters glowed for a second on the screen, then faded behind the phone's lock screen like a secret whispered and buried.

He scanned the vehicle again. No sign of anyone inside. No movement. No sound except the wind working its way through the dry treetops, making them whisper to each other in brittle voices.

Around the vehicle, the long, yellowing grass was beaten flat in a wide circle, as if someone had danced a slow, grim waltz around it. Caleb's eyes followed the trampled trail, his mind tracking the logic of the movements like a hunter. The grass was disturbed in a clear line leading up the hill, weaving between ghost gums and stringy barks, vanishing into thicker scrub at the crest.

That's where the driver had gone.

And unless they were a bird, they hadn't flown off the top.

Caleb moved forward, following the path like a hound on the scent. Each footstep was measured. Each breath shallow. He felt like he was walking into something, some shape just out of sight, something that might already be watching from up there in the trees.

From the crest of the hill, Caleb eased up like a ghost rising from the soil. The sun was low and hot on his back, and as he peered through the veil of sparsely scattered gums, the land fell away before him in a long, quiet sigh. About three hundred and fifty metres below, right where the slope of the hill exhaled into the flat, sat the weather-beaten worker's cottage, hunched and silent like it was ashamed to be seen in the daylight.

It was the same place he'd visited last week with his parents. The same place that stank of ammonia and secrets. It looked peaceful now. But Caleb knew better. Some houses carried their evil on the inside, like a tumour growing under the floorboards.

As his gaze swept the scene, something snagged his eye, a tiny flash, a spark in the corner of his vision like the flick of a match. Instinct kicked in like a boot to the gut. Caleb dropped into a crouch, his spine folding low, elbows brushing his knees. Marine training. Muscle memory. A lifetime of moving unseen.

He scanned again, slower this time.

There. Twenty metres ahead, nestled near the base of a skinny, half-dead tree, something glinted faintly in the filtered morning light. He squinted, reached for the binoculars, and brought them up with steady hands.

What he saw made his stomach knot, not in fear exactly, but in a kind of cold, surgical alertness. The kind a man feels when he's walking blindfolded and suddenly smells gas.

A spoon.

More specifically, a silver soup spoon, wedged just-so into the bark of the tree. Caleb understood its purpose immediately. He'd seen the trick used before, once in the Hindu Kush by a Russian merc with no fingers on his left hand. The curved bowl of the spoon was turned outward, catching just enough sun to serve as a rear-view mirror for someone who didn't want to be seen.

He adjusted his angle slightly and froze.

Lying prone in the dry leaf litter just to the left of the spoon's reflection was a man in full camouflage, the paint on his face cracked and flaking like old plaster. He was barely more than a shadow stretched over the earth, but the tripod and telescope gave him away. A professional setup. Patient. Silent. Watching the cottage.

Watching something.

Caleb's breath came slower now, each inhale deliberate. A bead of sweat rolled from his temple and curved around his cheekbone like it knew better than to fall.

He wasn't alone out here.

And whoever the man was, whoever had parked that LandCruiser and crawled up the hill, he wasn't just some hiker or stray hunter.

He was waiting.

Watching.

And worst of all, he was good at it.

Caleb's eyes never left the figure lying prone behind the telescope, but then a faint sound, the soft rustle of disturbed leaves, the almost imperceptible crunch of dry twigs, pulled his attention sharply to the right. A shadow detached itself from the gloom, a second figure emerging cautiously from behind the tree line. Like the first, this one was swathed in dark camouflage, the dull fabric blending into the undergrowth, the only giveaway the unmistakable shape of a military-style rifle cradled in his hands.

The man moved awkwardly, as if returning from something private, a bathroom break in the wild, Caleb guessed, and now he was edging back toward the first figure's position. Caleb's heart kicked hard against his ribs. He had been damned lucky to catch the man at the telescope first; had he arrived a moment later, the second one would've spotted him instantly.

"What the hell are these people doing here?" The question burned hot in Caleb's mind. His breath slowed, measured, silent.

With the practiced stealth of a hunter, Caleb slipped to the opposite side of the tree. His boots barely whispered against the dirt, his body low, his hands ready. He wasn't about to let this get out of hand.

Caleb's voice broke the heavy silence, low but clear enough to carry.

"Are you guys looking for someone?"

The second figure froze, then spun like a coiled snake, rifle swinging around the tree trunk and pointing dead at Caleb's chest. For a moment, time froze. The rifle's barrel was a cold steel promise inches from his face.

But Caleb was ready. His hands darted out and gripped the barrel, fingers locking around the cold metal like iron clamps. Using the tree for leverage, he wrenched the rifle from the man's grasp and twisted it around, forcing the barrel toward the ground.

"Take it easy!" Caleb barked, voice firm, no room for argument. "Stand still! Take it easy... both of you!"

He trained the rifle's muzzle on the man at the telescope. "Stay on the ground."

Then he turned back to the now disarmed soldier. "You! Get on the ground!"

The men hesitated, caught somewhere between shock and the instinct to fight. Caleb's fingers flicked the safety switch on the rifle, a small, but distinct click echoed sharply in the quiet.

"Both of you, hands in front. Slowly, take off those service belts."

The men obeyed, sliding their Glock 19s and extra magazines off as Caleb studied them carefully.

"Same mechanism as the Colt M4," Caleb muttered with a grim smile.

After disarming them, Caleb ordered the men to remove their headgear. Their faces emerged, young, hard, eyes sharp but wary.

"Now," Caleb said, voice calm but steely, "time to tell me who you are and what you're doing here."

He paused, then added with authority, "I'm Caleb Ahrens. Part owner of this property."

A flicker passed between the two men's eyes, radio chatter, Caleb was sure of it. He spoke loud enough for them to hear.

"Tell your supervisor to get up here. Pronto."

Minutes ticked by with agonizing slowness. Then, from just beyond the crest of the hill Caleb had ascended earlier, the faint roar of an engine broke the silence. Caleb crouched behind the tree, watching, waiting.

Two more figures appeared, moving cautiously down the slope. Like the others, they wore camouflage uniforms, but these two carried themselves differently. Their weapons were lowered, their postures less hostile.

Caleb called out, voice sharp, commanding:

"Lower those weapons! We don't want any injuries here today. Identify yourselves."

The response came quickly, clipped and professional:

"Senior Inspector Colin Suthons and Inspector David Hughes, Australian Federal Police. And you are?"

Caleb stood a little taller, the weight of ownership settling firmly on his shoulders.

"I am Caleb Ahrens, owner of this property," he answered, voice steady but resolute. "And I want to know what the hell you're doing here."

"Show your identification, please," came the curt reply.

Caleb met the inspector's gaze evenly.

"At this stage, Inspector, I'm calling the shots," he said firmly. "Now, both of you, put your service belts and that rifle there, right in front of me."

The men complied without hesitation.

"Good," Caleb said. "Now, have a seat."

The air hung heavy, charged with questions, unspoken threats, and the faint, metallic taste of danger that never quite left a man who knew how to survive. The real story was just about to begin.

Both officers sank down onto the hard ground, settling beside their two still-standing colleagues, whose identities Caleb hadn't yet pressed for. The early morning sun sliced through the trees, casting long, skeletal shadows across the dirt like fingers reaching to clutch the men in place. The air hung thick with silence, punctuated only by the occasional birdcall, distant, unaware.

"May I show my identification?" Suthons asked, voice low but respectful.

Caleb's gaze didn't waver. "Just move nice and slow," he said, the words sharp as broken glass.

The senior inspector's hand moved deliberately, pulling from a battered black leather folder the small, authoritative emblem of his office, the police badge and ID. Caleb's eyes flicked over it quickly, then he placed the rifle carefully on the ground in front of the officer.

Suthons nodded slowly, the faintest trace of a grin breaking the tension in his eyes as he stood. "Looks like you caught us out big time," he said, the kind of half-joke that's really a question. "Who exactly are you?"

The three other men now moved as one, coming upright and watching Caleb with a mix of curiosity and caution. Caleb met their gaze steadily and, pulling out his wallet, showed the newly issued driver's license with his name and the property address printed clear as a beacon, Kimbarry.

"I'm also a former US Marine RECON," Caleb added, his voice calm but unmistakably carrying the weight of hard-earned respect.

The officers exchanged looks, respect mingled with a new wariness. The check over and search that followed was quick but thorough. Then, the senior inspector filled Caleb in. They'd been running surveillance on a suspected meth lab hidden in the worker's cottage. The aim was to find the kingpin, the person pulling strings behind the scenes. "We couldn't tell anyone for obvious reasons," Suthons admitted, a faint edge of frustration in his voice. "You did well to find us."

Caleb nodded slowly. "I was on my way to do the same thing," he said quietly. "Last Friday, I suspected the cottage was a meth lab when I went out there with my parents."

He didn't spare the details, the two dogs snapping viciously under the house, the agitated occupant who'd nearly come at him with a knife. He promised to keep the whole encounter quiet, to steer clear of the area until he heard back from them.

As Caleb turned to leave, the officer who had lost his rifle called out, half-joking, half-serious: "You're lucky I didn't shoot you!"

Caleb chuckled, the sound low and dark. "You're lucky you were sleeping," he said over his shoulder as he walked back toward the Land Rover.

The kitchen was warm and smelled like fried eggs and freshly brewed coffee when Caleb returned. Joanna called out cheerfully, "Good timing!"

Eggs sizzled in the pan, and his parents were already seated, sipping coffee in quiet morning ritual. Joanna smiled, holding a plate out to him. "Eggs?"

"No thanks," Caleb said, rubbing the back of his neck. "Just coffee. I think I really need to lose some weight."

His mother's eyes narrowed playfully but with motherly concern. "You also need to eat, Caleb."

He sank into a chair at the kitchen table beside his father, who looked up from his mug just as Caleb's mind flicked to the office. "Hey, Dad… have you seen the map I left in the office? It's not where I left it."

Wesley lifted his eyes, thoughtful. "I saw it on Friday morning. It was on the desk under the compass." He shrugged. "I suspect it won't be too far away."

Caleb nodded slowly, a quiet unease settling under his skin. Something was off, but the morning still held its fragile calm. Outside, the sun climbed higher, and the day waited to reveal its secrets.

Contrary to what he had told the police, Caleb didn't hold back with Joanna and his parents. He recounted his morning encounter in full, his voice steady but tinged with a strange undercurrent of disbelief. Joanna's eyes widened, and his parents exchanged uneasy glances. The house, normally filled with the warm hum of routine, suddenly felt a little colder, the shadows longer than before.

"The cops were casing the cottage," Caleb said, rubbing his chin thoughtfully. "They suspect it's a meth lab."

Adina nodded, her voice soft but certain. "Well, it did smell like one the other day when we drove past."

Caleb shrugged, a thin smile playing at the corners of his mouth. "On the strength of the police being around, I don't think we should go treasure hunting anytime soon," he said, voice dropping to a murmur as if admitting a private thought. "I wonder what happened to that map..."

He pushed back from the table and stood, the faint creak of the old floorboards echoing in the quiet kitchen. His footsteps, usually so confident, carried a note of hesitation as he made his way back to the office. He needed to resurvey the area where the map had last been, the spot on the desk, under the compass.

Kneeling, Caleb scanned the floor. No sign of the map. That was impossible anyway, given the heavy compass had been resting squarely on top of it. He checked the desk drawers one by one, fingers probing the dark wood's worn edges, but the map was nowhere to be found.

Then his hand brushed against the bottom drawer, the one where he'd stashed his Smith and Wesson automatic handgun. His eyes flicked to the lock. He needed to secure it, so he reached for the keys.

The keys.

They were never far, always kept together on a solitary key ring with the safe key. Usually tucked out of sight, hanging on a small hook under the desk beside the drawers. But when Caleb reached to grasp them, his fingers met only empty air.

He bent down, squinting into the dim underside of the desk. The hook was there, a sliver of cold metal gleaming faintly in the morning light, but no keys. Nothing.

A cold prickle ran down Caleb's spine. They were just the four of them at the homestead, he, Joanna, and his parents. Apart from the 'drugo' at the meth cottage and the old man Kerry, who lived in the other worker's cottage, no one was within miles. No one else could have taken the keys or the map.

"Strange," Caleb thought, the word whispering in his mind like a warning.

He shook it off, swallowing the unease like a bitter pill. They had bigger plans, Wesley's new 'Cruiser' waited outside, promising an afternoon of exploration and fresh air. For now, the missing map and vanished keys were just mysteries to be shelved, buried beneath the wide Queensland sky.

They gave the 'meth' cottage a wide berth, skirting the ragged edges of that place like it was a wound still oozing something foul. The land around Kimbarry was dotted with tracks, animal prints, tire ruts, and something else, something less natural, like footprints that didn't quite belong. One trail led them to the second worker's cottage, a squat, weather-beaten structure nestled under the gaunt shadows of gum trees.

Kerry was there, his lanky frame silhouetted against the clothesline, pinning sheets that snapped and flapped in the dry breeze. As they pulled up in the Cruiser, his voice floated across the yard, rough and familiar.

"The kettle's just boiled," he called out. "Yous'll be wantin' a cuppa, yeah? Or maybe somethin' a bit stronger, medicinal, eh?" He chuckled, the sound rough but warm.

Joanna smiled, her hand resting lightly on Caleb's arm. "Too early for us," she said, her voice light but firm. Then she introduced Wesley and Adina, Caleb's mum and dad, to Kerry.

They filed inside the cottage, the air thick with the scent of aged wood and old stories. The kitchen was vast, the kind of space that had seen decades of meals and conversations, the walls worn smooth by time. The place was clean, almost obsessively so, and despite its age, it felt alive, like a stubborn heartbeat in the rural quiet.

Kerry poured tea with a practiced hand, offering cups to each of them, and though none really wanted the brew, they sipped politely, no one dared offend the old man's hospitality.

He led them on a tour of the place: three bedrooms, a lounge room heavy with threadbare furniture, and a combined kitchen and dining area that smelled faintly of linseed oil and memories. The walls bore the patina of decades, and everywhere there was evidence of Kerry's diligent care. They praised him, genuine admiration shining through their words.

"Have you had a chance to look at the other cottage yet?" Kerry asked, his voice dropping a notch, a bitter edge sneaking in. "It's a disgrace. Don't rightly know what nationality the folks are, but judging by the horrible cooking smells waftin' out, I'm guessin' Indian."

Joanna's brow furrowed. "You don't know the people then, Kerry?"

"Nah," Kerry said, shaking his head. "They just showed up one day and took the place over. Sometimes it's just one big bearded bloke, but other times, I see cars, quite a few. Always looks like a mess on the outside, so you can only imagine the inside. Reckon the only way to fix that dump now would be with a gallon of petrol and a box of matches."

A silence settled, heavy and uncomfortable, before Adina spoke up. "Kerry, why don't you come around for dinner this evening? You can tell us all about Kimbarry."

Kerry's eyes lit up, and a rare smile cracked his weathered face. "I could think of nothin' better, ma'am. But only if you're sure you wanna be bored shitless by an old man."

"Dress as you are, and bring nothing but yourself. You got transport, Kerry?"

"Oh, yeah. Got an old Landy, like the one you've got at the big house. It's locked up in the shed 'cause I don't trust those Indians over at the other cottage," Kerry said with a laugh, following them outside. His voice dropped a little quieter, a flicker of something sharper beneath the humour. "What time should I be there?"

"Come 'round about five, five-thirty," Adina called as she climbed into the Cruiser, the engine rumbling to life. "We'll have a drink first."

She turned to Wesley with a grin. "Which reminds me, we'll need to stop at the pub in Bigga, don't think we've got enough drinks at home."

Joanna waved through the open window. "See you later, Kerry."

As the Cruiser rolled away, Kerry lingered in the dusty yard, watching them go. There was something about those new arrivals, something more than just neighbours. The land held its secrets tight, but Kerry had learned that sometimes, secrets claw their way out no matter how deep you bury them.

Kerry arrived at the homestead dead on five o'clock, punctual in a way that spoke of a life shaped by routine and respect. In his hands, he carried a full carton of Victoria Bitter like a peace offering from another time, green aluminium soldiers ready to be deployed. He grinned, sheepish, as Adina met him on the wide stone porch, arms folded, an eyebrow cocked.

"I told you to only bring yourself," she said, smiling but firm, like a mother shooing a boy away from the cookie jar.

"We'll use 'em for reserves!" Caleb called from the rear courtyard, already holding a beer of his own. His voice was warm and teasing, and Kerry chuckled, tucking the carton back into the tray of his old Land Rover, locking it like he was guarding treasure.

The sun had almost dipped behind the hills when Kerry joined them out back. The beer garden and BBQ area stretched like an open stage beneath the late winter sky, every breath coming with a curl of steam. Wesley had a roaring fire going in the stone-ringed pit near the grill, flames licking upward with a life of their own, throwing shadows that danced like spirits from long ago. They all stood there for a while, holding drinks, swapping light talk, wrapped in coats and the brittle chill of country air.

But as the night deepened, the cold clawed in earnest, slipping fingers under cuffs and collars.

"Middle of winter," Kerry muttered, rubbing his hands together and glancing toward the darkening landscape. "It's no wonder the bones start rememberin' the years."

They retreated indoors, into the old house that sighed as they entered, the timber expanding and contracting like lungs that hadn't quite exhaled in decades. In the main dining lounge,

Max Barrington

high-ceilinged, timber-beamed, and filled with a warm amber glow, Kerry paused just inside the threshold. He looked around with an expression caught somewhere between nostalgia and something else. Grief, maybe. Or memory grown heavy.

"Been a long time since I was in here," he said, his voice quieter now, as though the walls were listening. "I remember Mr. and Mrs. Hewson when they lived here. I was only five years old then. I used to come in here all the time, like I was one of their own. Then the news came…"

He trailed off, eyes losing focus.

"I didn't understand it, not then. Everyone in the valley was so sad. There was this weight in the air you couldn't see but you could feel, like thunder that never came. The Hewson boys, David, Colin, Robert, and Patrick, they weren't coming home. That's what the grown-ups said. Just like that. 'They're not coming home.'"

He shook his head, took a drink, and stared at the fire flickering behind the glass screen in the lounge hearth.

"Of course, I didn't know what it meant. Just knew that after that, Mrs. Hewson never let me in the house again. Like the laughter of kids reminded her too much of what she'd lost. I stopped coming by after that. Didn't want to see that look in her eyes."

Adina rested a hand gently on his forearm. He looked up, startled for a second, like he'd forgotten he was speaking aloud.

"It wasn't until Donal bought the place from his uncle… that would've been, God, around 1960, maybe '61, I'm not sure. That's when I first came inside again. I was twenty then. I remember that clearly."

"Why?" Adina asked.

"Because I remember being shocked that someone younger than me could own a place like this." He let out a soft laugh, more breath than sound. "Donal was just a few months younger. Not even a full year. But he was already a very rich young man. His father, Barry's brother, left it all to him. The house. The land. Everything."

"And yet you became good friends?" Wesley asked, curious.

Kerry nodded slowly, eyes gleaming with the reflection of the fire.

"We did. Donal was a good man. A man who carried the weight of things without complainin'. That's rare, you know. There's something about this place, Kimbarry. It doesn't just sit quiet on the hill. It remembers. It holds on."

No one spoke for a moment. Outside, the wind picked up, brushing the walls like fingers dragging along old scars.

And inside the house, the past stirred softly, as if waiting for the rest of the story to be told.

Kerry's eyes had gone misty with the sort of remembering that seeps in through the cracks of the years, slow and stubborn as groundwater. He leaned forward slightly in his chair, both hands wrapped around his beer like it was the only warm thing in the room.

"It was maybe a year after Donal bought the place," he said, his voice low, catching in places like it was brushing against barbed wire. "Dad told me to come up here with him to help air the place out. It was a proper mess by then, shut up for years like a sealed tomb."

A log cracked in the hearth. Outside, the wind shifted again.

"I was just a kid, barely shaving, but even then I knew there was something… wrong. Not evil, nothing like that," Kerry went on, choosing his words the way a man might tiptoe through broken glass. "Just sad. Real, deep-down sad. The kind that gets in your bones and stays there."

He looked across the room, past the flickering light and the glow of the stove, into the shadows as if the old memories were standing just beyond them.

"I was opening windows. Dust everywhere. Could see the sun filtering through like it was trying to make sense of the place. I went into the boys' rooms, the Hewson boys. And I swear to God, it was like they'd just left the day before. Beds made. Clothes still hanging in the wardrobes. One of the dressers had watches lined up neat as soldiers on top, like they were waiting to be claimed. The rooms were still. Too still."

Kerry took a long swallow of his drink, and when he set it down again, there was a faint tremor in his hand.

"It was spooky," he admitted. "Not jump-out-at-you ghost story spooky. No chains rattling or cold spots. Just... you got that sense. You know what I mean? Like someone was watching you open their windows, someone who didn't quite know they were gone. Like the house itself didn't know either."

Nobody spoke for a moment. The fire hissed and popped. Even the shadows seemed to lean in.

"Donal showed up while Dad and I were still airing the place. Young bastard, still can't believe he owned the whole thing at twenty. But he was alright. We hit it off right away, like we'd known each other for years. Stayed mates too, until he lost interest in it all. Found other things to throw his energy into. This place... it wore on people, eventually."

Kerry's eyes flicked to the kitchen. "D'yer know? I swear, that's the same damn furniture I saw back then. Even those skillets on the stovetop, those were there the day I opened the windows."

Everyone turned to look, half expecting to see something move. The heavy black pans gleamed under the stove light like relics from another world.

"Yes, well, it was just as you see it now when we bought it," Caleb said, shrugging. "The drawers were full, cutlery, plates, a full service for twelve. Even the beds in the main bedrooms were made, with fresh-looking bedding. Well, fresh-looking enough, I should say, we changed it, obviously."

"But the other four bedrooms are bare," Joanna added, glancing at Kerry. "Totally empty."

Kerry's brow furrowed, and something in his face shifted, like a door inside him creaked open.

"The boys' rooms?" he asked, voice quiet now. "Bare?"

They both nodded.

"Nothing in them at all. Just the curtains and drapes."

Kerry leaned back in his chair and stared into the fire like it might answer him. "That's... strange," he murmured. "That's real strange. I remember them clear as day. Beds, of course. But also two big wardrobes, filled. Clothes. Uniforms. Civilian stuff. And a dresser. There were watches, cufflinks, bits of jewelry in trays, like someone had laid them out to choose from. And..."

He trailed off again, the silence swelling like a tide.

"Is the gun cabinet still in the office?" he asked finally.

Caleb shook his head. "Nope. No cabinet. Just a big old desk, a safe, a drafting table and cupboard. And an empty bookcase. That's it."

Kerry didn't say anything for a long moment. Just nodded slowly, like that missing gun cabinet carried more weight than anyone wanted to ask about.

It was Adina who broke the silence, her voice clear but gentle, like wind rustling through dry grass. "Come on," she said, brushing her hands on a dish towel. "Let's eat."

She moved to the wall where a long, oak sideboard stood like an altar, and from the double oven pulled a whole roast rump, the aroma rolling into the room like a tide of warmth and memory. She placed it on the board with reverence. Joanna followed, heaving a cast-iron pot from the opposite oven and setting it beside the meat. She lifted the heavy lid with a grunt, and a great steam of rosemary, garlic, and roasted earth rose into the air.

The dining table loomed in the middle of the room, twelve chairs with high backs, thick with history. As everyone gathered around it, something about the number struck Kerry.

"Twelve chairs," he said under his breath. "Twelve places."

He didn't finish the thought. But he didn't have to.

The conversation over dinner drifted like smoke, lazy, slow-moving, but not without sparks. Kerry's stories of life on Kimbarry unfolded with the relaxed cadence of a man long used to wide paddocks and quiet nights. In return, he inquired politely, but persistently, about the saloon in San Francisco. Caleb, sharp as a splinter under the skin, noticed the pattern in Kerry's questioning and, with discreet glances and subtle shifts in tone, signalled the others to steer the discussion in safer directions, away from the saloon, away from whatever shadows it might cast.

And then, like the snap of dry kindling underfoot, Kerry looked up, his gaze crawling toward the pressed tin ceiling, and asked, quite calmly, "What's in the upstairs rooms?"

The question hung in the air like the echo of a gunshot in an empty street.

Caleb paused, his fork halfway to his mouth. "Upstairs rooms?" he asked, brows narrowing. "There are no upstairs rooms here."

Kerry pointed upward, his expression almost dreamlike, eyes fixed on some space far above. "Right up there," he said softly. "There used to be ten single rooms, two bathrooms. It was the Cobb and Co. Inn, remember? The stairs were through that door there, just beyond the office."

Joanna looked at him as if a ghost had spoken. "There are no stairs there," she said gently, the way you might speak to someone who's just awakened from a vivid dream. "Maybe you're confusing this place with the pub in Bigga?"

Kerry didn't even glance at her. "Inns like this didn't always have windows up top," he murmured, half to himself. "Guests would sleep during the day, ride out under moonlight. Do you mind?" He was already rising, heading toward the door he claimed once led to the stairwell.

They let him go. Something in his voice had stilled their objections.

Kerry pushed through the door and stood staring into the space beyond. The ceiling was low now, modern, false, hiding whatever may once have been above. It hung at a regulation eight feet, or thereabouts, neatly boxed in, as if someone had been desperate to forget what had come before.

"All covered over," he said at last, voice laced with something old and uncertain. A memory not quite aligning with reality. "But the stairs were here. I remember them. Clear as anything. Turned at a landing halfway up."

Adina followed quietly, resting a hand on the edge of the doorway. "Are you sure you're not thinking of another place, Kerry?" she asked. Her tone was kind, but there was something careful in it, too. Measured. Like one might speak to a man who's seen too much.

Joanna was less delicate. "There's no trace of stairs," she said. "Not even marks on the walls."

Kerry turned back, confusion tightening his brow. "It doesn't make sense," he said. "I remember… wardrobes, beds, even luggage up there. The hallway had these oil lamps in glass holders, just like a steamer ship."

But there was no hallway. No lamps. No upstairs. Just the smooth false ceiling and the soft hum of old timber keeping its secrets.

They returned to the table in silence, the atmosphere dulled now, like a storm had passed just out of sight. Adina and Joanna poured drinks, port, brandy, and a heavy Shiraz, and Caleb threw a few fresh logs on the fire, the flames licking up with a crackle that sounded, for the briefest moment, like footsteps on a wooden stair.

"Let's take our drinks into the lounge," Caleb said, his voice easy but just a bit too light. "The fire's going strong. Bit of warmth wouldn't hurt."

They rose as one, moving like people in a dream, leaving behind the heavy table with its twelve tall chairs, and the room where the past had tried, just briefly, to claw its way through the ceiling.

They settled in like old souls in the quiet after a storm. The fire spat softly in the hearth, casting an amber glow across the timeworn timber walls. Shadows flickered like dancers along the high ceiling beams, and for a moment, the whole room seemed to inhale and hold its breath.

Wesley leaned forward, the leather of his chair creaking with the weight of his curiosity. His voice broke the silence, low and deliberate.

"Hey, Kerry... you ever hear of a bushranger named Frank Gardiner? They say he used to haunt these parts."

Kerry, already halfway through a beer, paused. He didn't answer right away. Instead, he took a long, thoughtful sip, like he was savouring the taste of something far older than hops and barley. Something like memory.

He set the glass down with a quiet thump on the oak side table beside him. "Believe it or not," he said, eyes catching the firelight, "Australian Bushrangers are my thing. I mean really my thing. I've got shelves full of books, half of them out of print. If it's ever been written about Gardiner or any of the others, I've read it. Frank... yes, I know Frank. Or at least, the many names he wore like masks. Francis Clarke. Frank Christie. The Dark Highwayman. He had more aliases than a politician under oath."

Adina passed him another beer without a word, and he accepted it with a nod, cracked the top, and let the hush in the room settle again. The others leaned in slightly, like plants bending toward sunlight, hungry for the story.

Kerry's voice dropped an octave, took on a weight. "Frank's story starts in the early 1860s, Australia wasn't the sun-soaked paradise tourists think of now. The colonies were raw then. Harsh. The kind of place that didn't forgive weakness or forget a grudge. Roads were long, isolated veins through the bush, and the spaces between towns were dark and dangerous. The sort of dark that felt... watching."

He paused. Outside, a wind brushed the eaves like a whisper, and the fire gave a sharp crack. Kerry glanced toward the window before continuing.

"Frank started as a convict, like a lot of them did, but somewhere along the line, the man inside turned cold. Smart as hell, too. He wasn't just some dumb brute with a musket and a grudge. He had a mind like a fox and a silver tongue. When he spoke, men listened. And when he planned, people bled."

Caleb shifted uneasily in his chair. The shadows behind Kerry seemed to ripple with the weight of the tale.

"He formed a gang, all rough bastards, most of them with prison stink still on them. But Gardiner... he gave them purpose. They didn't just rob, they orchestrated. Banks. Coaches. Gold shipments. Hell, he even hit a governor's private courier once, or so the legend goes. But the big one, his masterpiece, was Eugowra."

He looked around. Every face was fixed on him, silent and pale in the firelight.

"Eugowra, 1862. A gold escort coming through the Central West, armed and guarded, moving slow through a gully flanked by ironbarks and sandstone. Frank and his boys ambushed it like ghosts out of the trees. They hit hard and fast, and when the dust settled, they were gone with over fourteen thousand pounds in gold and cash. That's millions today. It was the biggest heist in the country's history at the time, and it spooked the colonies. People stopped trusting the roads. Mothers started keeping their kids closer. Newspapers printed his name in bold black ink, like a warning or a prayer."

Adina crossed herself subtly. Maybe she was Catholic. Maybe she just didn't like the way Kerry's voice had changed, like the words themselves were conjuring something.

Kerry's voice lowered even further. "And some say he left something behind out there in the bush. Not just gold. Something... darker. A part of himself. Because men like that, they don't just vanish. They stain the land."

He took another long sip. The fire flared and hissed as a log shifted in the grate.

"I'll tell you this," he said, leaning back, his eyes glinting with something more than firelight. "Frank Gardiner may be buried in another country... but out here, in these hills and gullies, his ghost still rides. You don't need a grave to haunt a place. Just blood and memory."

No one spoke for a moment. Even the wind outside seemed to fall still.

And somewhere, faint and far off, a floorboard creaked, upstairs.

Kerry let the fire warm his words as he leaned into the heart of the tale, the room still caught in that hush where every sound seems bigger than it should be.

"The Eugowra robbery," he said, swirling the neck of the bottle before raising it to his lips, "was the moment Frank Gardiner stepped out of history... and into folklore. It cemented him, like a fossil in sandstone, as something more than just a man with a gun and a grudge. He became a living myth, an outlaw who rewrote the rules while the colonies were still fumbling for their own."

The logs shifted again, giving off a low groan that sounded eerily like a sigh. Somewhere, a moth fluttered against the glass.

"To some," Kerry continued, "he was a goddamned hero. A bush Messiah with a revolver in one hand and a code of his own scribbled in blood. They said he was the people's man, a stick-it-to-the-man rebel who robbed from the rich and, if he didn't give to the poor, at least gave them something to believe in. To others... well, he was a predator. A manipulator. A man who wore his charm like a snake wears its scales, slick, silent, and always ready to strike."

Adina's brow furrowed slightly. Maybe she was thinking of someone she knew who fit that description all too well.

"But like every flame that burns too bright," Kerry said, his voice darkening, "Frank's light began to draw attention. The kind that didn't just watch, it hunted. The very traits that made him such a legend, his intelligence, his organization, his charisma, they painted a bloody red target on his back."

He set the bottle down with a soft thud, like a headstone gently placed.

"The manhunt that followed was... biblical. We're talking months of sweat-soaked lawmen on horseback, tracking him through the scrub, the gullies, the ghost towns. They didn't stop. They couldn't. Not until the legend was broken. And in 1864, the trap finally snapped shut. Someone close, someone who knew too much and owed too little, sold him out."

Kerry paused as Joanna moved quietly among them with a tray of drinks. No one reached for theirs until she'd stepped back. The room had shifted. You could feel it. The temperature hadn't dropped, but it felt colder.

"Captured in New South Wales. Shackled. Stripped of his pride. He stood in a courtroom like a man already buried, and they sentenced him to thirty-two years of hard labor. Thirty-two years. That wasn't justice, that was erasure. A message from the Crown to every would-be Gardiner out there: 'Play your games, and we'll grind your bones to dust.'"

Kerry's eyes flicked to the shadows dancing at the edge of the firelight.

"But Frank..." he said softly, "Frank didn't vanish. Not yet."

He leaned forward, voice dropping as if someone outside might be listening.

"He did ten years. Ten long, mean years. They say the prisons back then were worse than hell, rats, chains, work that broke the body and starved the soul. But Gardiner, he didn't break. He waited. He planned. And then... he vanished."

No one breathed.

"They say he escaped in 1874. No one knows how. Some say bribery. Others whisper about sympathisers in the walls, guards who still believed in the myth, or maybe just hated their own masters more than they hated the man in chains. Either way, when the dust cleared, Frank Gardiner was gone."

Wesley sat forward, beer untouched, eyes like dinner plates.

"Where did he go?" he asked, his voice barely more than a breath.

Kerry smiled, not kindly. More like a man who's seen too much to believe in fairy tales.

"He slipped back into the bush, and the bush took him in. There were sightings, flickers of a man with a familiar gait, a glint of gold teeth in a shadowed face. Some claimed he was living out west, off the map. Others swore he made it to Queensland. But there were rumours, too, darker ones. Ones that said he was dead, but walking. That something came out of Eugowra that day alongside the gold. Something that didn't sleep."

Adina shivered.

"But the most persistent rumour," Kerry went on, "is that he left Australia altogether. That by the 1880s, Frank Gardiner was living in the United States, in San Francisco, of all places. A man with too many names and not enough past. But there were no records. No photographs. Just stories. Whispers. Ghosts in the wind."

He leaned back, drained the last of his beer, and stared into the flames.

"And that's how it ends. Frank Gardiner, thief, rebel, legend, died in obscurity. Or maybe he didn't die at all. Maybe he just faded out of time, like smoke after a gunshot. All that remains are the stories. And one last little fact…"

He looked around, eyes narrowing slightly.

"The gold? From the Eugowra heist? Never recovered. Not a single ingot. And that, my friends… that's where the legend becomes something else. A promise. Or a warning."

The fire cracked again, loud as a pistol shot.

Kerry excused himself with a mumble and a wry smile, rising from the lounge with the slow, deliberate gait of a man who'd told too many stories and drank just enough to need the bathroom. The old timber floors groaned beneath his boots as he disappeared down the dark hallway, the flickering firelight throwing long shadows that moved like memories across the walls.

The moment he was gone, Wesley leaned in, his voice low and urgent, like a child about to confess to stealing something holy.

"Why don't we tell Kerry about the map?" he whispered, eyes flicking to the hallway. "I mean… not everything. Just enough. We don't have to tell him that we've already found some of the gold."

Joanna's head tilted, her face unreadable in the soft firelight. "I don't think we know him well enough to trust him. Not yet," she said slowly, her words as careful as someone stepping through a minefield. "We barely know his story. And stories… well, they're easy to wear and just as easy to change."

Caleb looked up sharply. "Joanna," he said, "did you… did you take the map from the office desk?"

Joanna blinked, her voice edged with concern. "No, I didn't. Is it missing? Or just… misplaced?"

Caleb's brow tightened into a hard knot. "It's gone. I checked twice. No one else has been here since the last time we were all together. And now it's just, vanished."

A sudden creak came from the hallway as Kerry re-entered the room, still buttoning the cuff of his sleeve, muttering to himself.

"I do remember now…" he said absently, like someone caught in the web of a half-remembered dream. "She came back to live here. After the old fella died."

Caleb blinked, caught off guard. "Who? Sorry, Kerry, you've lost me."

Kerry sat heavily in his chair, staring at the fire as if it held the answer. "Mrs Hewson… Kimberly. I remember now. After Barry passed away, she moved back in for a while. Six months or so. Donal was around on and off, but then he went to England. And she stayed. I think she had the boys' furniture moved. But why? And where the hell to?"

Joanna leaned forward. "Would she have had the stairs removed? And the ceiling installed? Is there another way into that space above it?"

Kerry shrugged. "Who knows? And…" he sighed, rubbing his face, "who really cares?"

But Adina did. She stood up sharply, a tension in her limbs that hadn't been there moments before. Her voice cut through the room like a cold wind. "I think we've had enough for tonight. It's getting late."

She began gathering the empty glasses scattered around the lounge, her fingers moving with a touch too much force, as if trying to keep control of something deeper just under the skin.

"Are you okay to get yourself home, Kerry?" she asked, a trace of steel in her tone.

Kerry nodded, already moving toward the door, his silhouette framed against the hallway's dim light. "I'm fine, thank you. And thanks for dinner, it was amazing."

The old Land Rover growled to life a few minutes later, its engine coughing like a sick animal before fading into the darkness down the gravel drive.

Only when the night swallowed the sound did Adina speak again.

"Something's not right around here."

Her voice was low. Firm. The kind of voice that didn't ask for permission.

"We need to check above that ceiling, where Kerry said the stairs used to be. First thing tomorrow."

No one argued. The fire snapped once, a single ember flying loose and vanishing midair like a warning.

They all nodded in silence.

Tomorrow, they would find out what lay above that ceiling.

And maybe, just maybe, what had been waiting for them.

It was just after eight in the morning, and the sun outside was already beginning to warm the dew off the verandah railings, but inside the kitchen of the old homestead, the air still carried a chill that settled in the bones. Caleb stood barefoot on the cold tiles, one hand wrapped around the warm handle of the coffee pot as the machine hissed and sputtered to life behind him.

His mobile rang, the sound abrupt and startling in the stillness. The screen flashed a number he didn't recognise, local, but unfamiliar.

He swiped to answer. "Caleb Ahrens."

A voice, clipped and official, responded.

"Mr Ahrens? This is Inspector David Hughes," the man said, his tone polite but distant, as if reading from a script he didn't particularly like. "Just a courtesy call, sir. I'm phoning to inform you that we've concluded our operation involving surveillance on a cottage situated on your property, Kimbarry, I believe it's called?"

Caleb blinked. The name, spoken by someone else, gave him a strange feeling. Like hearing your house mentioned on the news.

"Yes, Inspector. What is it I can help you with?"

"We're satisfied that there are no illegal activities currently taking place at that location," Hughes continued. "If you require any further information, please don't hesitate to contact me."

And with that, the line went dead. No questions. No pleasantries. No warmth. Just, click.

Caleb stood frozen for a moment, phone still to his ear, the coffee now burning slightly on the bottom of the pot.

What the hell was that?

Something about the call gnawed at him, too brief, too convenient. The kind of neat little conclusion that sounded more like the end of a lie than the end of a case.

He grabbed the worn contact card from the noticeboard near the fridge, the one belonging to Senior Inspector Colin Suthons, and punched the number in with fast, precise fingers.

The call picked up after the second ring. "Inspector Suthons," came the voice on the other end.

"Good morning, Inspector. Caleb Ahrens here, from Kimbarry, the property where we met," Caleb said quickly. "Look, I've just received a brief call from Inspector Hughes, and, "

He didn't finish. Suthons cut in, his voice laced with something sharper. Frustration. Or was it something darker?

"He's with me now," Suthons said. "We raided the cottage last night. Nothing. Clean as a damn whistle. We think the bastard was tipped off, or maybe he's just that slippery. But either way, we've got nothing. No drugs, no weapons, no tech, not even a dirty rag out of place. He knew we were coming, or suspected it. That much is clear."

Caleb felt a leaden weight drop in his gut.

"We would've loved to arrest the smug bastard," Suthons went on, "but we've got no grounds. Be careful with him, Caleb. If he's still hanging around, I'd advise you, strongly, to get him off your property. I wouldn't want someone like that living near my family."

"I understand," Caleb said, his voice low, his thoughts already racing ahead. "Thank you, Inspector. I'll look into it immediately. And just for the record, I told no one about your surveillance. You can be sure of that."

"Good," Suthons said flatly, and ended the call.

Caleb stood there in the quiet kitchen, the air now warm but somehow less comforting. Outside, the birds chirped merrily in the trees, but their songs felt false, like actors reading from a script written by someone who didn't understand joy.

He poured his coffee, black and bitter, and stared out the kitchen window toward the shadowed tree line where the cottage lay, half-hidden behind a veil of mist and gum leaves.

Whoever he was, whoever that man in the cottage had been, he was still out there.

And Caleb had just been warned.

After breakfast, the search began, not with urgency, but with a low, determined hum. Like a group of kids who had dared each other to poke around in the attic of a haunted house. Only this wasn't a game, and the stakes, though still murky, were beginning to rise like mist from a forgotten grave.

Their target was the right wing of the homestead, a part of the house that had always seemed quieter than the rest, as if it were listening instead of speaking. The layout was simple, but the atmosphere held weight, like something waiting just out of reach.

The group entered through the kitchen-dining door, the familiar clink of the latch sounding louder than it should in the hush of mid-morning. Beyond lay the corridor, dim despite the growing light outside, with shadows pooling in corners like spilled ink. To their right was the storeroom, a squat, dusty chamber that doubled as a pass-through to the kitchen, lined with shelves of pickling jars, rusting tools, and the occasional spider that darted at the sound of footsteps.

They moved on, past the open doorway that marked the beginning of the corridor proper. The office came next, Caleb's old haunt, and the place where secrets had already begun to whisper from the walls. The ceiling here, like the rest of the house, was a soaring 2.7 metres high. Joanna's eyes scanned upward, and there it was. The panel.

Rectangular, dusty, inconspicuous, yet it might as well have been a portal to another world. Just above the entry doorway, it seemed to taunt them with its placement, as if the house itself had grown tired of their probing and decided to dangle the next clue just out of reach.

Further along the corridor sat the bathroom, tiles cold and curling at the edges, the mirror slightly tarnished with age, and beyond that, the bedroom Caleb and Joanna had claimed. None of these rooms held the answer. Not on the ground, at least.

Back in the office, Caleb returned with the folding steps they'd found in the garage. The metal frame creaked as he extended them fully. They rose to a modest 1.8 metres, but once opened and locked into place, the platform barely reached 1.5 metres off the ground.

He climbed up, tested the wobble of the steps beneath his boots, and reached up, stretching, straining, but came nowhere near touching the panel.

"No good," he muttered, stepping back down. "We'd need another metre, at least. Maybe more."

They all stared upward. The access panel remained stubborn, silent.

"What the hell's up there?" Joanna asked, her voice quiet, not really expecting an answer.

Adina, arms folded, said, "Something someone didn't want easily found. You don't install a ceiling that high with no ladder unless you want to keep people out."

Caleb looked from the panel to the others. "We need a proper ladder. Or a scaffold."

"Or a boost," Wesley offered, grinning. "But I'm not volunteering."

They chuckled, but the laughter didn't stick. The panel still loomed.

And somewhere above it, in that unknown space between ceiling and roof, something was waiting.

Something that had outlived the builders. Outlived the Hewson's.

And now, it was watching them.

The plan was simple enough, a run into Cowra for essentials: groceries, beer, and, thanks to the morning's disappointing reach for the ceiling panel, a detour to the hardware store. Caleb had scribbled "step ladder, 2m platform" on the shopping list in block letters, then underlined it twice, as if that would help them get through whatever secrets the house might be keeping up there.

They piled into Joanna's Jeep mid-morning, its roof rack soon burdened with a new, gleaming aluminium ladder that glinted in the sun like a loaded weapon. With the errands handled and the heat beginning to stretch long shadows across the pavement, they agreed that lunch sounded like a damn fine idea. The Imperial Hotel, perched on the main drag like an old but not-yet-forgotten cowboy, beckoned with its creaking timber verandah and promise of cold beer.

Inside, the air was cool and still, the kind of stillness you get in places that have known generations of whispered deals, weekend brawls, and stories best left unspoken.

They had barely taken their first sips when a man approached Caleb's table. He wore jeans and a flannel shirt, a sharp contrast to the starched blue uniform Caleb had seen him in just two mornings prior. For a moment, Caleb stared, trying to place the familiar face without the badge and authority.

"Bit of a giggle the other morning," the man said, grinning with something that wasn't quite humour.

Caleb blinked. Then the memory clicked. The telescope. The slight smirk. "Ah, yes! Sorry, I didn't recognise you without the... formal attire."

The man chuckled. "Carl Holgate," he said, extending a hand.

"Well, no hard feelings, I hope," Caleb replied, standing to shake it. "Let me get you a beer."

Introductions were made, drinks were bought, and Carl joined their table with the ease of someone who had already made up his mind that these folks were good people. Caleb and Carl fell into easy conversation, the others turning inward to discuss their ceiling expedition with that low, buzzing anticipation of an adventure just out of reach.

Carl's voice dropped after a while. "You know we raided that cottage last night, right?"

Caleb nodded. "Yeah. Got a call from Inspector Hughes this morning. Said the place was clean."

"Clean," Carl muttered, taking a pull of his beer and setting the glass down harder than necessary. "That's a laugh. We all know what that guy's up to. Has been for months. Meth. We're not talking theories, we're talking stench, movement, patterns... we even had a tip from a school liaison officer. But no evidence, apparently. Not enough for a conviction."

His eyes were hard now, the tired fury of a man who'd been watching a slow-motion train wreck without the power to stop it.

"Budget's blown out. Surveillance team's been pulled. He'll be cooking again by next week, mark my words. And it's the kids that'll pay. They always do."

Caleb felt something churn in his gut. Not fear, something deeper. Something colder. He glanced at Adina, who had been

                    Max Barrington

listening from her end of the table. She slid her chair closer, her expression unreadable, but her voice calm and clear.

"I used to be on the job," she said. "California. We had the same problem. Guys we knew were guilty, walking because the law's hands were tied behind its back. Courts don't want to hear your gut, they want a smoking gun."

Carl gave a bitter smile. "That's the truth."

What followed was something rare, a connection, built not on small talk but on shared disillusionment. They traded stories, frustrations, gallows humour. By the time the glasses were empty and the heat of the day had begun to mellow, Adina had Carl's number in her phone and plans were made. A BBQ out at Kimbarry. Families. Beers. Maybe a break from the weight they all carried, if only for a few hours.

The drive home was quiet. Joanna took the wheel, she wasn't drinking, knowing she had ten straight days of duty starting the next morning. The new ladder was strapped to the roof like a promise, or maybe a challenge. But the shadows were long now, and by the time they rolled through the front gates and into the gravel drive, the house had already started to settle into its twilight hush.

"Too late for ceiling games," Caleb said, stepping out and stretching his back. "Tomorrow."

Joanna smiled, weary but supportive. "Just don't go falling through the plaster while I'm gone."

They laughed, but it didn't erase the unease. Because whatever was waiting above their heads, it had waited this long.

oanna had only one shift left before the clock ran out on her career. Ten days, that was all that separated her from the life she'd been living and the one she was about to step into, irrevocably changed. The resignation had been filed and accepted, and the wheels were turning fast, spinning her out of Washington, out of the uniform, out of the chapter she'd known for so long.

She would have to officially retire from service there, the place where her posting was registered, where the badge had meant something, and the city had held memories both dark and bright. It wasn't just a job ending; it was the closing of a door that had once felt like home.

But home was shifting beneath her feet now, folding itself into a new shape. Australia. Bigga. Caleb's world. The promise of fresh starts and sun-soaked horizons. And for a moment, it didn't feel like a surrender, but like a chance to rewrite her story.

There was the trip back to the States to come. The long flight crossing oceans, slicing through time zones, back to the place where her parents waited, her mum and dad, the steady constants in a life that had spun too fast. She wanted to see them, to hold their hands and tell them everything: about the house, the strange things stirring in the shadows, and the future she was chasing.

Maybe, she thought, she'd invite them to Australia for a holiday. To see this place she now called home. Maybe even a wedding. A new beginning stitched together with old ties. It was a thought that warmed her, a light she hadn't allowed herself in months.

Caleb was going with her. Not just as a travel companion, but as someone who would stand beside her, who would meet her family and share the quiet moments between the formalities and the laughter. It felt good, having him there, not just as support, but as a part of the life she was stepping toward.

Money, too, was no longer a shadow looming over every decision. There was enough now, and maybe more on the horizon. It wasn't just about the dollars; it was about freedom, the freedom to choose, to dream, to live without chains tightening around her every step.

But even as she let the possibilities roll through her mind, Joanna knew that beneath the surface, something else waited. The past clung stubbornly, the unknown whispered just beyond the edges of the light.

Ten days. Then the leap. And whatever came next, there was no going back.

Joanna had left just before dawn, slipping out at five o'clock to start her shift at eight. Caleb had been up early too, moving quietly so as not to wake his parents. The steps were off the roof rack of Joanna's Jeep and now carefully positioned beneath the access panel in the office ceiling. The house was still wrapped in the soft silence of early morning, his mother and father still asleep, their breathing slow and steady.

Caleb didn't want to climb up alone; he knew better than that. So he waited until the kitchen came alive with the smells and sounds of breakfast. When the clatter of plates and the murmur of voices reached him, he took it as a signal, time to go.

After breakfast, while Adina cleaned up, Caleb and Wesley slipped quietly into the ceiling void. Each carried an LED lantern, their pale beams cutting through the thick darkness overhead. Without those lights, they might as well have been groping at shadows. They crawled carefully over the network of roof framing, the rough timber beams pressing into their palms and knees, inching toward the kitchen side of the house.

Here, the ceiling vaulted to about three metres at its peak, a new extension, Caleb realized. The original building, the heart of the three connected structures, rose at least a metre higher, its roofline a stubborn sentinel against the sky.

At the end of the new wing, the solid stone brick wall loomed ahead. This had to be the original outer wall of the house. There was no way forward, just cold, unyielding masonry.

They dropped down to the kitchen entry door, the reality settling between them. The wall they'd found above was the boundary, the perimeter. That meant their only way deeper into the mystery was through the ceiling corridor ahead, just past the storeroom.

"Let's do it," Wesley said, eyes gleaming with a quiet, stubborn resolve.

Caleb hesitated. The old house had secrets, and not all were meant to be disturbed. "Are you sure we should?"

Wesley didn't answer. He was already climbing the steps with a hammer in hand, tapping out the joists above the ceiling, the faint tap-tap echoing in the stillness. When he found the right spot, he began chiseling at the pine planking, splinters scattering quietly in the gloom. Soon, a square hole six hundred by six hundred millimetres yawned in the ceiling.

Wesley hauled himself through the opening. He landed on what felt like newer joists, solid and unyielding beneath his boots. From here, he craned his neck forward, toward the front of the building. There it was, a door, hanging just beneath the ridge of the roof like a secret waiting to be opened.

The door was standard-sized, nothing fancy, but the bottom edge sat about six hundred millimetres above the floor joists Wesley stood on. The handle was out of reach, at least two metres away, too high for him to reach without a proper ladder.

The smaller set of steps didn't fit through the ceiling opening either. They had to be adjusted, trimmed by two hundred millimetres on one side before they could be maneuvered into place.

Once the steps were settled under the door, Wesley climbed up, lantern in hand, and reached out to the handle. It turned smoothly, without resistance, and the door creaked open inward.

Caleb stood at the foot of the steps, shining his lantern into the dark cavity beyond just as Wesley's light flickered from the second step. What stretched out before them was a narrow corridor, running parallel to the front entrance below. Doors lined both sides, closed tight, hiding who knew what beyond.

The air inside was stale and cold, carrying a faint, almost imperceptible scent, dust, old wood, and something else. Something forgotten.

The house had revealed its first secret. And Caleb could feel the weight of many more waiting in the shadows.

Wesley climbed down the small steps carefully, his boots making soft thuds against the timber joists. Together, they shifted the ladder aside to clear the narrow corridor entrance. The air was cooler here, heavier with dust and memories. Caleb took a deep breath, steadying himself before following Wesley back up, this time stepping fully into the long, dimly lit corridor.

Their boots echoed quietly on the old wooden floorboards, the thin planks creaking beneath their weight. The corridor stretched out before them, narrow, almost claustrophobic, with doors evenly spaced on either side, each pair facing one another like silent sentinels.

The first door on the left gave way easily to the turning of a knob. Caleb and Wesley pushed it open together, the beams of their lanterns spilling into the room beyond. The space was small, just under two and a half metres wide, nearly three deep, empty, save for a faint layer of dust that danced in the shafts of light.

They moved down the corridor, opening the door directly opposite. This room was almost full to bursting with furniture, aged and worn, a forgotten trove of old chairs, tables, and cupboards shoved close together as if stacked in a hurry. Next door was empty again, followed by another across the hall, stuffed with belongings.

It became clear, room by room, a pattern emerged. Every second chamber held the remnants of a life once lived, packed away in the shadows of this hidden space. The bathrooms, functional and cold, stood empty, stark as forgotten tombs.

When they climbed back down to ground level, a quiet realisation settled over them both. The old lady, the one who'd lived here long before, had moved the contents of her sons' bedrooms up into this loft. And then, in a final act of grief or protection, had tried to seal it all away, removing the stairs, closing off the space with a makeshift ceiling, as if to lock those memories out of reach forever.

Later, when they told Adina what they'd found, her face went pale. Without hesitation, she ordered them to restore the ceiling, to cover the entrance as if putting a lid on something sacred.

"We'll honour Mrs. Kimberly Hewson's wishes," Adina said firmly. "Her children were lost in the war. This space up there, it's a sanctuary now. No one goes up there again. It's hers, and it will remain that way."

The words hung in the air, heavy with the weight of respect and sorrow. The house, with all its secrets, had just whispered one of its deepest.

That afternoon, Caleb picked up the phone and called the builder he'd hired to handle the final repairs before they moved in. The man was familiar with the old place and its quirks, someone who knew how to work quietly, without stirring up more trouble than necessary. Caleb gave him the details: the ceiling in the right wing needed to be reinstated, sealed back up tight, like a tomb.

The builder didn't ask questions, just promised to come out by the next day and do the job. Caleb hung up, feeling the weight of the decision settle on his shoulders, the house was closing itself off again, burying its secrets for another generation.

Wesley and Adina had driven Caleb to Canberra early that morning, the day Joanna's final shift as the US Military Attaché at the embassy was to begin. The air was crisp, the sky a hard blue, the kind of morning that felt too sharp, too clear, like the last breath before something changed.

They had loaded Joanna's clothing and personal effects carefully into both her Jeep and their old Land Cruiser, the weight of it all pressing heavier than the suitcases and boxes suggested. The plan was simple enough: Wesley would take Joanna's Jeep back to Kimbarry, the old family property, and Adina would follow in the Cruiser. A quiet convoy back home after a day steeped in farewells and final goodbyes.

Later that evening, they returned to Kimbarry, the house looming like a patient sentinel in the fading light, waiting for their stories to unfold.

Joanna's farewell party had been a formal affair, beginning with a luncheon at the embassy laid on by the American Ambassador himself. The room had been filled with dignitaries, Australian Ministers, the Governor General, faces etched in official smiles and polite nods. But once the official guests had departed, the Ambassador opened the doors to the embassy staff and the Marines not on duty, turning the event into something warmer, human. Caleb and Joanna slipped out afterwards, spending the night at the Lakeside Hotel on the Ambassador's generosity.

The next morning, they caught the flight to Washington, Joanna's official discharge from service hanging in the air like a closing chapter. Three days were spent in the city, the capital's cold formality pressing in, before another flight carried them south to Midland, Texas. There, at last, they would meet Joanna's parents, George and Marlee Martinez.

Midland was a sun-baked city in the heart of West Texas, a place where the earth seemed to sweat oil. It thrived on the pulse of the Permian Basin, the vast, dusty cradle of the nation's oil fortunes. Here, oil rigs dotted the horizon like silent steel sentinels, pumping dark liquid wealth from the earth's bowels.

George Martinez was a man shaped by this harsh landscape. A senior engineer for Texaco, he had worked the oil fields for nearly fifteen years. His hands bore the calluses of hard work, but his sharp eyes reflected the sharp mind that had made him both respected and wealthy. The family lived in a company home, modest but well kept, the kind of place where every detail whispered a story of pride and perseverance.

For George, Midland wasn't just a job site. It was a second home, a relentless heartbeat beneath the vast Texas sky. Conversations here circled endlessly around oil prices, drilling forecasts, and the promise of black gold. Outside, the horizon stretched out like a challenge, endless, unforgiving, but full of possibility.

And now Caleb was here, standing at the edge of that horizon, ready to meet the family who'd shaped Joanna's past, and perhaps the future they would build together.

On one crisp Monday morning, George pulled into Texaco's Midland office, his old truck coated in a thin film of red dust, the kind that clung stubbornly, a badge of honour earned under the relentless West Texas sun. The landscape outside was scorched and bare, but the hum of industry was constant, a pulse beneath the stillness.

On his desk sat a project marked **URGENT**, the kind of label that made a man's spine straighten. A cluster of aging wells needed reengineering, not just to squeeze more oil from the earth but to do it while toeing the line of ever-tightening environmental regulations. A balancing act George had grown accustomed to, where his knack for solving problems met the reality of dwindling resources and mounting pressure from watchdog groups.

The Longhorn site was the troublemaker of the day. George arrived to find it buzzing like a hive, workers swarming the platform beneath the merciless sun. The air vibrated with the clang of steel and the hoarse shouts of men locked in a struggle with stubborn machinery. The pump jack's slow, steady rhythm was a heartbeat against the heat.

George nodded greetings as he passed the crew, their faces bronzed and weathered like the cracked earth beneath their boots. He climbed onto the platform, the wood creaking underfoot, and began his inspection.

The problem was just as he'd suspected, a stubborn blockage in the pipeline, a hard pack of mineral deposits choking the flow. But as George dove into the data, his brow furrowed. The pressure readings whispered secrets, something the initial surveys had missed. There was a new pocket of oil, just beyond reach, lurking beneath the parched soil like a hidden vein of promise.

That evening, back at his modest ranch-style home, the Texas heat replaced by the cool desert night, George sat on his porch, the faint smell of juniper in the air. He couldn't shake the implications. A new oil pocket could mean big money for Texaco, a shot of lifeblood for Midland's tired economy. But it also meant pushing deeper into land where the environment was already gasping, where every new drill drew protest and whispered warnings.

George's mind turned over the choices. More drilling, more profit, but at what cost? The desert held its silence, watching, waiting.

The next morning, George walked into Texaco's glassy office like a man carrying the weight of a promise. In his hands, the blueprint of a future, directional drilling, a technique that could thread through the earth without ripping apart the land above. "We can access it without disrupting the surrounding ecosystems," he said, voice steady, eyes sharp. He laid out the full draft proposal, every calculation and contingency in place, like a soldier mapping out a battle plan. "This could put us on the map, responsibly."

His supervisor listened, nodding with measured interest. The oil game was always a balancing act, but George's idea had the smell of something new, innovation tempered with conscience. Weeks later, George stood at the Longhorn site, the sun beating down on the sweltering platform, watching the new rig hum with life. The drill bit bit deeper, carving a silent tunnel beneath the earth. Pride swelled inside him, not just for the job done, but for doing it right, for threading progress through the needle's eye of responsibility.

In Midland, a town both blessed and cursed by oil, George's work became a symbol of something more than profit, a fragile bridge between old ways and new. His success brought not just dollars but a nod to stewardship, a hope that the desert could endure. And with it came a healthy reward for his years of labor.

At home, Marlee's world was quieter but no less complex. A devoted housewife, she spent her days volunteering at every charity and cause Midland had to offer. Their daughter, Joanna, carried the family's hope and scars. She had a brother, lost too young, swallowed by the shadow of a drug overdose at nineteen. The silence about him in their household was a wall built high and thick. Joanna had warned Caleb before, telling him her parents never spoke of the boy, a ghost between them all.

Midland was no stranger to such ghosts. The oil roads that fueled fortunes also ferried darker things, drugs, violence, whispers of trouble that followed like a shadow at dusk. It was a place where hope and hardship tangled in the dust.

After just one week in Midland, Caleb and Joanna found themselves restless, their hearts tugging back to Australia, their new life, their adventure waiting just beyond the horizon. They had invited Joanna's parents to visit down under, and the plans were already taking shape, small sparks of excitement in a landscape heavy with history.

But two weeks out from Australia, the homesickness crept in like a slow-moving storm. The bright promise of new beginnings dulled beneath the weight of memory and longing. The road ahead was still long, and the past, with all its shadows, was never far behind.

Carl Holgate had kept in regular contact with Adina by phone, updating her on any movement at the 'drug cottage', just as she had requested. Now, he had suggested they meet in person to observe the cottage together from the same vantage point the police had used during their surveillance. He gave her rough directions to the meeting spot and promised to drive her the rest of the way.

Perched side by side, they trained their binoculars on the small, weathered cottage nestled against the slope. It was clear from the sight that only one person was present, besides the two dogs Adina had noticed during her last visit. Those dogs had burst from under the house, tails whipping through the air, before a gruff voice had sent them scurrying with a harsh volley of abuse.

"There's just the one guy in there, from the looks of it," Adina whispered, her voice low.

Carl nodded, eyes sharp behind his own binoculars. "Yeah, usually he's alone when he's cooking. From what we've recorded, he keeps it up for about four days straight, cooking, packaging, maybe making pills, who knows exactly. Then, two others show up, drop off more gear, and haul away the finished product."

Adina mulled over the timeline. "So… he's cooking now, which means no visitors for at least two days, right?"

"That's what it looks like," Carl confirmed, his voice steady.

Adina's mind raced as she visualised the cottage's layout, the twin to Kerry's place, identical down to the last detail, as Kerry had explained during their walkthrough. Their binoculars scanned the back door, which opened onto a small laundry, then a narrow corridor leading into the lounge. That lounge, they surmised, was where the cooking operation was underway.

A quiet tension filled the air between them. Each detail was a piece of the puzzle, small, yet vital. The long wait ahead would demand patience, but both knew the stakes were high. The quiet hill behind the cottage offered a hidden vantage, but beneath the stillness, danger pulsed like a heartbeat in the shadows.

When Adina had driven up to the front of the cottage a few days ago, the dogs had erupted like an alarm bell, fierce, sharp, unyielding. No sooner had their snarls sliced through the heavy air than the man appeared at the front door, his shadow flickering in the weak sunlight like a warning sign. Quick as a cat, he'd dashed inside. But here was the thing, he couldn't get to the back door as fast as the dogs could raise hell. The hallway and the cramped laundry room forced him to slow down, gave her an edge.

"That'll work," she muttered under her breath, the words almost swallowed by the thick silence around them.

Carl, standing a few feet away, had no idea what she meant. He looked at her, puzzled.

"What'll work?" he asked.

Adina didn't answer right away. She reached into the waistband of her pants, fingers deft and steady, pulling free the sleek Smith & Wesson .22 LR auto. It gleamed faintly in the fading light, already fitted with a suppressor, and loaded with ten rounds of subsonic stinger ammo, silent but deadly.

"I'm about to show you how we take down a drug lab back home," she said, voice low, almost a whisper. "Are you armed?"

Carl blinked, dumbfounded. "You can't be serious."

"Are you armed?" she repeated, eyes narrowing.

He fumbled in his jacket and pulled out his Glock 9mm. "Yeah. Got this."

Adina nodded once. "Good. You shouldn't need it. Hopefully. We don't want any shots ringing out. You stay behind me. Backup. Try not to shoot."

Carl's face tightened. "You're crazy. There's just the two of us. We don't even know how many are inside, or if anyone's gonna show up while we're in there. This is reckless, Adina."

"Just stay calm. Follow me." Her voice was iron-clad.

And like a lamb to the slaughter, Carl followed. His mind raced with doubts and questions, but she moved with a purpose, a strange, fierce purpose, that left no room for argument.

They crossed a shallow gully, half-choked with trash and stinking rotten. The smell was vile, but it was nothing compared to the chemical stench drifting from the cottage: that sharp, sickly-sweet odor of meth cooking, a poison that seeped into the bones.

"Get ready," Adina whispered, eyes flicking up to the back door as she moved quickly, silently.

The dogs exploded from beneath the house, barking and snarling like demons unleashed. They charged straight at her, wild and furious.

Two shots, almost a whisper, and both dogs collapsed, their bodies hitting the ground with soft thuds.

Adina raised the laser sight, aiming dead centre at the dark opening of the back door.

One shot cracked softly.

A figure at the doorway jerked, then crumpled backward like a rag doll dropped from a great height.

Before the body could even touch the floor, Adina slipped through the door, cold and precise, and fired again, a 32-grain stinger round, right to the head. The man's body went limp, the fight gone before it had even begun.

The room fell into a heavy silence, but Adina's breath stayed steady. This was only the beginning.

Carl stood frozen where the two dogs had fallen, his heart pounding loud enough to drown out the sudden silence. He hadn't expected Adina, of all people, with her silver hair and calm demeanor, to sprint like a predator, her shots ringing out so quick and true. The world felt unreal for a moment, the cottage's shadow swallowing the noise, leaving only the thudding of his own breath in his ears.

Slowly, almost cautiously, Carl crouched and edged forward, gripping his Glock with both hands, the way they'd drilled into him at the academy. His eyes darted, searching for any sign of movement, any trap. Then Adina appeared, slipping through the back door like a ghost, her face calm but sharp.

"All clear," she said, voice low but steady. "I need your help now."

Without hesitation, she pushed the Smith & Wesson back into her pants pocket, as if it was no more than a casual accessory.

"Drag the body into the lounge, right next to where he was cooking," she ordered, voice cold as steel. Carl hesitated a moment, then bent down and began hauling the man's uncouth, filthy, stinking body across the floor, the smell rising like a rotten fog.

Adina vanished into the kitchen, reappearing moments later with an almost full two-litre container of methylated spirits clutched in her hands.

Carl, his nerves jangling, followed her orders again. This time she pointed toward the shallow gully, the rubbish dump where the two dead dogs lay.

"Get those gone. Quick," she said without looking back.

As Carl dragged the limp, lifeless dogs toward the foul gully, Adina moved with purpose. She poured the methylated spirits liberally over the body, soaking it in the burning chemical scent.

Her eyes scanned the room with practiced precision, no trace left behind. Then, like a final act of judgment, she picked up a Bic lighter from the table, flicked it, and touched the flame to the man's soaked clothing.

The fire caught instantly, the sickly orange glow swallowing the body, flickering shadows dancing on the walls as the cottage filled with the acrid stench of burning flesh and chemicals.

Carl stopped mid-drag, swallowed hard, and realised this was no ordinary woman he was following. This was a force of nature.

Methylated spirits, they burn slow. No sudden flash, no roar like petrol or gasoline. Just a steady, creeping fire, licking and smoldering, devouring everything in its path without making a scene. And the way Adina had mixed it with those other chemicals? No forensic lab would find a trace, not in the ashes or the embers. It was clever, almost surgical. The kind of thing that slipped past the prying eyes of cops and lab techs alike, leaving behind nothing but charred secrets.

They stopped and looked back, about fifty meters from the cottage, halfway up the hill where they had been watching it like vultures. The cottage was changing before their eyes, black smoke billowed from the back door they'd carelessly left open, a yawning mouth coughing out death. Through the grimy windows, the dull glow of flames flickered, a dark reddish-orange dancing in the shadows. Then, suddenly, like a beast waking, the fire leapt to the roof, flames twisting upward, clawing at the night sky.

By the time they'd reached the ridge where they'd started the descent, the cottage was a raging furnace, fully engulfed, a twisted monument to destruction. They turned again to watch, hearts pounding, as a deafening explosion ripped through the building, tearing most of the roof from its fragile bones. A plume of smoke and fire roared skyward, the smell of burning wood

     Max Barrington

and chemicals thick in the air, mingling with the cold night breeze.

Exhausted, they collapsed onto the grass, the heat washing over them in waves, the inferno before them a monstrous beast consuming everything it touched.

Carl stared at Adina, his mind struggling to grasp what he'd just witnessed. For six months, the police had been dancing around this place, stalking, waiting, gathering evidence like timid children afraid to touch a sleeping bear. They'd hoped to catch the man inside red-handed, to nab him, charge him, maybe even put him away for life. The law was clear: produce and distribute, mandatory life sentence in Australia. But all those months, all the caution and paperwork and court dates, it had come to nothing.

And here she was. This woman, this force of nature, had just done what took the entire system half a year to plan, all in ten minutes. No trial, no hearings, no appeals. The sentence was carried out swift and brutal, final as the grave. The case was now closed.

Carl's voice cracked with disbelief, a mix of shock and something darker simmering beneath. "This is justice. This is how it should be done, none of that endless bullshit with legalities and smart-arse lawyers who twist everything to set scumbags like this loose, despite the charges the cops lay down." His excitement edged into urgency, then dropped as reality clawed back in. "But… what happens now?"

Adina's eyes flicked over him, steady and unreadable. "Meaning what?"

Carl swallowed hard, anxiety threading through his words like a creeping chill. "Meaning… there's gonna be an investigation, right? Like, someone's going to poke around, find out what happened. We need to cover our arses, now."

Adina's voice was calm, almost a whisper, but it carried the weight of iron. "Relax, Carl. Settle down. Just keep walking with me to your car, okay? We weren't here. You understand that? We were not here."

The words hung in the night air between them, heavier than smoke. They reached his Nissan Patrol, the same one he'd left parked there days ago, near the spot where Caleb had caught them off guard. Carl slid into the driver's seat, the engine rumbling to life as he steered them back toward where Adina had first met him.

"Look," she said, voice as even as the steady hum of the engine, "meth labs, they blow up. It happens. A lot. And often, the people inside don't make it out. This lab? It just exploded. The guy inside, he was killed in the blast. The fire consumed the place and his body. It's doubtful anyone will dig any deeper than that."

Carl blinked, the knot in his gut loosening, replaced by a flicker of relief. His mind cleared, the fog of anxiety lifting like morning mist. Adina caught the shift and allowed herself a small nod.

"I'd imagine the local bush fire brigade will be heading out there right now," Adina said, eyes scanning the dark horizon.

Carl shook his head slowly, the faint authority of experience returning to his tone. "Probably not. They're volunteers, mostly. Takes time to get them organized. And remember, they're geared for bushfires, not structure fires. They don't respond with the urgency a burning building demands."

He glanced over, voice steady. "But the color of that smoke? It'll tell them a building's involved, make them move faster. They'll call the ambulance, the cops… all the right people."

Adina offered a sly smile, the flicker of something almost human in her eyes. "Might look better if you're at my place having a coffee when the smoke shows up on the horizon."

Carl laughed, a sound equal parts nervous and relieved, driving into the night, the flames burning far behind them.

The smoke rose thick and dark, visible even from the rear of the Kimbarry homestead, curling up over the rise like a living thing, slow and sinister. Inside the house, Wesley and Adam, the carpenter sent by the builder to finish the ceiling, were putting the final touches on their work. The light was fading, and sawdust hung in the air like a fine mist.

Adina and Carl stepped inside quietly, coffee cups in hand, breaking the concentration with news heavy on their tongues.

"Smoke," Adina said, her voice low but urgent. "Over the rise, behind the house. We think we should take a look."

Wesley's eyes narrowed, the lines of his face deepening with concern. "I'm coming with you," he said without hesitation.

In moments, they were packed into Wesley's Land Cruiser, the engine growling to life as they made their way toward the plume.

By the time they arrived, the cottage was lost, no hope left to save it. The volunteer fire brigade's battered old truck sat at the edge of the clearing, its lone driver standing by. The rest of the brigade was nowhere to be seen.

The cottage burned with ferocity. Curtains had curled into blackened skeletons and crumbled to ash, brittle and defeated. Furniture groaned and snapped under the heat, walls blistered, floors blackened, the ceiling sagging as flames licked every surface. The hearth that once promised warmth and comfort was now a furious inferno, an uncontrollable beast tearing through the place.

Windows shattered with sharp, violent pops, showering shards of glass onto the scorched earth below. Flames clawed outwards, escaping their prison, reaching hungrily for the garden fence and scorching the nearby shrubs. The air was thick with the choking smell of burning wood mixed with acrid chemical fumes, the sour stench of melted paint and singed fabric.

The heat shimmered in waves, distorting the view as the small group stood powerless. The fire spoke in crackles and roars, each snap and boom signalling another beam's collapse or an object exploding under pressure.

And then, as the fuel began to run out, the flames lost their strength, flickering and sputtering like a dying animal before finally beginning to falter.

By the time the police and ambulance rolled onto the scene, the fierce, bright orange blaze had faded to a dull, sullen red, the fire's angry heartbeat slowing to a mournful pulse. Smoke no longer billowed thick and heavy; instead, it drifted in thin, ghostly wisps that twisted and curled into the cool evening air like lost spirits unwilling to leave. The cottage was nothing more than a skeletal ruin: blackened beams stood jagged and broken, surrounded by smouldering ruins and the heavy haze of smoke and destruction hanging low over the scorched earth.

The ground itself seemed wounded, scrubby bushes still burned here and there, and the creeping flames had found their way to the narrow gully behind the cottage, starting to snake along its dry, cracked floor. It was a slow, relentless hunger that could not be stopped, only contained.

There was nothing left to do but watch. Stand and watch as the last, trembling bones of what once was settled into silence and ruin.

Senior Constable Robert Black from the Bigga Police Station had spotted Carl in the gathering crowd. Recognizing him, Black approached, his boots crunching on the ash-littered soil. "You know what happened here?" he asked, voice low, carrying the tired edge of long nights and hard calls.

Carl nodded and introduced the Ahrens as the owners of the cottage, part of their sprawling property at Kimbarry. Black turned to Wesley, the carpenter, his expression sharp and expectant.

"What happened here?" he asked.

Wesley shook his head, hands raised in honest ignorance. "Totally clueless, mate. We just saw the smoke, so we came over. There was a squatter living here, though."

Carl stepped in, his tone steady but quiet. "Federal Police have been watching the place. Suspected meth lab. I'm seconded to their operation."

Black's eyes narrowed. "Think anyone was inside?"

Carl lifted his hands, the only answer he could give. "Who knows? Looks like it'll be a long time before anyone gets close enough to find out."

The volunteer fire brigade had arrived in force by then, old trucks rumbling in and men springing into action. They were busy dousing the scattered embers in the grass around the ruins, determined to snuff out every flicker that might spread the fire further. At the gully's edge, they worked to isolate the blaze, choosing to let it burn itself out where it was contained, nature's own cleansing fire, stubborn and relentless.

The night was thick with the smell of smoke and silence. The cottage was gone. And with it, some piece of the past, swallowed by fire and shadow.

The smell lingered like a ghost, sharp and acrid, a brutal chemical punch that clawed at the back of your throat and made your eyes water. It was the unmistakable stench of a methamphetamine lab, a harsh blend of solvents and burnt plastic that hung heavy in the air, refusing to be washed away even long after the flames had died down to cold, ashen bones. It was a smell that turned your stomach, repulsive but eerily distinct, like the faint trace of something terrible that refuses to let you forget.

Constable Black moved with methodical precision. He stretched the blue and white police tape around the blackened skeleton of the cottage, cordoning it off like a crime scene from some low-budget horror movie. Then he called in forensics, specialists who'd sift through the ashes for anything, evidence, clues, maybe even body remains. There was the grim possibility, one that settled uneasily in the pit of everyone's stomach.

Black had already done the rounds, a quick preliminary interview with anyone who might have seen or heard something. But there were no witnesses. No one. Wesley and the carpenter had been working inside the homestead on the ceiling, oblivious to the slow build of disaster just over the rise. Adina, sitting on the porch with a cup of coffee in her hands, had been the one to spot the smoke curling above the trees. She'd been planning a BBQ with Carl, who was visiting for the day, when the first tendrils of grey appeared on the horizon, thin and wispy, but unmistakable.

It all felt like the calm before something darker, the kind of quiet that presses down just before the real nightmare begins.

Wesley and Adina had been on the road for three long hours, cutting through endless miles of highway, chasing the slow crawl of the sun across the sky, until finally they pulled into the sprawling, chaotic expanse of Sydney International Airport. They were there to meet Caleb and Joanna, fresh off a long-haul flight from the States. The car hummed along the freeway on the way back to Kimbarry, the air inside thick with a mixture of anticipation, relief, and something darker that neither wanted to say out loud.

The conversation, when it came, circled relentlessly around the burnt-out cottage, one of the two little workers' shacks that had stood on their land. Now it was just a skeleton of charred timber and ash. The police had found something awful inside: the remains of a badly burned body, so destroyed by the flames it was impossible to say who it had been. Forensics said the fire hadn't been a simple accident. Chemicals had exploded, mixing under heat in a deadly dance that ended in a sudden, violent blaze. According to the cops, that was the end of it. Case closed.

Adina, however, wasn't about to let it go that easy. She had already checked the insurance policy they'd carefully put together through a broker, every building on Kimbarry covered, every risk accounted for. The assessor was due next week, and she wanted to make sure no corner was left unturned.

Meanwhile, Caleb and Joanna, still bleary-eyed from jetlag, were glowing with the kind of relief that only comes from finally being home. Joanna, in particular, looked lighter, freer, now that she no longer had to drag herself through the endless grind at the embassy in Canberra. For the first time in a long time, life at Kimbarry promised a kind of peace.

That night, over dinner, the conversation took a sharper turn. It was time to get serious. The treasure hunt, their real reason for being here, couldn't be put off any longer. There was still plenty of gold left, safely stashed beneath the floorboards in Caleb and Joanna's bedroom, hidden under a doormat that had never raised suspicion. They had time, yes, but not forever.

The hunt was on again, shadows lengthening around them as the past burned away into ash and smoke.

The mention of the gold, safely tucked away beneath the floorboards, pried open a cracked door in Caleb's mind. The missing drawer. The vanished safe key. And, most troubling of all, the lost map. It was a knot of unease tightening in his chest. He looked up, locking eyes with his parents across the table. "Have the keys or the map turned up yet?" His voice was steady but edged with urgency.

Adina and Wesley exchanged glances, their faces reflecting the fog of distraction. "Honestly," Adina said, "we'd completely forgotten about those keys and the map. There's been so much going on with everything else, they just slipped out of mind."

Wesley nodded, rubbing the back of his neck. "No reason for us to have touched them. We haven't needed to."

The three of them fell silent, the weight of the missing pieces settling like dust in the corners of the room. The keys and map weren't just misplaced; they were gone. Someone else had taken them. But who? And why?

The uneasy topic churned in Caleb's thoughts until it pulled him back to something else, a book he'd picked up during his trip to America. Rising abruptly from the table, he excused himself and disappeared into the adjoining room. Moments later, he returned clutching the worn volume, a small flicker of something, hope or perhaps curiosity, playing in his eyes.

Pouring himself a drink, he settled back into his chair, cleared his throat, and opened the book. The room hushed, the kind of silence that feels like holding your breath. Then, with a calm, measured voice, Caleb began to read aloud a short story from the pages, as if the words themselves might illuminate the shadow that had crept over them all.

The Bushranger's Refuge

By the 1870s, San Francisco was a city of ambition and vice, where fortunes were made and lost in the blink of an eye. Down a crooked alley near the Barbary Coast stood The Southern Cross, a saloon unlike any other. Its battered sign bore the emblem of Australia's iconic stars, and its proprietor, Frank 'Darkie' Gardiner, had a reputation as colourful as the patrons who frequented his establishment.

Frank had come to San Francisco under a cloud of infamy. Once a notorious bushranger in the wilds of New South Wales, he had fled Australia after narrowly escaping the gallows.

The gold rush of California offered him a second chance, and he seized it. Frank wasn't a man to let his talents go to waste; the skills that once made him a feared outlaw, charm, cunning, and a knack for reading people, now made him the perfect saloonkeeper.

'The Southern Cross' was more than a saloon; it was a haven for outcasts and adventurers. Miners fresh from the Sierras, sailors from distant ports, gamblers down to their last dollar, all found solace under Frank's roof. The air was thick with the scent of whiskey and tobacco, the din of laughter, clinking glasses, and the occasional shout of a card game gone wrong.

But The Southern Cross had its secrets. Frank kept a sawed-off shotgun under the bar, a relic from his bushranging days in Australia, and a hidden backroom where deals were made in whispers. Some said he ran a smuggling operation; others claimed he'd buried gold somewhere in the hills in Australia near a town called Forbes. Frank never confirmed or denied these rumours, preferring to let his enigmatic smile do the talking.

One stormy night, a stranger walked into the saloon. He was tall and lean, with a face weathered by years on the trail. His coat dripped rain onto the wooden floor as he approached the bar.

"You Frank Gardiner?" the man asked, his voice low and rough with an Australian accent.

Frank sized him up. "Depends who's asking."

The stranger slid a piece of paper across the bar. Frank picked it up, his eyes narrowing as he read. It was a wanted poster from Australia bearing his name and likeness.

'You've come a long way,' Frank said evenly, setting the paper down.

'Ten thousand pounds,' the stranger replied. 'Enough to make the trip worthwhile.'

The saloon grew silent as the tension thickened. Frank leaned on the bar, his fingers inching toward the shotgun hidden beneath. 'You reckon you'll collect?' Frank asked.

The stranger's hand moved to his hip, but before he could draw, a sharp click echoed through the room as Frank's shotgun was pointed squarely at his chest.

'Listen here, mate, Frank said, his voice as smooth as silk. 'I didn't survive the bush, the gallows, and the Pacific crossing just to be taken down by the likes of you. So why don't you turn around, walk out that door, and forget you ever found me?'

The stranger hesitated, his eyes darting around the room. The patrons, a motley crew of rogues and roughnecks, stared him down. One by one, they stood, forming a silent wall of solidarity behind Frank.

The stranger nodded slowly, backing toward the door. 'This ain't over, Gardiner,' he muttered before disappearing into the storm.

Frank lowered the shotgun and called after him, 'None shall have, 'The Darkie's Gold' the tension easing as the saloon returned to life.

He poured himself a whiskey and raised his glass. 'To old friends and new beginnings,' he said with a grin, earning a raucous cheer from the crowd.

That night, as the rain lashed against the windows, Frank sat by the fire in the corner of the saloon, his mind drifting to the eucalyptus-scented hills of home. He was a long way from Australia, but here in San Francisco, among his chosen family of misfits and dreamers, Frank Gardiner had carved out his own legend.'

They all sat in silence, the heavy quiet thick enough to press against their skin after Caleb's voice faded. The story lingered like smoke in the room, an echo of a past long buried, yet stubbornly alive in the corners of their minds.

Caleb finally broke the silence, voice steady but carrying a flicker of excitement. "Apparently, the bloke who wrote it knew Frank Gardiner himself. The forward says he was there in the saloon that night when the wanted poster was slid across the bar. He wrote other stories too, about Australian bushrangers who, hearing that Gardiner was making good in San Francisco, escaped and joined him there."

Adina's impatience cracked through the calm like a sudden gust. "Where the fuck is Forbes?" She glanced at Wesley, who was already leaning toward his laptop, fingers poised like a pianist about to play.

Wesley didn't hesitate. "About two hundred kilometres, or one hundred and twenty-five miles, as we reckon it," he said, his eyes fixed on the screen.

Adina snorted. "I don't think our map is from Frank Gardiner. That's a six, maybe seven-day ride on a horse loaded down with weight. And this book talks about the 'Southern Cross' saloon, ours was called the 'Twilight Star.' And don't forget, there's always been some confusion over the names of the streets and the saloons around here."

Caleb shrugged, unphased. "Doesn't matter who hid the gold. We have the map. We've already proved it's accurate."

Wesley cut in sharply, shaking his head. "No. We don't have the map. Remember?" He looked around the table, eyes serious. "We're missing it. Someone stole the map. And the safe key, too."

A cold chill crept through the room, the kind that has nothing to do with the weather outside.

"Why?" Adina whispered.

Wesley's voice dropped lower. "To open the safe. Someone knows we have gold. Our gold."

The air thickened with unspoken dread, the past closing in on them like a storm rolling over the hills.

"Well, that's a no-brainer," Caleb said, voice sharp enough to slice the silence. "Alex. Fucking. Gregory. Him. Them. Of course it's them. Carol included. They know about the gold, hell, they probably knew before we did, and don't forget, Carol's the one who handed over the keys to the house after settlement. Wouldn't take much for her to keep a set for herself. Or make a new one."

Joanna's brow furrowed, her voice cautious, like she didn't want to jinx something already spiraling. "But when could they have been here?"

And then, softly, she answered her own question. "I guess… we've been bouncing around Sydney and Canberra a bit lately. When exactly did you first notice the map was gone, Caleb?"

Caleb didn't need to think. "The day after we came back from Canberra with Mum and Dad's new car."

"That was… we left Saturday. Got back Sunday. Two days. One night." She said it as if trying to convince herself it couldn't have been enough time. But deep down, they all knew it was more than enough.

"Carol's got a business to run," Caleb continued, his voice low and bitter. "So a Saturday visit makes sense. They knew we were away. She's been in that house before. I'd bet she's been watching it. Waiting. That bastard Alex wouldn't hesitate to snoop around. He never did."

Adina crossed her arms, her eyes narrowing with the kind of fire you didn't want aimed your way. "So now what?"

Caleb sank into thought, the kind of thought that looked like it might dig a tunnel straight through his skull. But it was Joanna who broke the pause, words clicking into place with the clean precision of a lock engaging.

"The desk key, the safe key, doesn't matter. Nothing of real value in either. The map? That's another story, but we've got it on our iPhones, laptops, and even the original, if you count the digital scan. The real issue, the big one?" She leaned forward, her voice low but urgent. "They know. They know there's gold. They've got the scent. And they're on our land."

Heads nodded around the room. Agreement settled like dust in the air. No one liked the weight of it, but it was there all the same.

"And let's face it," Joanna continued, "those second and third targets haven't been easy to pin down. Every time we've tried to hit them, we've come up empty. Just guesses and wrong holes. But we covered the site where we did find gold, backfilled, scattered brush, hid the mess. They don't know it's already been taken. And that first site? It's the easiest of the three."

"I'll bet they've already been digging there," she added grimly.

"So it's a race now," Wesley said, his voice quiet, almost defeated. "A race to beat them to the other two spots."

"Bullshit, it is!" Adina's voice exploded across the room like a shotgun blast. She slammed her hand against the table, rattling empty mugs. "This isn't some bloody scavenger hunt. It's our property, and our gold. There is no fucking race, my dears. Those pricks are not setting foot on our land again. End of story."

"I agree," Caleb said, steel returning to his voice. "I'll look into wireless game cameras. Motion sensors. Whatever we can get. We're going to set them up, catch them in the act if they come back. But first..." He stood up, a new determination in his posture. "We need to focus on finding those last two sites. Nail them down. Get ahead of this."

With that, he left the room, heading for the office where his laptop waited, ready to spit out another version of the map.

Wesley, silent until now, pulled his phone closer, tapped through the screen, and found a locksmith in Cowra. He typed quickly, requesting a full rekey of every lock on the property, and hit send on the email with a grim sense of satisfaction.

Outside, the wind picked up, whispering against the windows like someone breathing through their teeth. And just for a moment, it felt like the house itself was holding its breath.

Waiting.

The insurance assessor had arrived precisely when his email had said he would, 10:00 a.m. sharp. His SUV crunched up the gravel drive with a slow, deliberate rhythm, the way people drive when they're already planning their report before stepping out of the vehicle. He was met at the front door of the homestead by Adina, who'd been up since dawn, sipping coffee from an enamel mug and watching the horizon for his arrival like she was waiting for bad weather.

He was a thin man, polite to a fault, with a clipboard under one arm and a retractable tape measure hooked to his belt. He nodded as Adina gave him the short version of what was about to happen, then obediently followed her in his car as she drove the old Land Rover out to what remained of the southern paddock.

The burned-out cottage, or rather, the place where the cottage had once been, was quiet now. A scorched rectangle of ash and crumbled brick, the ghost of a home that had once stood upright and useful. The smell of it still lingered, acrid and ghostly, no matter how many days had passed since the fire. The wind moved through the place like a whisper from a darker chapter.

The assessor stepped out, quietly professional. He got to work without fanfare, moving through the blackened footprint with the solemnity of a coroner examining a corpse. He measured out the perimeter, noted the collapsed structure's boundaries, and made a point of walking the seven metres or so to the cracked cement lid of the septic tank, mumbling to himself as he counted the number of pipe inlets.

Adina crossed her arms and waited until he straightened up, brushing ash off his slacks.

"How are we looking?" she asked, her voice clipped, like someone bracing for bad news from a doctor.

"When we estimate the replacement cost of a home that's been completely destroyed by fire, as in this case," the assessor began, speaking with the carefully neutral tone of someone used to delivering just-bearable disappointment, "we use a systematic approach. It ensures our calculations are accurate and align with the provisions of your policy. And in your case, you're covered for replacement value, not just market value, which is fortunate."

He adjusted his glasses, peering at her from behind bureaucratic lenses. "Do you have any recent photographs of the building? Exterior or interior? And do you happen to have a current furniture inventory?"

Adina didn't hesitate. "No photos of the ruins, but I've got something better." She gestured back toward the Land Rover. "Follow me again."

They drove along the narrow track that sliced through the paddocks like a scar, winding toward the other cottage on the property, the one still standing. It sat beneath a lonely pepper tree, its walls whitewashed and its tin roof dull with dust. Kerry's place.

She parked and knocked on the door, firm and authoritative. A moment passed before it creaked open, and Kerry appeared, rubbing the sleep from his eyes. He looked like he'd been dreaming of somewhere far away, and reality hadn't quite caught up yet.

"Morning," Adina said, cutting through his haze. "Sorry to barge in. I've got the insurance assessor with me. The cottage that burned was identical to yours, in every way. Layout, furniture, fittings. Would you mind if he takes a quick look around for reference? It's for the claim."

Kerry blinked a few times, scratched the back of his head, and gave a half-nod.

"Yeah, alright," he said. "Just... give me a minute to clean up a bit."

The assessor waited politely, staring at the doorway like he could already see inside. Behind him, Adina stood rigid, arms crossed again, her gaze fixed not on the cottage, but on the smudge of black smoke still staining the sky in her memory.

The place might be gone, she thought, but what had started the fire, and what came next, was still smouldering, just beneath the surface.

The assessor moved like a ghost through the cottage, his tape measure dragging behind him like a tail, clicking and coiling as he moved from room to room. Outside on the verandah, under a roof just beginning to blister under the late morning sun, Adina sat with Kerry, her hands curled around a porcelain cup of strong, bitter coffee that he'd made with a polished chrome machine sitting proudly in his kitchen. The aroma alone had curled into her soul like a cat settling in for a nap, and she'd already scribbled in her battered notepad: Buy coffee machine. Sick of that bloody instant.

She watched the assessor through the flyscreen door for a moment, then turned back to Kerry. He was barefoot, his feet on the railing, his gaze drifting beyond the hills. Adina spoke first, her voice quiet, almost reverent. "Caleb brought back this book from the States," she said. "It's about Frank Gardiner... apparently he ran a saloon called The Southern Cross in San Francisco. Back in the 1860s."

Kerry grunted, nodding slowly. "Barbary Coast," he said, chewing on the words like old tobacco. "Heard that story, or something close to it. Supposedly had a joint there, yeah. But Frank Gardiner, he was always good at vanishing."

Adina leaned forward. Her eyes gleamed like someone reaching for a match in the dark. "Do you think the gold from the Escort Robbery could be hidden somewhere around here?"

Kerry didn't speak right away. He smiled instead, the kind of smile that carries weight, like an old photo found in a drawer you'd forgotten existed. Without a word, he disappeared into the cottage, and returned just as the assessor announced he was done and would be in touch with the final report. Adina nodded, barely hearing him, as Kerry laid a weathered book on the table between them.

He opened it with care, like it might crumble. Then he began to read.

The Cobb & Co. Mystery at Bigga

The coach stop at Bigga had long since fallen into ruin, its timbers sagging like a drunkard at the end of a long night, but back in the late 1880s, it had been alive with motion. Dust devils danced across the hard-packed road, and the inn was warm with the smell of woodsmoke, stew, and the sweat of men who had spent too many hours in the saddle. It was there that Samual Baker and William Squires had arrived, two Americans, wide-eyed and hungry for adventure.

Sam, the excitable one, carried a yellowed parchment. A map. "Bought it from an old sailor in San Francisco," he claimed, waving it like a relic from the Ark. "Said the treasure's buried near Bigga, by an old Cobb & Co. stop."

Will, quieter, more cautious, had squinted at the crude ink lines. "Hope it's not just someone's idea of a joke."

They arrived at the inn just as the coach pulled away, hooves hammering the road like thunder. Inside, they found warmth, a plate of stew, and Mary, the innkeeper with sharp eyes and a sharper tongue.

"Treasure?" she said, raising an eyebrow. "Plenty have come sniffin'. All they've found are blisters and snakebites. Still… there's a spot, just north of the creek that runs to the river. Folks say it's cursed. Noises. People disappearing."

Sam had only grinned. "Sounds like the place for us."

Adina sat bolt upright at that. "A creek…" she murmured.

Kerry didn't pause, but his eyes flicked toward her.

The next morning, the Americans set off. Shovels. A lantern. And the map.

The grove they found was twisted and overgrown, trees leaning in like gossips. The creek whispered behind them, winding its way toward the river, and the air felt… strange. Thick. Watchful.

They dug. Time passed like a dream. Shadows lengthened. Then, clang. A hard sound. They struck something.

A chest. Small. Rusted. The lock was brittle as bone and snapped easily. Inside: coins. Old. A pistol, its silver long gone to tarnish.

Sam whooped. Will only frowned.

Then came the whistle.

It was low. Sad. Like a song that had forgotten its words.

"Wind?" Will asked.

But they both knew it wasn't.

The lantern flickered, then died. In the dark, there were footsteps. Circling.

They ran, the chest clutched between them, the whistle pursuing them like breath on the back of the neck. At the inn, they told Mary. She laughed, but her eyes were not laughing.

"That's the bushranger's gold. The Darkie's Gold, they call it. Spirit guards it. Kills for it, they say."

The Americans didn't sleep. They sold the coins in Sydney and sailed for home. They told no more stories.

But the pistol, they left that behind. It's still there, above the mantle at the old inn, for anyone to see. The treasure? Still buried. Still guarded.

Kerry closed the book and looked up at Adina, whose fingers had tightened around her coffee cup until her knuckles showed white.

"It's just a story," he said. "But you know what they say, every story starts with a seed of truth. And this story? It's about this Cobb & Co. stop. Your homestead."

Adina's voice came out soft. Almost a whisper. "So the Escort gold could be around here…"

Kerry chuckled, standing and stretching his back. "That's not the only one I've heard. Just the only one I've read. My grandfather told me another. Almost the same. Two men. A creek. But they didn't tell anyone. Not before. Not after. Just caught the next coach out."

He stepped inside, glancing at the old clock above the kitchen sink.

"It's ten o'clock somewhere," he called over his shoulder. "Time for something stronger."

And on the verandah, Adina sat alone, the coffee cold in her cup, eyes turned toward the distant creek, and something in the breeze, a sound just faint enough to question, just clear enough to remember. A whistle. Low. Haunting. Carried on the wind like a secret not meant to be told.

Adina tapped Wesley's number while Kerry vanished into the cool shade of the cottage to retrieve their drinks. The line clicked, and she spoke quickly, her voice calm, almost offhand, as if trying to disguise the electricity prickling at the base of her skull.

"I'm having a beer with Kerry. I'll be home soon."

They clinked bottles a moment later, foam hissing quietly in the dry country air. Kerry lowered himself into the chair across from her again, the weight of old stories hanging between them like the scent of distant bushfires.

"It was Matt Cross running the Inn back then," Kerry began, his voice a low drawl soaked in memory and time. "He's the one who told my grandfather about those two Americans. Quiet blokes, he said. Kept to themselves."

Adina leaned forward, her beer untouched.

"The Americans asked Matt about hiring horses, two riding horses, bridles, saddles, and a packhorse rigged with a saddle tree. Matt sorted it. They rode out the next day. Didn't say much. Just left."

He paused, glancing out toward the gnarled trees that marked the edge of the yard.

"While they were gone, one of the furriers at the stables noticed something missing, a heavy shovel and an iron bar we used for cutting drain channels. Disappeared, just like that. They turned the place upside down looking for 'em. No luck. Then the men came back, stayed one more night, and left on the Sydney coach. All they had were the same two carpetbags they'd brought with them."

Adina said nothing. Her heart was ticking louder now, an internal metronome keeping time with every unfolding thread.

Kerry went on, his voice steadier now. "Nearly a year later, this bloke Charlie Jenkins, a regular at the Inn and a keen ferreter, was out chasing rabbits for the butcher. He stumbles on the missing tools, half-buried near a big rock close to the creek. Says there were diggings, fresh ones, several of 'em. Like someone had been looking for something but didn't finish."

He took a long pull from his beer, eyes narrowing against the light. "Charlie turned in the shovel and the pick. Got a pint for his troubles."

Adina exhaled slowly. "So both stories mention the creek that runs into the river."

Kerry nodded. "Aye. And I've heard others, most of 'em nothing but whispers and beer talk. But these two? They stick. And they both circle back to the same place."

Adina stood, thanked him for the coffee, the beer, and, perhaps most of all, the stories that had stirred something deep inside her. Then, as if her mind couldn't let go, she asked the question before it could fester.

"Would it be hard to find that big rock? The one near the creek where it meets the river?"

Kerry didn't flinch. He set his beer down, gave her a long, quiet look. "Not hard... if you've got a map. Which you people do."

Adina froze. Her throat tightened as her heartbeat seemed to miss a beat.

"What are you saying?" she asked, her voice lower, sharper now.

"I know who you are. I know why you're here. And I know you have the map," Kerry replied, his tone calm, devoid of malice, just a man stating facts that had long since settled in his mind.

Her composure cracked, but not for long. Adina's instincts kicked in, honed by years of unspoken things and sharp observations. She recovered fast.

"You'd better come to the homestead this afternoon," she said. "Now, in fact. We need to talk. All of us."

She opened her iPhone, her fingers moving fast. "Wesley? Tell Caleb and Joanna to cancel anything they had planned. Light the BBQ, stock the fridge. Kerry's coming back with me. Cancel everything."

"What's going on, Mum?" Caleb asked as she swept through the back door of the house, grabbing a beer from the BBQ fridge like it was ammunition.

"Something urgent," she said, her voice clipped. "I'll explain when everyone's here."

Moments later, Kerry arrived, nodded a silent greeting, and followed her outside. He glanced at the fridge, then at her.

She nodded.

He pulled out a beer, popped the cap with the edge of the bench, and took a long drink.

The shadows were growing longer, stretching across the paddocks like reaching fingers.

Something was shifting in the dirt beneath their feet, and in the silence between every word that followed.

The afternoon sun hung low in the western sky, fat and bleeding orange through the treetops, casting long fingers of shadow across the rough timber deck of the homestead. The heat had finally broken. A warm breeze played in the gum trees like a whisperer stirring old ghosts.

At the outdoor dining table, four drinks sweated in sync with their owners. Glasses clinked idly, hands fidgeted with labels and coasters, but the tension was knotted and thick as blood pudding. Wesley. Caleb. Joanna. And Adina, the matriarch now perched like a hawk above them all, her eyes hard and her voice flint-sharp.

"Kerry seems to think he knows everything about us," she said. Her tone didn't invite contradiction. "So I thought it best he comes here today to tell us all about what he thinks he knows. Please… Kerry… the floor is yours."

And just like that, the eyes of the room, four hard gazes, turned on the old man.

Kerry looked like someone had just pulled the ripcord on his stomach. He took a sip from his beer, the bottle trembling ever so slightly in his hand, and stood. His shadow loomed long behind him, slanting toward the paddock beyond.

"If I'm gonna tell it, best I start at the beginning," he muttered, his voice gravelly with age and something else, regret, perhaps, or maybe fear. No one said a word. He went on.

"My real name's Kevin Albert Kerridge," he said. "My folks called me Bertie, but around Bigga, everyone just stuck with 'Kerry.'"

He talked about his childhood, grainy sepia images forming behind his words. The red dust roads of Bigga. Primary school memories that smelled of chalk and wet wool. Then high school in Cowra, three hours a day on a wheezing school bus that crawled through paddocks and mist. He told them how he was just a bush kid, good with horses, tractors, and broken things. Then, in the dry grip of the summer of 1967, the letter arrived. Government-issue. Cold. Official. He was being conscripted.

"They took me from the paddocks to the barracks," he said. "Turned a farmhand into a soldier."

His voice darkened as he described boot camp, the screaming of sergeants, the stench of sweat and fear, the weight of a rifle heavier than conscience. But beneath it all, he found something: a talent. For reading things. Patterns. Shadows. Motives.

"I had a knack," Kerry said, shrugging with a humility that didn't quite hide the pride. "Could spot a lie faster than I could skin a rabbit. The army saw it, and soon enough I wasn't just a soldier, I was gathering intel. Watching. Listening."

He was plucked from the front lines and placed in military intelligence. Surveillance. Analysis. Dark rooms and darker missions.

"When I got out in '70, ASIO came knocking," he said. "Offered me a job before I even took off my boots. That's how I spent the next twenty years, working in the shadows. Following people who didn't want to be followed. Listening to voices not meant to be heard."

They stared at him now, not like a man they'd shared beers with, but like a ghost who had just stepped into the room and told them he'd been watching them all their lives.

Kerry went on. How he tracked foreign agents in Sydney, disrupted a Soviet leak, earned quiet praise from the brass without ever appearing in a single news clipping. And then, he'd retired. Not with fanfare, not with parades. Just faded back to Bigga. Back into the dust. Like a man burying something, maybe even himself.

He took another swig of beer and accepted a fresh one from Caleb. The boy's hand shook slightly as he passed it over.

"After Hewson sold this place to you lot, I got curious," Kerry said. His eyes, no longer mild, now bore into them like drill bits. "Didn't take long to figure out you weren't just here for the serenity."

He turned to Caleb. "You, a USMC Recon Master Sergeant. And your mate, a decorated Marine Major. You suddenly buy a ten-thousand-dollar metal detector, then this property. Doesn't that sound strange to you?"

His gaze flicked to Wesley and Joanna. "A brilliant surgeon and a top homicide detective from San Francisco. Both of you, burnt out in a crumbling saloon that wasn't making a dime. Then you vanish, quietly, and turn up here. Flush with cash. Like magic."

No one spoke. The gum leaves rustled like gossip overhead.

"I did some digging," Kerry said. "Found out about Gardiner. Frank bloody Gardiner. Used to run a saloon in San Francisco. Same place you folks did. And he was part of the escort robbery, the biggest haul this country ever saw. Gold. Still missing."

He leaned in, his voice a blade now.

"You found something back in San Francisco, didn't you? A map, maybe. Something that led you here. You came chasing gold buried by ghosts. And from where I'm sitting… you already found some of it."

Adina's face remained unreadable, carved from stone.

"But here's the part that matters," Kerry said, straightening up. "I know you're not done looking. I know there's more out here. And I want in."

Silence.

Even the birds seemed to hush.

Kerry finished his beer and placed the empty bottle down with a soft, final thud.

"Whatever ghosts are still whispering under that soil out there, I reckon they'd talk to me too."

He looked each of them in the eye, one by one.

"Time to decide," he said. "Am I in the circle? Or am I a problem to be… managed?"

And for a long moment, no one moved. No one even breathed.

Out in the bush, far beyond the fence line, a crow gave a single caw. And the sky darkened just a little more.

And now, there were five

Wesley read the letter twice before he slid it across the worn timber of the breakfast table. The paper made a dry, rasping sound as it passed under his fingers, like dead leaves blown across asphalt. It came to rest beside Adina's plate, where a wedge of uneaten sourdough sat congealing beside a smear of poached egg.

Adina picked up the letter and read it without a word, her face carved from stone. Outside, the wind moved through the trees with a low, whispering hum that sounded like voices if you let your mind drift just far enough.

It was from the insurance company. Regarding the recent destruction of the secondary dwelling known as "The Cottage," we regret to inform you… And so on. The usual corporate condolences, followed by the real kick in the guts: the claim was denied. No payout. Not now, not ever. The reason? The structure had allegedly been used in the manufacture of illicit drugs. A meth lab. An icebox. A chemical coffin waiting to go off. Take your pick.

"Well, that's that then," Wesley said finally, the weight of it hitting his shoulders like a wet wool coat. He reached for his coffee but didn't drink. "Shame, too. I had plans for that little patch of ground. Figured we'd build something decent. A proper place for the two of us. Clean. Quiet. New."

Adina didn't answer at first. She kept staring at the letter, as if the weight of her glare might make the ink bleed, curl, vanish. Finally, she dropped it on the table like it was something diseased.

"This is bullshit," she snapped. "How the hell can they say it was a drug lab? Where's the proof? The police couldn't prove it.

They couldn't even say it was a lab. Just suspicion. Shadows and whispers."

Across from her, Caleb had been quietly chewing his way through scrambled eggs, his laptop open beside his plate, one eye on the screen, the other half-listening, like a predator in tall grass. At Adina's outburst, he stopped chewing, fork held mid-air, and turned his head toward her.

"What do you mean?" he asked, tone casual but eyes sharp. "You're saying the cops couldn't prove it was a lab? I thought they knew, they just didn't have the physical evidence. That's what I heard. Where'd you get your info, Mum?"

There was a beat. Then another. A silence thick enough to carve meat from.

Adina felt the floor shift under her. Caleb was too quick. Always had been. A quiet boy who saw too much, remembered more. She realized, just a second too late, that she'd said too much. Shown a card she didn't mean to reveal. And she didn't like the way her son was now looking at her, like she was some strange puzzle piece that didn't quite fit the picture.

She waved a hand like brushing away a fly. "I'll give it to my legal people," she said, standing. Her voice was tight now, clipped. "They can sort it out."

And with that, she changed the subject like slamming a door.

"What time is Kerry coming round?" she asked, loudly enough that the question filled the room and pushed out the ghosts.

Joanna, who had been lingering near the kitchen sink, answered without turning. "One o'clock."

That hung in the air like a countdown.

From outside came the call of a magpie, low and strange. Caleb watched his mother for a long moment before returning to his eggs, though they'd gone cold now. He didn't look away from her as he took the next bite.

And Wesley… Wesley was staring at the letter again, as if somewhere between the lines was the truth they all kept dancing around. Or maybe something darker still.

Something that hadn't yet come to light.

But soon would.

They had held the family meeting the evening before, just after Kerry's revelation had detonated across the kitchen table like a stick of lit dynamite. The room had gone still after he'd finished, eyes darting, coffee cooling in forgotten mugs. In the end, after all the voices had been raised, all the tempers soothed and egos patched back together, they'd come to a consensus. It was in their best interest to allow Kerry to join them, not just as a consultant or a hanger-on, but as a partner.

An equal partner.

But Kerry had stood, arms folded and face unreadable, and said, "That's not fair. Not to the four of you. I won't do that."

And he meant it.

He had instead proposed two partnerships, two shares each. Still unequal, but weighted more toward those who had laid the groundwork. He argued he'd only just arrived, hadn't swung a pick or risked a jail term (not yet anyway). What right did he have to cut the same slice of pie as the rest?

Yet, as the discussion had wound into that grey hour when even the walls seemed to lean in and listen, the others disagreed, forcefully. Adina most of all.

In the end, Kerry relented. He reminded himself of the calibre of people sitting around that table. He may not have trusted them entirely, particularly Adina, with her hawk's eyes and that cool, too-smooth voice, but he wasn't stupid enough to make enemies out of all of them. Not yet. Not when he was still so deep in the shadows of the fire, the dead man, and the secrets that seemed to whisper out from Adina's very pores.

So, he accepted it. One-fifth. An even share.

And now, here they were, today, back around the same table in the cool interior of the shed that doubled as a meeting room, planning the next move. The search for the remaining two sites, the recovery of whatever gold, or whatever secrets, still lay buried.

The tension had thinned, though not entirely dissolved. It hung in the air like a faint odour no one could quite name.

Kerry, punctual as ever, leaned forward and stared at the map laid out on the trestle table. His index finger traced the faded paper like a diviner searching for water. "There are three sites marked here," he said, more to himself than anyone else. "I thought there were only two."

Caleb looked up from where he was sipping instant coffee from a chipped mug. "What made you think there were only two?"

"Because I know," Kerry said, turning to face him, "that you struck gold before you bought Kimbarry. I assumed you bought the property to keep digging. Makes sense. Two sites."

Caleb blinked. Just once. He hadn't expected Kerry to be quite so sharp. Most people they dealt with were blunt instruments, easy to read and easier to manipulate. But not Kerry. This man had a mind like a steel trap, and every time he opened his mouth, it snapped a little closer.

Have to be careful with him, Caleb thought. Don't underestimate him. Not for a second.

Kerry tapped the first marked location on the map. "So where exactly did you hit gold?"

Caleb hesitated, then pointed. Kerry leaned in, studied the position, then sat back slowly, his face unreadable.

"That's State Forest now," he said finally. "Jesus, you lot are lucky you didn't get caught. If a ranger had stumbled on you digging there, you'd be swapping stories in a prison yard right about now."

No one spoke. It was true. They all knew it. The gold they had found came with risk like rust on iron.

Kerry studied the map again. His brow furrowed in thought, the lines on his forehead deepening like cracks in old wood. He pointed back to the marked site. "These numbers here, '98 x 10', I'm assuming that means a bearing of 98 degrees from this star here?" He touched a hand-drawn five-pointed star encircled in red. "And you measured ten yards?"

Joanna nodded, brushing a lock of hair behind her ear. "Yes. Well… I think so. I mean, when the metal detector went off its brain at ten, ten metres or ten yards, I don't know, we didn't really measure." Her voice carried a hint of unease now, like she was unsure whether to be embarrassed or defensive.

Kerry's eyes didn't leave the map. "And these numbers, 0601?" he asked, his voice calm but sharp, like the edge of a scalpel.

Joanna gave a small shrug. "No clue. The whole thing is cryptic. To be honest, I was just guessing with the bearings. I think we were bloody lucky to find anything at all. That big rock was the only thing that made sense, it looked like the one sketched on the map. But the other two sites?" She shook her head. "We couldn't even find the right area, let alone a matching rock."

Kerry said nothing. His finger moved again, hovering just above one of the remaining circled sites like a priest preparing to exorcise a demon. He was quiet for a long time.

Then, very softly, he said, "Maybe the map isn't the only thing that's cryptic."

Nobody asked what he meant.

But Adina was watching him now. And for the first time, her smile didn't quite reach her eyes.

Kerry squinted at the map under the lamp's pale circle, his finger tracing the crude notations like they were scars on an old man's skin. "I know this place," he muttered, almost to himself. "Looks damn near the same as where my grandfather took me once. Rabbiting. I was ten. He said this was where Charlie found the missing tools from the Inn. Said the Yanks were digging here. Showed me the ground, soft, pocked, like a giant had dropped his fingertips there."

The others leaned in.

Kerry tapped the spot marked with an X, beside the numbers 112 x 20, and just below that, a circled X with 0604 underlined. The ink looked like it had bled from the past.

"So," he said, turning to Joanna. "One-twelve. That's the reversed bearing for the circled star, right? And the twenty? Twenty metres from the cross on the rock, in that direction?"

Joanna nodded, hesitant. "I think so… Yeah. That's how I read it with the last one. Worked for me."

Kerry didn't smile. "How much gold did you find?"

A quiet crackled through the room like static.

Adina didn't blink. "None of your fucking business, Kerry," she said. Her voice was calm, flat. Dangerous. "Your share starts now. What we find from here on in. Get that straight."

Kerry raised his hands and leaned back, all innocence. "Just wondered."

The fire in the hearth hissed softly as if it was listening in.

Then Wesley leaned forward. His face was drawn tight, like he'd been chewing on something sour for weeks. "There's something you need to know, Kerry." He pointed to the map between them. "A copy of this… was stolen. Five weeks back. We were out of town, in Canberra. Whole thing stinks."

He told him everything, the break-in, the missing keys, the gut feeling that the people they'd bought the house from had come back for seconds. Real estate agents. Charming, helpful. Now, just ghosts with a spare key and a thirst for treasure.

Kerry raised his brows. "For gold?"

"Yeah," Wesley said. "And they didn't just take the map. They took keys, one to the safe, one to the desk drawer. Lucky for us, both were empty."

Kerry, now chewing on a corner of thought, offered this: "That site in the State Forest, it's too easy. Anyone with half a clue will go there first. And we already cleaned that one out, right? So let 'em dig. But we need to move. Fast. Frost's coming in tonight. Stars will be sharp as razors."

A decision settled over the group like dusk.

They agreed to head out by four. Metal detector, picks, shovels. LED lanterns for the return trip, no one wanted to stumble back down that hill in the dark, not with rocks that seemed to shift just when you weren't looking.

Kerry led the way in his battered old Land Rover. The others followed, tyres crunching on dry gravel. He took them up a trail none of them had seen before, a narrow cut behind the ridge they'd always looked at, but never beyond.

And the wind through the pines whispered secrets that hadn't been told since the war.

The track gave out like a dying breath, just crumbled into the river and vanished. No warning. No signs. Just water where a road used to be. The bush thickened on either side, as if trying to erase the memory of what had once passed through.

Kerry's Land Rover came to a halt so abruptly that dust rose behind it in a lazy spiral. He backed it around slowly, its headlights now facing the way they'd come. In his mind, he was already retracing his steps, wondering if he'd taken a wrong turn somewhere back at the fork near the leaning gum tree.

The others pulled up behind him and killed the engine. Gravel popped under cooling metal. For a moment, no one moved.

Then Kerry stepped out into the quiet, his boots crunching across the loose shale. He walked back toward them as they were climbing down from their vehicle. "Get the map out," he said, without ceremony. "Put it on the bonnet."

Joanna unfolded the worn page and flattened it against the steel hood of the Cruiser. The lamp hanging from the bull bar swayed in the breeze, casting shadows that seemed to crawl across the map like something alive.

Kerry stabbed a calloused finger at the bottom edge. "Right here," he said. "See where the river ends? That used to be a bridge. Long gone now, washed away in a flood, years ago. My grandfather told me this used to be part of the Cobb & Co route. There's an arrow, right there. Points to where the bridge once stood."

The group leaned in closer. The map's edges curled slightly, like it didn't want to give up its secrets.

"Now," Kerry continued, lifting his head, "if you look up that slope, you'll see a bit of crag sticking out. Shift around a little and you'll see how it lines up with that big bastard of a rock. That's our mark. That's where I think we're headed."

They turned their eyes uphill. A long silence fell, broken only by the soft slosh of the river and the faint rustle of leaves. Then, one by one, they nodded. They could see it.

Adina tilted her head. "You said you'd been up here with your grandfather."

Kerry shook his head. "Not this site. Different one. Easier to get to, too, we passed the turnoff earlier. Could make that tomorrow's target, if we're still standing."

"Gee," Joanna said, folding the map back up. "You picked that out quick. Hope the next bit's just as easy."

Kerry gave her a dry smile. "Those other numbers… they're still rattling in my head. They're not just there for decoration. They mean something. We'll figure it out." He turned and looked them over, each a silhouette in the waning afternoon light, each carrying something. Caleb had the detector and a shovel. Joanna held two LED lanterns like sacred relics. Wesley gripped a long-handled pick and a shovel. Adina cradled a length of poly pipe, her snake stick. And Kerry? He had a pack of sandwiches, ham and mustard, and a growing sense of unease.

"Let's be off," he said, and started up the hill. Adina fell in behind him, the others trailing close behind. The bush swallowed them up.

They got back to the homestead a little after two in the morning. No one spoke. No one even undressed. Boots thudded on floorboards. Doors creaked. Beds groaned. Sleep hit them like a sedative.

Kerry had been handed a copy of the map before he left. He didn't say much, just tucked it into his jacket like it might disappear if left alone too long.

But before sleep claimed him, he sat alone at his kitchen table, the map spread out in front of him like a riddle written by ghosts.

He couldn't shake the feeling. Something gnawed at him, something small, but sharp.

"Doesn't make sense," he muttered to himself. "You don't bury gold in a place like that. You wouldn't even camp there, let alone stash something valuable. It's all wrong."

He rubbed at his jaw. The silence in his house felt thick, like it was watching.

Whatever they were chasing, it hadn't been put there by someone who wanted it found.

And Kerry knew, deep down, that maps don't always lead to treasure.

Sometimes they lead to something else.

Adina's cottage, was now nothing but ash and blackened memories. The insurance company refused to pay out. Their cold, clinical denial had thrown a shadow over what little hope she had left. But Adina wasn't one to back down. She and Wesley had thrown themselves into the fight, hiring solicitors who tore into the insurance company's excuses like wolves on a carcass.

The battle had been dragged all the way to the courts in Sydney, which was no small inconvenience for Adina. Between the endless paperwork and the crushing weight of court dates, the city felt like a steel trap closing around her. Still, she and Wesley decided to turn the grim business into something else, a small, bitter holiday where they could watch the drama unfold in the courtroom itself.

Sydney had its usual hum beneath the cloud-heavy sky, buses groaned past, distant sirens wailed, and somewhere, the river gleamed cold and indifferent. But inside the high, glass-walled courtroom, the air was thick with something far heavier than the outside world's noise.

Their legal champion was Carmen Phuels, a fierce Vietnamese barrister whose calm, razor-sharp intellect cut through the opposition like a blade through silk. The insurance company's legal team tried to weave their usual tangled web, but Carmen methodically unraveled it with cold, surgical precision.

She had gone over the insurance policy with the meticulous eye of a hawk. The question wasn't just about fire damage, it was about the fine print, the words buried in legalese that could make or break them. The insurer claimed the loss was drug-related, that illegal activities voided the policy. But Carmen knew the burden of proof was theirs. It wasn't enough to throw accusations like stones into the dark, there had to be proof, hard proof, that drugs had caused or significantly contributed to the fire.

Standing before the court, she laid out the argument like a master storyteller. "The language of this policy," she said, voice steady and cold, "is ambiguous, unclear. And where there is ambiguity, the law demands that it be interpreted in favour of the insured."

The judge listened, eyes sharp but unreadable. Carmen's voice carried weight. She hammered on the point that finding traces of drugs in the debris was not the smoking gun the insurer wanted it to be. "Traces," she said, "do not equal cause. They could be coincidental. They do not prove involvement in the fire or its ignition. Mere presence is not causation."

The room held its breath as she called on the insurer to prove the link, a direct, undeniable chain from drugs to flame. The fire investigation report, she argued, failed to establish this connection. Without it, the insurer's denial was not just flimsy, it was unjustified.

Outside the courtroom, Sydney's streets went on, unaware. But inside, a quiet reckoning had begun. Adina sat with Wesley, their hands clenched tight in their laps, waiting for justice to tip the scales. And somewhere in that waiting was the hope that the law, no matter how tangled or twisted, could still see the truth in the smoke.

Carmen's voice cut through the courtroom again, colder this time, edged with a quiet fury. She didn't just accuse the insurance company of hiding behind loopholes and empty words, she laid bare something darker. Bad faith.

"If this company continues to deny this claim," she told the judge, "without proper, thorough investigation. If they use evidence unrelated to the fire, evidence twisted to fit their narrative rather than the facts, then this is not just a breach of contract. It is bad faith. It is a betrayal of trust that the law cannot, and will not, allow."

There was a charged silence. The kind that makes the hairs on your neck stand up. The magistrate's eyes narrowed slightly, the weight of Carmen's words settling like a cold fog across the courtroom.

Then, suddenly, the gavel came down with a sharp crack.

The case was terminated.

All costs awarded in favour of Adina and Wesley Ahrens.

A hush of disbelief mixed with relief washed over the room. It was over. The victory was theirs.

A few days later, the Ahrens's brief holiday in Sydney folded up like an old map, and they found themselves on the flight home, spirits high and a sense of hard-won triumph warming their bones. Their lawyers had told them that the insurance company had already appealed the judgment, but reassured them not to worry. The law had spoken. Justice had been served.

But outside the warmth of their relief, unseen and unknown, a shadow moved.

The insurance company had quietly enlisted one of Australia's best private investigators: Russell Cox.

A man whose reputation was carved from relentless pursuit and cold calculation.

A man who didn't lose cases.

And so the game was far from over.

Wesley and Adina had barely unpacked their bags, barely shaken off the chill of Sydney's courthouse, when Kerry's call came through like a sudden crack of thunder. His voice was tense, urgent, a warning wrapped in a riddle. They had to meet. Now.

So, despite the biting cold that seeped through the old homestead walls, they gathered around the large wooden table, its surface scarred and worn like the secrets it was about to witness. The fire flickered weakly in the hearth, shadows dancing and stretching, as if listening in.

The early moments were polite, casual. Small talk. Cigarette smoke curling lazily into the night. But then Kerry cut through the murmur with a question that dropped like a stone into a still pond.

"What, roughly, was the date you found the gold in the State Forest?" His eyes locked onto Caleb.

Adina snapped back immediately, her voice sharp as broken glass. "That first find was none of your business, Kerry. Not yours, never was."

But Kerry just sighed, a sound heavy with frustration. "Alright," he said slowly, eyes moving around the group, "let me try this another way. The stars you're using to take bearings from the rocks…" He paused, as if measuring the weight of his own words. "…those stars only line up the same way twice a year."

The room held its breath.

No one moved. No one spoke.

Then Joanna's eyes widened like she'd just cracked a code. She looked at Kerry, face flushed with sudden understanding. "Yes… yes! Of course! The bearing's only accurate when the star is in the exact same position it was when the original bearing was made."

Kerry nodded, his voice low but sharp. "And those numbers, the ones that baffled us, what if they're not random? What if they're dates?"

A ripple of murmurs spread through the room, disbelief giving way to dawning realisation.

Caleb broke the silence, almost whispering, "It was just after Christmas… when we found the gold." He leaned forward, tracing the underlined numbers on the map, 0601. "January 6th… that would be close to the date we struck it."

The fire snapped, sending a flurry of sparks into the hearth's dark throat.

Kerry folded his hands, his gaze darkening. "The next star phase we can use will be September, then October. It's June now. That means we're looking at three months before we can search the peak again, the one we failed at recently. And four months before we can hit the site I know. The one we haven't even tried yet."

The cold air seemed to close in tighter around them, as if the house itself held its breath for what was coming next.

Because time wasn't just ticking. It was counting down.

A long breath finally escaped the room, carried by the warmth of the fire and the clinking of glasses. Relief rolled over the group like a slow tide, washing away some of the tension that had gripped them since Kerry's revelation. Drinks were poured, the rich amber liquid catching the firelight and glowing like a small, defiant beacon against the cold.

Caleb leaned back in his chair, a faint grin tugging at the corners of his mouth. "And another thing," he said, eyes flicking around the table. "Don't worry about that stolen map just yet. Whoever's got it can't do squat with it until those dates come around, if, that is, they're smart enough to crack the encryption."

A ripple of laughter, tentative but genuine, broke out. The heaviness that had settled moments before began to lift.

Then Kerry leaned forward, his voice dropping to a conspiratorial whisper. "Oh! That reminds me…" He glanced around, making sure their circle was tight. "A good mate of mine at ASIO, yeah, one of the real ones, has a son working with National Parks. I mentioned something about some prospecting going on around here. Just a casual chat, you know. Well, yesterday, he told me his son and a colleague busted a couple out in the park. Metal detector, digging holes everywhere. These fools didn't even try to hide it."

Kerry smirked, a little darkly. "Their gear and car got confiscated, and they're staring down fines up to a hundred grand each, or maybe prison. Guess they'll think twice next time."

More laughter, this time with a sharper edge, relief, but also warning.

Caleb nodded, pulling out his phone with a satisfied flick. "And good news for me too," he said. "I'm finally cancelling that bloody lease on the surveillance cameras. Those cursed things were linked to my phone and kept going off day and night, false alarms every five minutes. I thought I'd lost my mind."

The fire cracked and hissed, shadows stretching long against the walls like silent watchers.

For a moment, the homestead felt less like a trap and more like a sanctuary.

But somewhere, just beyond the warmth and the laughter, something waited in the dark.

Something patient. Something hungry.

Russel Cox was a man carved from steel and shadows, born in the restless heart of London, where the city's pulse never slowed and danger lurked beneath every flickering streetlamp. He started out as just another police constable, walking the cracked pavements of Soho, where the neon buzz of clubs masked whispered secrets and the heavy scent of fear hung thick in the air. But Russel wasn't like the others. His mind was sharp, his patience relentless, and he saw patterns in chaos that others missed.

Before long, he was climbing the ranks of New Scotland Yard, chasing down killers and unravelling the tangled webs of organized crime. By the time he hit thirty-five, he wore the mantle of Chief Superintendent, a man who commanded respect not by shouting but by quiet, unshakable authority. His investigations were masterpieces of precision, peeling back layers of deceit until the raw, ugly truth lay exposed.

Then came MI6. The whisper of the British Secret Intelligence Service was like a siren's call, and Russel answered without hesitation. They wanted a mind that could untangle the darkest riddles, a soul that could keep steady when the world tilted on its axis. His new life became a shadow dance across continents, one moment embedded deep inside South American drug cartels, the next slipping through the frozen wastelands of Eastern Europe, always walking the razor's edge between life and death.

The faces he wore, the lies he told, the alliances forged in danger, all became part of his identity. There was a rush to it, the kind only men like Russel knew: the adrenaline, the weight of secrets, the knowing glance that said everything and nothing. But time is a cruel master. At fifty, the cold hand of MI6's mandatory retirement policies closed around him, pushing him out into the fading light of a career he still loved.

Retirement wasn't an end. It was a new beginning, a chance to wield the same relentless will and uncanny insight as a private investigator. Australia called to him, vast, sun-drenched, and wild, a stark contrast to the grey streets he knew so well. Sydney's sprawling skyline and endless horizons promised freedom, but Russel knew better than to believe in easy answers.

In this sunlit land, he would chase truth in the shadows once more, a man forever haunted by the ghosts of his past, yet never willing to let the truth slip away.

In Australia, Russel Cox wasted no time carving out a niche for himself as the go-to private investigator, the kind of man who didn't just look for the truth but hunted it like a predator stalking through the underbrush. His years with MI6 and Scotland Yard were more than just credentials; they were the foundation of a reputation built on precision, patience, and a stubborn refusal to accept anything less than absolute certainty.

The game had changed. No longer operating in the shadowed alleys of international espionage, Russel found himself navigating a quieter but no less tangled world of insurance fraud, corporate deception, and carefully crafted lies. His clients ranged from nervous CEOs clutching their balance sheets to private citizens desperate to expose a false claim. And in every case, the truth was buried beneath layers of smoke and mirrors, numbers fudged, stories rehearsed, motives concealed.

Russel's methods had evolved. Instead of tailing agents in foreign capitals or decoding secret communications, he poured over forensic accounting reports, grilled reluctant witnesses under fluorescent interrogation rooms, and kept silent watch on suspects from behind rented car windows and hotel room curtains. But his spirit, unyielding, exacting, relentless, remained unchanged. Each case, whether a multi-million-dollar scam or a petty insurance swindle, was a puzzle demanding the same clinical dissection he'd applied for decades.

Now in his late fifties, Russel stood at the apex of this second career, the lines on his face deepening like the grooves in a well-read map of truth and deception. Sydney had become his domain, its sprawling urban maze peppered with the unexpected bursts of nature's wildness, offering a strange sort of peace, a quiet counterbalance to the shadows that always lurked just out of sight.

But beneath the calm, the same fire burned. Russel Cox was an investigator born to dig, to pry open every secret until the last stone was overturned. Driven not just by duty, but by an insatiable curiosity and a raw, stubborn integrity that refused to let the truth slip away.

Russel Cox pulled his car quietly onto the dusty gravel drive of the Kimbarry property, eyes narrowing as he scanned the perimeter. The silence inside the vehicle was almost too perfect, no electronic buzz, no telltale beeps from the surveillance camera detector perched on the front passenger seat beside him. That lack of signal set off a flicker of unease in his gut. In an era where biosecurity rules clamped down hard on vehicle access, surveillance was usually everywhere, cameras like silent sentinels, watching, recording, waiting.

Still, he allowed himself a brief, tight-lipped smile. That absence was strange, but it worked in his favour. Russel reached over, dragging the camouflage net from the back seat, its mesh of green and brown designed to swallow the car whole against the scrub and trees. With practiced care, he draped it over the vehicle, smoothing it down until the headlights and roof vanished beneath the patterned shroud.

Stepping back a few meters, he crouched low and surveyed his handiwork. From this angle, the car was nothing more than a blot of shadow stitched into the landscape, a ghost waiting to be forgotten. His backpack shifted comfortably on his shoulders, weighted with the tools and gadgets he always carried: notepads, cameras, a pocket knife, and a small first aid kit. More importantly, it contained the patience and vigilance born of decades chasing secrets in shadows.

He pulled the map from his jacket pocket, a creased, weathered thing marked with faint pencil lines tracing tracks and ridges, and folded it carefully in half. His eyes traced a path behind the burned-out shell of the cottage he was investigating, to a hill that loomed beyond it. According to the topo, a rough track wound its way behind that hill, a perfect place to begin.

With one last glance back toward the netted car, Russel turned and started walking, his boots crunching softly on the dry earth. The wind whispered through the dry grass, carrying the faint scent of charred wood and something older, something buried.

Senior Inspector Colin Suthons rose as Russel Cox entered, extending a solid handshake that spoke volumes, years of hard-won trust and a shared history of cases cracked wide open. There was a rare ease between them, an understanding that wasn't spoken but felt in every measured glance and subtle nod. Colin's office was a modest, functional space cluttered with case files and fading photographs pinned to a corkboard, a shrine to battles fought and sometimes lost.

But today, Colin's usual steady confidence was tempered by the weight of recent failure. The sting was fresh, raw enough to taste bitter on his tongue. The raid on the meth lab, a sequestered cottage nestled on the outskirts of the Kimbarry property, near the sleepy, timeworn town of Bigga, had slipped through their fingers like smoke. The criminals had vanished moments before the assault, taking every scrap of evidence with them. The only trace left behind was a smouldering ruin, the echoes of an explosion that wiped the operation clean off the map.

Colin's jaw tightened as he poured a cup of coffee, the dark liquid trembling slightly in the cup. Rumours circled the station like vultures, each whisper a fresh wound on his reputation. The explosion, the loss of the lab, the missed chance, it all threatened to unravel the threads of his career.

"Russel," Colin began, voice low but edged with a wry smile, "good to see you. You always seem to show up when I'm up to my neck in shit. Not that I'm complaining." His chuckle was forced, a brief release of tension, but the frustration lingered like a shadow in the room.

He gestured toward a worn leather chair across the desk. "Sit down. I need your eyes on something... and maybe your magic touch."

Russel nodded, settling into the chair, sensing the gravity beneath Colin's bravado.

Russel eased back into the worn leather chair, the kind that creaked under a man's weight as if warning him not to get too comfortable. His eyes, sharp, cold, and endlessly watchful, swept the cluttered office like a hawk circling its prey. The faded paint on the walls, the scattered files, the faint smell of burnt coffee mingled with stale smoke, all of it spoke of battles fought quietly in the shadows.

"My client, the insurance company underwriting the property," Russel said, cutting straight through the thick fog of tension, "they've shared what they know about the cottage." He paused, voice low but steady. "Sounds like a real mystery, Colin. And from what I gather, you think there's more hiding beneath the surface."

Colin leaned back, fingers massaging the bridge of his nose as if trying to erase the headache that had settled there weeks ago and never quite left. "Disaster doesn't even begin to cover it." His voice dropped to a conspiratorial whisper, like he was afraid the walls had ears. "The lab going up in flames? Too damn convenient. We had intel on this operation for months. Then, just before we move in, poof, they vanish. Like they knew we were coming." His eyes narrowed. "And that explosion? No accident. Someone cleaned house. Made sure nothing was left behind, no evidence, no traces."

Russel nodded slowly, the wheels turning behind his calm facade. "You think there's a mole."

Colin's grim smile was a razor blade. "I'd bet my badge on it. But proving it, that's the nightmare. That's why I need someone outside the station, someone who won't stir the hornet's nest. Someone I trust."

A faint smirk tugged at Russel's lips. "You know I'm never one to shy away from a challenge." He folded his hands, leaning forward like a predator ready to stalk its quarry. "Tell me everything you've got. Let's see if we can flush out this rat."

Colin's shoulders eased for the first time that day. A flicker of hope sparked in his eyes, a rare thing in a job soaked in smoke and failure.

He reached across the desk, grabbing a battered file and sliding it toward Russel with a quiet thud. "It's all in there. Everything."

Russel flipped open the file, his mind already piecing together fragments of a puzzle that was far more complex than a busted meth lab or a burnt-out shack. This was something deeper, a dark thread weaving through lies and betrayals that would take all his skill to unravel.

Colin sighed and admitted, with a reluctant edge, how his career had taken a hit that day he crossed paths with Caleb Ahrens. "The higher-ups called it 'an unfortunate encounter', 'One doesn't expect to bump into a United States Marine RECON officer wandering the bush around Bigga,'" he recited with a bitter chuckle. But no matter the words, the incident was etched into his record, a stubborn stain he couldn't scrub away.

The room seemed to close in around them, thick with secrets and unsaid fears. Somewhere in the ruins of Kimbarry and the shadows of Bigga, the truth waited. And Russel Cox intended to find it, no matter what it cost.

From the moment Colin Suthons had crossed paths with Caleb Ahrens, an uneasy knot had settled deep in his gut. The man carried an aura that didn't sit right, too smooth, too precise, like a shadow that didn't belong in the daylight. Colin's superior's words echoed through his mind, sharp as a whip crack: You don't expect to meet the US Marines' very best wandering the bush around Bigga. It was as if fate had thrown two worlds together in a place where they didn't quite fit.

His first task was clear: find out why Caleb Ahrens was in Australia at all, and more importantly, how he'd come to own or co-own such an expensive patch of land. Simple in theory, but the closer Colin dug, the murkier it became. The trail was tangled with gaps, unanswered questions that screamed for attention.

Colin was well aware of a gold transaction tied to the purchase, something he intended to forward to both the Australian Taxation Office and Immigration. But deep down, he knew this was just a drop in a much larger ocean. The scent of a bigger catch hung heavy in the air, elusive but undeniable.

He had stumbled across a report detailing the sale of a saloon in San Francisco, owned by Caleb's parents. They'd sold the place at a loss but were living it up on this side of the world, wallets fat without the burden of honest work. It was a detail that didn't escape Colin's keen eye, and one he was eager to share with Russel Cox. Help was not a question; it was a promise.

With Colin's directions and a hastily sketched map guiding him, Russel found himself stepping into a landscape that felt eerily familiar, a former police surveillance site, hidden in plain sight. Only a trained eye could catch the faint, distinct impressions in the dirt: two sets of footprints weaving away from the site, tracing a path down towards the ruins of the burned-out cottage. Russel moved with quiet purpose, senses stretched taut, searching for clues others would overlook.

The trail led him to a shallow gully, blackened earth cracked and scarred from a recent fire. Ash and scattered debris lay like a jigsaw puzzle waiting to be solved. As Russel prepared to cross, a faint, cloying scent clawed at his nostrils, the sickly-sweet stench of decay. Peering down into the gully, his eyes locked onto the charred remains of a skull.

To anyone else, it might have been little more than a grim curiosity, but Russel recognised it instantly, a dog's skull, blackened but eerily intact. Nearby lay a second skeleton, similarly scorched, bones bleached by fire but preserved enough to tell a darker story.

It was the second skull that held his attention, a neat, round hole punctured its cranium. A bullet hole. A quick glance at the first skull revealed the same sinister mark.

Both dogs had been shot.

Russel crouched lower, letting the weight of the discovery settle around him like a fog. "Had both dogs been shot?" he murmured, voice low and steady, almost to himself.

Pulling a small ziplock bag and disposable gloves from his backpack, he prepared to gather what evidence he could. Whatever the story was here, it wasn't just about fire and ruin, it was about violence, and someone trying to erase every trace of it.

And Russel Cox knew better than most that the truth has a way of clawing its way back, no matter how deep it's buried.

He crouched low, turning each skull slowly under the fading light, searching for exit wounds that might tell a fuller story. But there were none, no clean punches through the bone, no telltale shards kicked outward. Instead, nestled amid the blackened fragments inside the skulls, Russel found shattered pieces of metal. Bullet fragments, battered but still holding their shape, bases and jagged sides glinting faintly against the ashen remains. Carefully, almost reverently, he gathered the fragments into the small ziplock bag, treating the shards like keys to a locked room. Each piece he photographed meticulously, documenting evidence that might otherwise be lost to time and fire.

When he finally approached the skeletal remains of the cottage, Russel slowed his pace, moving with the caution of a man stepping through a crime scene frozen in time. He mapped out the skeleton of the building with an expert eye, the ghost outlines of where the front and back doors once stood, the skeletal frame of walls long collapsed. His boots settled on scorched hardwood and softwood alike, the difference visible even beneath the ash.

His gaze caught on a particular patch where the charred ruins suggested a large table had once dominated the lounge room, a centerpiece strangely out of place amid the wreckage. Unusual spot for such a large table, he thought, brow furrowing in quiet intrigue.

Russel's eyes then drifted downwards, catching a section of flooring that wasn't just blackened, it was gone, stripped clean in a jagged strip about 1.8 meters long. The missing planks lay adjacent to where the table had stood, a glaring void amidst the ruins. He knelt, letting his fingers hover just above the ash-covered ground, feeling for clues invisible to the eye.

Accelerant, his mind whispered. The burn patterns told their own brutal story, sudden, intense, and focused. This wasn't the random spread of a wildfire or a careless spark; it was a calculated inferno designed to erase, to destroy evidence.

He snapped more photographs, the broken bones of the table, the ragged hole in the floor, the fine details that might unravel the story locked within these ruins. The fragments of the puzzle began to fit together in his mind, though thick questions still clung to the edges of his thoughts like smoke in the air.

And those two dogs, shot and burned, there was no mistaking it now. Their deaths were no accident. Too deliberate, too cruel. Someone had wanted to bury secrets in fire and blood.

Russel stood, shoulders tense but determined.

As dusk bled into the horizon, Russel turned away from the smouldering remains, the heavy silence of the ruined cottage lingering like a weight on his shoulders. He retraced his steps with measured care, the shadows stretching long and thin as he made his way back toward the camouflaged car. The night air was thick with the scent of burnt wood and something darker, unspoken threats and secrets that clung to the land like a second skin.

The long drive back to Sydney would have to wait. Not tonight. Tonight, the images, the pieces of shattered bone and burnt timber, the jagged scars in the earth, they all needed to settle, to be wrestled with in the quiet hours. His mind churned with the fragments of evidence, fitting them together like a puzzle whose picture kept shifting.

He decided on the local pub in Bigga, a place that promised the soft hum of muted conversation, a stiff drink, and a bed for the night. Somewhere to gather his thoughts, to steel himself for the work waiting at dawn, the bullet fragments, the accelerant traces, the cold calculus of a fire set with intention.

Whatever dark story had played out in that cottage, Russel Cox was determined to unravel it.

Now, all the occupants of the Kimbarry homestead found themselves caught in the slow rhythm of waiting, three long months before they could set about retrieving more gold. The delay was a bitter pill, but beneath it stirred a quiet anticipation, a breathing space to turn their hands to other dreams and duties.

For Adina, time slipped away like the gentle turning of pages in a cherished book. She threw herself into designing the replacement cottage with a fierce and tender focus. This new home, she knew, would be hers and Wesley's sanctuary, a modest retreat woven perfectly to their needs and desires. The grand old house, with its sprawling rooms and echoing halls, was destined for the younger generation. Caleb and Joanna would inherit its vastness, and Adina's heart filled with a soft hope: that someday, those empty bedrooms would ring with the laughter of children. The dream of a family's roots spreading wide across the country air was a warmth she held close.

Wesley, ever the craftsman, had his own visions etched in wood and steel. His mind roamed to the workshop, a cavernous space packed with machines and memories, waiting to hum with life again. The building of furniture for the new cottage was not just work, it was a labor of love, a blending of practicality and artistry. With calloused hands and quiet satisfaction, he would craft each piece like a keepsake, a testament to their life unfolding here.

And Caleb, restless and eager, had his sights set on the old Land Rover, its engine whispering tales of journeys past. He dreamed of tearing it down, replacing the worn rings and battered bearings, bringing the stubborn machine back to life. Restoring it wasn't just nostalgia; it was a promise of freedom, the thrill of driving across the sprawling property under open skies. Next on his list was building a sturdy trailer, a faithful companion for the

Land Rover, ready to ease the hard work of the land and make each day a little smoother.

In the quiet between gold and dust, the Kimbarry homestead pulsed with hope and resolve, each occupant weaving their own thread into the tapestry of home.

Joanna, restless and bright-eyed, was already dreaming in green. She'd marked out several patches of earth around Kimbarry, prime real estate for vegetables and flowers alike. Her notebook bulged with lists: seeds, tools, fertilizer, and a few secret indulgences she wouldn't share just yet. For Joanna, gardening wasn't just dirt and sweat; it was a ritual, a slow dance with nature that promised quiet victories. She pictured riotous bursts of color, sunflowers towering like sentinels, tomatoes ripening in the sun, roses climbing the trellis with wild abandon. Each leaf, each petal, a testament to her care, her patience.

But Joanna's mind was a restless one, and while she waited for sprouts to break through the soil, another plan took root. She wanted to write a book. Not some dry history or a dusty memoir, but a living chronicle of her great Australian adventure. She imagined pages soaked with the sunburnt landscapes, the long dusty roads, and the people who'd woven themselves into her story. Every memory, sharp and strange, would find a home in those pages, a way to make sense of the chaos and beauty she'd stumbled into.

The whole family buzzed with a quiet certainty, as if some invisible thread was pulling them forward. They were happy here, convinced that the wild gamble of moving halfway across the world was the right choice. And when they thought back, it was almost unbelievable, how everything had begun with an old, weathered map, its edges frayed, its secrets waiting to be uncovered. A map that had led them not just to land or gold, but to a new life, tangled with hope and shadows, just waiting to be lived.

Russel Cox had finished his meal at the Federal Hotel in Bigga, New South Wales, a modest but warm place that somehow felt like a refuge from the weight of his work. The night was cool, the kind of cool that seeps through the cracks in the floorboards and settles in your bones, making the fire in the hearth all the more welcome. After a few drinks, he settled into his room and switched on his dictation recorder, fingers steady despite the day's fatigue.

His voice filled the quiet space, calm and measured, as he recounted the findings at Kimbarry. He painted a picture not just of charred wood and ash, but of a carefully concealed crime, arson, deliberate and cold. His words traced the outlines of suspicion and dark intent, weaving the facts into a narrative that suggested something far more sinister than a simple fire. Somewhere between the ashes, a story of greed and deception whispered.

As he finished, he flicked the switch, sending the report instantly to his secretary back in Sydney. He leaned back, eyes drifting to the window where the stars pierced the dark Australian sky, and for a moment, he allowed himself to imagine a different life. If he ever left the city, the rolling hills and quiet charm of Bigga, or perhaps the Kimbarry property itself if it ever came up for sale, might be the place he'd call home.

The insurance company read the report with keen interest. The suggestion of arson wasn't just a detail, it was a game-changer. They pushed for legal action, and the judge agreed, ordering the matter be handed over to the New South Wales Police for full investigation. The case file landed squarely on Senior Inspector Colin Suthons' desk, who wasted no time.

Within days, Suthons had a search warrant for the entire Kimbarry property, moving swiftly to uncover whatever secrets the land still held. The search turned up a cache of chilling evidence: a Smith & Wesson automatic .22LR pistol loaded with six Mini-Mag subsonic rounds, a .22 caliber suppressor fitted for the same pistol, a full box of forty rounds of Mini-Mag ammunition, and two bars of minted gold ingots weighing close to twelve kilograms, silent witnesses to the hidden wealth and darker dealings at Kimbarry.

Caleb Ahrens, already a figure of suspicion, was arrested on firearms charges. Under questioning, the pieces began to fall into place. Then, in a further twist, Joanna Martinez was taken into custody for the illegal importation of a firearm, an accusation that sent shockwaves through the tight-knit community.

The investigation was no longer just about a burnt cottage. It was a tangled web of smuggling, deception, and secrets buried beneath the scorched earth of Kimbarry. And for Russel Cox and Colin Suthons, the true depths of the mystery were only just beginning to surface.

The projectile fragments, tiny shards of metal torn from bullets lodged deep within the charred skulls of those two dead dogs, didn't just whisper secrets; they screamed them when they were sent to the ballistic lab. The technicians worked in near silence, their machines humming cold and clinical. But the conclusion was clear and unforgiving: those bullets had been fired from the very Smith & Wesson pistol unearthed during the Kimbarry property search. A pistol wrapped in shadows and lies.

The fingerprints on the cold metal, smudged but unmistakable, belonged to Adina Ahrens. When the police confronted her with the evidence, the quiet calm she once wore like a shield shattered. She was arrested, not just as a suspect but as a murderess, accused of the cold-blooded killing of those dogs, the symbolic sentinels of a darker crime, and of arson that had reduced the old cottage to ashes.

But the storm was just gathering.

Constable Carl Holgate, a man with a conscience heavy as chains, came forward. The weight of his silence had become unbearable, and with trembling hands, he delivered a statement that sliced through the tangled web of deception. Holgate confessed to the murder that had taken place at Kimbarry, the blood spilled beneath the scorched sky, and the fire set to cover it all. His admission branded him an accessory, and he too was charged with both murder and arson.

Meanwhile, the cold hand of the law tightened around Wesley Ahrens. The Australian Taxation Department uncovered a staggering nine million dollars in undeclared gold bullion that had slipped quietly into the country, a fortune hidden beneath layers of deceit and greed. Tax evasion wasn't just a crime here, it was a sentence, and Wesley found himself facing twenty long years behind bars, the weight of his crimes pressing down with relentless finality.

For Joanna Martinez, the noose tightened even further. The United States Embassy stepped into the fray, their diplomatic power wielded like a hammer. Joanna was extradited to America, where she faced grave charges, accused of using the embassy's diplomatic channels to smuggle weapons intended for violent crime on foreign soil. Amongst many others. The sentence was merciless: life imprisonment in a prison thousands of miles from the Australian sun.

As the courtroom drama unfolded, the fall of the Ahrens family became a public spectacle of ruin and regret. Adina's conviction for first-degree murder brought a life sentence that would stretch endlessly before her, a punishment compounded by a dozen more years for the arson she had ignited. Each day behind bars

                    Max Barrington

a reminder of the fire that had consumed more than just timber and memories.

Caleb's fate was sealed in harsher terms. Six years for the illegal possession of the Smith & Wesson, and another six for the silencer, a tool of silence in the bloody noise. The sentences were to run one after the other, an unyielding march to the end of his freedom. When those years were done, deportation would cast him out, a ghost to be sent away from the land where his family's sins had burned so bright.

The legal reckoning came swift and brutal, tearing through the shadows cloaking Kimbarry. The sins buried beneath the scorched earth were unearthed with a clarity that left no room for mercy. Justice, cold and unrelenting, closed its grip on every one of them. The story of Kimbarry had ended not in gold and glory but in fire, blood, and ruin.

During the relentless investigations that clawed at the heart of the Kimbarry case, one name kept clawing its way back to the surface: Kevin Albert Kerridge. Known to those who whispered in shadowed corners as simply "Kerry," he was more than just a shadow, he was a ghost with footprints in the dirt of every whispered crime. The tangled web of allegations painted him as an accessory, a man who wasn't just on the sidelines but pulled strings behind the scenes, his hands stained with knowledge, maybe even blood.

Witnesses, some shaken, others tight-lipped, pointed to Kerry as a linchpin in the twisted machinery of deceit. His name was uttered in hushed tones, linked to every illicit thread spun around the Kimbarry homestead. Rumors led the police to a lonely cottage nestled on the outskirts of Kimbarry itself, said to be Kerry's hideout, his base of operations.

When the officers finally arrived, the cottage offered nothing but silence and decay. The door creaked open to reveal a scene of chaos frozen in time, furniture splintered and overturned, heaps of rotting debris scattered like the remnants of a long-forgotten storm. The place smelled of dust and neglect, a tomb of memories left to rot. So dilapidated was the property that authorities condemned it as uninhabitable, a relic abandoned by the man who might once have called it home.

In the ramshackle garage, their flashlights caught the outline of what had once been a vehicle, Kerry's Land Rover, or so they thought. Now it was nothing more than a gutted husk, stripped of wheels and engine, balanced precariously on concrete blocks like a carcass picked clean by vultures. The empty shell seemed to mock the investigation itself.

Despite the grim tableau, tangible evidence tying Kerry to the crimes remained maddeningly elusive. The man was a shadow slipping through fingers, a name without a face. Refusing to be dismissed, the police reached out to the Australian Security Intelligence Organisation, ASIO, hoping to shed light on Kerry's murky past. Whispers had long suggested a connection, rumours of a man once woven into the secretive threads of intelligence, someone who knew the dance of lies and truths better than most.

ASIO's response was a stone wall. They neither confirmed nor denied Kerry's existence within their ranks, shrouding the truth behind a veil of operational secrecy. The silence was deafening, a deliberate refusal that only deepened the mystery.

Was Kevin Albert Kerridge the mastermind behind the chaos, or just a phantom, a Spector conjured to derail the investigation? If he had indeed danced with shadows within ASIO, did his involvement in the Kimbarry affairs bleed beyond mere criminality into something darker, more dangerous? The questions piled high like the debris in that ruined cottage, heavy and suffocating.

The enigma of Kerry lingered, a puzzle piece that refused to fit, leaving the investigators trapped in a maze with no clear way out.

There was something almost spectral in the old saying that kept slipping into hushed conversations and half-remembered stories: "None shall have, The Darkie's Gold." A cryptic warning, whispered like a curse, as if the treasure itself carried a shadow too heavy to bear. And now, with the gold bullion seized by the Crown and locked away from prying hands, the weight of that saying seemed to press even harder.

The gold, once gleaming with promise at the heart of the Kimbarry homestead, was now little more than cold metal, impounded, catalogued, and sent off for assay. Its value had to be known, quantified, stripped of mystery. But the whispers and speculation that this treasure was linked to the legendary Eugowra Rocks gold escort robbery, that infamous heist soaked in Australian folklore and blood, were quickly silenced. The assay revealed a truth that shattered those romantic notions: the bullion was minted, forged with precision and care, stamped with official marks of legitimacy.

This was no crude, cast bullion, the kind forged hastily by desperate hands in Forbes, the town where the gold had actually been mined. No, this was different. Clean, official, polished, the sort of gold that belonged to banks, governments, the weight of empires. It belonged to a world far removed from outlaw legends and daring robberies.

So, the dark lure of stolen gold faded into a cold reality. Yet that old saying lingered like a ghost in the minds of those who knew the story, a reminder that some treasures come with curses, and that the true story behind The Darkie's Gold was still buried in shadows deeper than anyone dared to dig.

Auction at Kimbarry

The property known as Kimbarry, once the scene of dark deeds and shattered lives, had been seized and claimed by the Crown following the tangled legal battles that unraveled its sinister secrets. Two years slipped by like a shadow passing over the sun, and finally, the Crown handed the estate to the Public Trustee, who resolved to sell it in an open auction. The sale would be held right there on the weathered grounds of Kimbarry itself, offering hopeful buyers the chance to walk the scorched earth, examine the property, and imagine what might yet be resurrected from its dismal past.

But fate had not been kind to the timing. The country's mood was tense, its economy wobbling on a knife-edge. A recent change in the Federal Government had unleashed a storm of uncertainty; interest rates climbed relentlessly, driving many wealthy buyers to retreat into caution. Investments that once seemed golden now shimmered with risk and doubt. And so, the crowd at Kimbarry was thin, just a trickle of serious bidders amid the restless wind that whispered through the cracked windows and broken beams.

Among those rare attendees were Russel Cox and Colin Suthons, two men forged by the ordeal of investigation and bound by a shared pursuit of truth. Their partnership had blossomed from mutual respect and countless long nights piecing together fragments of a dark puzzle. This auction was no mere transaction to them, it was a reckoning. They carried with them a curious relic from the past: an old, hand-drawn map, weathered and enigmatic, discovered in the course of their inquiries.

The map hinted at secrets hidden beneath Kimbarry's troubled soil, features or valuables long forgotten, buried beneath layers of dust and silence. As Russel and Colin stepped onto the land once more, the weight of history pressed against their shoulders. This was more than a property sale. It was a chance to uncover what shadows still lurked beneath the surface of Kimbarry, to find the truth that the fires and trials had failed to consume.

The bidding process dragged on like a dying campfire, occasional sparks of interest flaring up only to fizzle into nothing. Most of the attendees milled about with idle curiosity, more drawn to the aura of the infamous estate than any intention to buy it. They whispered among themselves, casting sideways glances at the historic outlines of the once-grand homestead, as though half expecting ghosts to rise from the foundations. The auctioneer's voice echoed across the dry paddocks, bouncing off hollow walls and cracked verandas, but it inspired little more than polite silence and the rustling of programs.

At one point, the silence stretched too long, and the auctioneer cleared his throat with theatrical frustration. It was obvious: the crowd had come to watch, not to buy. The word "passed in" hovered on his lips like a curse ready to be spoken.

That's when Russel Cox made his move.

From beneath the brim of his weathered Akubra, Russel raised his hand and calmly placed a single bid, one well below the reserve, low enough to be audacious, but not so low as to be insulting. The kind of bid that felt like an insult only because it was the only bid.

The auctioneer paused. A murmur swept through the sparse crowd like a ripple across still water. Eyes turned to Russel, some curious, others suspicious, but he didn't flinch. This was no impulse. It was a carefully staged manoeuvre. A play out of a longer game.

The hammer didn't fall, not officially. The bid hadn't met the reserve, and the auctioneer, somewhat deflated, was forced to declare the property "passed in." But that was exactly what Russel had been hoping for. Because now, by the rules of the game, he stood as the only registered bidder, and thus the only man legally permitted to negotiate with the Public Trustee.

The property was his to claim, if not by auction, then by strategy. And Russel held one more card in his hand: that hand-drawn map tucked into his coat pocket like a whisper from the past. It hinted at something hidden beneath Kimbarry's twisted soil, something valuable, something lost.

With the crowd beginning to disperse and the sun sinking lower over the hills of Bigga, Russel Cox remained. He stood not just as a bidder, but as a man on the edge of a mystery. The ghosts of Kimbarry were his now, and whatever they guarded beneath the earth… he would soon uncover.

It was late in the afternoon when Russel Cox stepped out of the Public Trustee's temporary field office, the freshly signed contract still warm in his hand, its ink barely dry. Kimbarry was his now, the land, the ruins, the secrets buried beneath both. The autumn sun hung low on the horizon, casting long amber fingers across the hills and paddocks, touching the old bones of the property like a final benediction.

With the deal sealed and the day nearly done, Russel turned to Colin Suthons and offered a suggestion wrapped in casual tones but laced with something more, a sense of occasion, perhaps. "Let's stay in Bigga tonight," he said. "That old pub's got some charm, and I wouldn't mind a decent steak and a proper drink."

The quaint hotel hadn't changed in decades. Lace curtains filtered the soft evening light, and the floorboards groaned with a century's worth of secrets. Dinner was hearty, simple fare, grilled lamb chops and mashed potatoes that tasted of childhood. Later, they settled into the dimly lit saloon bar with its amber-stained timber, mirrored shelves, and the subtle scent of old tobacco soaked into the walls.

Colin, never one to ignore a detail, wandered over to a wall cluttered with sepia-toned photographs. They lined the room like silent witnesses, snapshots of horse-drawn coaches, weather-beaten pioneers, and street parades long buried in memory. His gaze snagged on one image in particular: a large, strikingly crisp print of the original Bigga Cobb & Co. depot, its sandstone facade framed by gum trees and wagons.

"That's the original building Kimbarry was built around, isn't it?" Colin asked, beckoning Russel over with a tilt of his glass.

Russel joined him, studying the image in companionable silence. The depot had a sturdy, haunted look to it, as though it had withstood more than just weather. Then, almost at the same moment, both men leaned in, their eyes drawn to the inscription etched in clean, stark letters above the entryway:

'Kevin Albert Kerridge, Licensee 1853.'

The room seemed to still. Somewhere, a floorboard creaked. The air between them thickened with something that wasn't quite disbelief and wasn't quite understanding either.

Russel was the first to speak, his voice low and edged with something darker than curiosity. "That's impossible. That can't be right."

But the photograph didn't lie. The name that had surfaced time and again in their investigation, the ghost they could never quite catch, was etched right into the bones of the town itself. Kevin Albert Kerridge. Here. In 1853.

Colin swallowed his whisky hard. "Either it's one hell of a coincidence," he murmured, "or we've been looking at this all wrong."

Russel nodded slowly, his gaze never leaving the name above the door in the photo. "It's not just a crime scene anymore," he said. "It's a damn legacy."

Outside, the wind moaned through the alleyways of Bigga like a lost child, and somewhere in the darkness beyond the hills, Kimbarry waited, watchful, ancient, and still full of secrets.

Some weeks after Russel had taken possession of Kimbarry, after the dust of the auction had long settled and the contract formalities were buried beneath a pile of legal documents, he and Colin finally moved into the homestead.

It was a house with bones, thick timber walls that creaked at night like they were trying to speak, and furniture that looked as though it had been there for generations. The place felt still, but not empty. The kind of silence that listens.

One evening, after a long day clearing brush and taking stock of the property, the two men sat in the lounge kitchen at the massive wooden table that dominated the room. It was a beast of a thing, solid and dark with age, its top gouged and weathered, yet striking in its craftsmanship. The legs were carved with fluted designs, and the timber had the subtle lustre of something made to last.

Colin sat back with a sigh, swirling the last of his beer and letting the cool, quiet air settle over them. Then, almost absent-mindedly, he let his fingers drift across the tabletop. Beneath the pads of his fingertips, something subtle snagged his attention, a shift in texture, a shallow groove where the wood dipped ever so slightly.

He leaned in, squinting. "Hang on…"

"What is it?" Russel asked, setting down his glass.

Colin pulled out his iPhone, activated the magnifier, and hovered the screen above the worn timber. Slowly, the fine lines emerged from shadow, hidden in plain sight. Letters, carefully carved, timeworn but deliberate. He read them aloud, the words slow and heavy as stone:

"None shall have, 'The Darkie's Gold.'"

The room fell into a sudden hush. Outside, a breeze stirred the eucalypts, and the floor beneath them seemed to shift ever so slightly.

Russel leaned over, eyes narrowing on the faint inscription. "Jesus," he murmured. "That's the same line that kept cropping up in the old stories… the same damn phrase."

A chill crept in through the windows, or maybe it came from somewhere deeper inside the house.

The carving, hidden for who knew how long, wasn't just a scrap of folklore. It was a message. A warning, maybe. Or a claim.

Colin glanced at him. "It was here the whole time. Right in the heart of the house."

Russel nodded slowly, the gears in his mind already turning. "And maybe the map wasn't pointing to what's out there," he said, gesturing vaguely toward the surrounding hills. "Maybe it's what's in here. Maybe we've been walking over it."

The house, the land, the legend, they weren't just connected. They were bound together, sealed with whispers and blood and old, forgotten oaths.

And the deeper they looked, the louder Kimbarry seemed to speak.

Did you enjoy this book?...

If so please tell your friends and I would appreciate it greatly if you could rate it.

Thanks! ... Max

Other Books By Max Barrington

Woolgar River Park

Task

Dying To Find Gold

Harry Croft

The New March

Bad Company

The First Ten Years in Australia

Fifty Five More Years

You Couldn't Make This Stuff Up

The Writer & The Written

What's Mine is Yours

The Darkie's Gold

The Intrusion

The Premonition

Revelation at Narern

King to Spare

The Telephone

Going Backwards